ALSO BY IVO ANDRIĆ

Bosnian Chronicle (1963)

This is a BORZOI BOOK, *published in New York by* ALFRED A. KNOPF

 THE WOMAN FROM SARAJEVO

THE WOMAN FROM SARAJEVO

by

IVO ANDRIĆ

Translated from the Serbo-Croatian by
JOSEPH HITREC

New York: Alfred A. Knopf 1965

L. C. catalog card number: 64–19100

This is a Borzoi Book,
Published by Alfred A. Knopf, Inc.

FIRST AMERICAN EDITION

Originally published in Serbo-Croatian, in 1945, by Svjetlost
as *Gospodjica*.

THE WOMAN FROM SARAJEVO

One day toward the end of February 1935, there was a news item in all the Belgrade papers to the effect that the owner of house No. 16a in Stishka Street was found dead in her apartment. Her name was Raika Radakovich. Originally from Sarajevo, she had been living at the same house for some fifteen years in complete seclusion, leading the life of a lonely old maid with a reputation for stinginess and eccentricity. Her death was discovered by the postman. Having rung her bell without success for two days, he had walked around the house, peeped in through the courtyard window, seen the dead body of the old maid stretched on its back in the hall, and immediately notified the police.

As was the fashion of the times, coverage of crime news took up a lot of space in the daily press. The newspapers, without exception, made the most of murders, accidents, and cases involving bloodshed, so as to whet the curiosity of the public, tease its imagination, and, by serving up every last detail, increase the sale of the newspaper. And so this story of the death of the old woman was widely reported and was featured under the titillating headlines "Is it murder?" "Police inquiry started!" "Our reporter on the scene." This time, however, the papers were deprived of the chance of publishing long on-the-scene accounts larded with morbid details and photographs. The police, who promptly visited the house on Stishka Street, established quickly and beyond any doubt that there was no question of murder, that the old girl had died of natural causes, namely, of a heart attack, that nothing in the house had been touched or damaged, and that there was no trace whatever of robbery, violence, or theft.

Immediately after the announcement of her death, the aged

and well-known Belgrade merchant George Hadzi-Vasich and his wife came to the house in Stishka Street. They were the only relatives the dead woman had in Belgrade. They arranged the funeral and, being her nearest relatives, took over the house and all that was in it, pending the legal disposition of the property.

The name of Raika Radakovich dropped out of the newspapers for good and ever. Neither her life nor her death had been significant enough to attract further attention or arouse the imagination of the reading public.

when the blaze of this sun, setting in the plain between the two rivers under Belgrade, glances away into the high bowl of the sky, to break there and scatter itself in a red shimmer over the whole far-flung town. At such moments, even the most godforsaken back alleys of Belgrade light up unexpectedly and the sun kindles even house windows which ordinarily lie fallow and colorless.

One day, toward the end of February in the year 1935, this russet glow spread over the façade of a small and neglected house in Stishka Street. The street was one of those that had sprung up and developed much too rapidly, causing a mixup in the city's numbering system, so that there were suddenly two numbers 16 and one of them had to be designated 16a. Such, then, was the number of this squatting yellowish house that was hemmed in and all but lost between two modern tall apartment houses of more recent vintage. The ungainly one-story building dated back to a time before the Balkan wars, when the district had been referred to as lying "beyond the back of God," and the price of land was one dinar per square meter, when houses on this street had been few and far between and all alike, squat and divided by large gardens, either jutting into the street or else set well back, depending on the mood or the needs of their owners. In those days house numbers were not a thing of importance. One knew what house belonged to whom and most people knew one another at least by name or by sight. When they didn't, they left one another alone, and still, in an emergency, they seemed to get together much more easily than is the case nowadays.

In the outlying streets of Belgrade there still exist quite a few houses of this "ante bellum" type. They are all the same, not so much in size as in shape and construction and in the arrangement of space, interior layout, and appointments. Two or four windows look out on the street, depending on whether the house has three or four rooms. Below the window line the stucco decorations proclaim some sort of turn-of-the-century motif or else a crude geometrical ornament from the never-varying mold of some "master" from Crnotrava. The iron gate, the upper half of which is made of wire netting adorned with sharp spikes along the top, admits one to a small court-yard paved with tiny cobblestones, which has a narrow flower bed along the wall and a grapevine or rambler rose sprawl-ing over the wall itself. Here, in the middle, is the entrance to the house, with one or two stone steps roofed over by a small wooden canopy, which, if the owner is a person of means, is usually made of thick frosted glass. In the back, beyond the house, there is a garden with a walnut tree in the center, often with a water well beside it, and along the fence which separates the house from neighboring gardens and courtyards there are early-flowering plum and apricot trees. Indoors the layout is always the same: a large foyer and around it three or four rooms and a kitchen.

Similar in so many ways, the houses can now be distin-guished only by their outward appearance. Some are white-washed, obviously well kept and properly maintained: the iron swing gate in the courtyard painted a bright color, the windows shiny clean and curtained with thin muslin. They show that the inmates are keeping in step with the times, that they are working hard and being rewarded for it, that they ask and get certain things out of life. The other houses, by contrast, are neglected and unlovely. Their eaves have chipped away, the tiles on the roof are displaced, the paint faded or peeling, the crude stucco decorations crumbling. The wall beneath the windows is spattered with the mud of the street and full of scribbles by the small fry and their awkward exercises in the newly learned alphabet. Through the glass panes a glimpse may be had of the neglected interiors, of poverty, or simply the absence of any personal needs on the part of the owners.

House No. 16a is of the latter kind. It has only two windows facing the street. Conspicuous in the windows are thick iron bars, which give the whole house an austere and prison-like air.

Judging by its appearance, one might think of it as a house that has been abandoned or one that is waiting for a buyer who might take it not because he wants to live in it but simply to raze it and build a new and bigger one, perhaps similar to the two houses that now hem it in from the left and right. But if you peer at it more closely, you will notice, behind one of those uncurtained and flowerless windows, an older woman sitting in a chair, bent and motionless, wearing the absent and preoccupied expression one often sees in the faces of women busy with their embroidery. Her name is Raika Radakovich.

The older inhabitants of Stishka Street, those who settled here before the new, many-storied houses sprang up and a strange new crowd of people moved in, know her by name, but all of them, for many years past, have simply referred to her as "Miss."

She moved in right after the liberation of 1919, having come from Sarajevo; she bought the house and lived in it with her mother, who died two years later. Since then she has lived alone, without relations and servants, and is hardly ever visited by friends. On what does she live? (This is usually the first and main question people here ask and tirelessly repeat about everyone else, until such time as the answer is either found or invented.) A long time ago, the old settlers at Stishka Street discovered that she lived on savings and rents. Some claimed that she was wealthy and absolutely rolling in money, others that she was hard up and had to struggle. Be that as it may, it is now many years since anyone has paid any attention to the solitary old maid, especially since the influx of so many colorful new people into the neighborhood.

Lately she is hardly ever seen outside. From time to time she goes to the market at Kalenich, or, in winter as now, comes out to clear the snow from the pavement in front of the house. She is a tall, thin old girl in her fifties, with a sallow face generously lined with wrinkles. The wrinkles are unusually deep; on her forehead, directly above the nose, they come together and form a perfect triangle, which connects two bushy eyebrows. Along the bottom of each of these creases there lies, like an inky sediment, a thin, elongated shadow. This gives her whole face a somber and exhausted air, which the look in her eyes does little to dispel, for they too radiate gloom. But she holds herself straight and in her bearing there is not a trace of that wavering uncertainty which lonely, ailing, and poor people reveal in their every move, and her walk is quick and brisk. In her black jacket and her unusually long skirt, which is of a kind no one today wears any more, and in her threadbare shoes and thick stockings, with a little woolen cap on her graying hair, she appears dressed in a manner that is beyond time or fashion. The people of today, whose life is conditioned by speed and whose habit is to rush around instead of walk, scarcely ever notice the tall strange form of the thin dark woman.

In the early evening of this February day, Miss Raika sits by the window mending her stockings. Earlier in the afternoon, she had had to go out on some business, but had returned while there was still daylight, soaked and frozen by the February wind which always brings snow and rain together. She had pulled off her old galoshes and taken off the long black winter coat made of a coarse, almost military fabric, now sopping with water. Taking the ancient coat rack from the corner of the hall and setting it in the middle of the room, she slung the coat around it so that it would dry out more quickly. The thing stood there like a tall headless human being who had just entered the house and stopped in the middle of the foyer. Then she walked into the room, which seemed warm to her because she was frozen, and picked up her mending basket and sat down.

That evening blush which seems to hover longer and glow more intensely above Belgrade than above other cities, also kindles the windows of Miss Raika's house. One has only to sit close to the window to be able to go on working in this last rose light of the invisible sun; for at the other end of the room it is already dusk. In that dusk one can make out a small iron stove surrounded by the modest furnishings of a clothes chest, a shelf, and a wooden bed covered with a coarse blanket of camel's hair. Everything in this room, from the walls to the furniture, bears the mark of apathy and neglect, as if the room were tenanted by a blind man or by someone utterly indifferent to material objects, who makes use of them because he has to, and only as often as he has to, who cares very little where any particular thing happens to be standing or what it looks like. This pink light of Belgrade's early evening has the effect of making poor, neglected rooms look even seedier, just as it makes neat, well-kept ones seem cozier.

In this joyless room Miss Raika spends most of her time, for it is the only part of the house that is heated. Here she sleeps and passes the day, here she works, and here, on the small stove, she cooks her frugal lunch which is also her supper. She doesn't spend much time on chores such as tidying up or cooking. Above all, she dislikes spending money; the very word—spending—in any shape or connection, fills her with repugnance. A different thing altogether is the work she is doing at the moment—mending. This is pleasant, useful work: it uses up much time and strains the eyes, it is true, but it helps to save all the rest; for time and eyes are things one has an abundance of, which can hardly be said of "all the rest." A stitch in time saves nine, she tells herself as she sits down by the window. Then, picking up her old stockings, which have been mended several times, she repeats the saying over and over again in her mind—a stitch in time. . . !—just as young girls at work feel impelled to hum the words and melody of a love song which, though meaningless in itself and picked up God knows where or how, nevertheless provides a vivid picture and an exact expression of their own deepest longings.

Mending! What a delight that is! True, it is also an endless and wearying struggle to outwit a powerful unseen enemy. In this struggle there are many dull, trying, and seemingly frustrating moments; defeat and faintheartedness are not infrequent; but there are also, more numerous by far, bright moments of devoted, holy service and victorious elation. It happens sometimes that a pair of old slippers or a piece of underwear becomes threadbare or torn at some spot or other, so that the whole thing is rendered useless, fit neither to be worn nor to be thrown out. And here, where any other woman might throw up her hands and give in to the irresistible power that frays and wears away all possessions, and dogs every human life and every moment, like the curse hurled down on human existence because of man's original sin, here, as far as Miss Raika is concerned, is where the real struggle only just begins, where the prospect of victory begins to open up, arduous and remote but potentially rewarding. With her quiet and invisible, her great and obstinate virgin's strength, she pounces on this object and will not let it out of her hands and sight until it is mended and patched for another long spell of wear.

"Every other woman in my place would have thrown this away, but I throw nothing away." This is how Miss Raika talks to herself as she gazes, with a kind of loving elation, at the slipper that has been saved and snatched from the jaws of that hostile power which gnaws, bores, eats away, and tears everything that people wear or touch. True, the slipper is no longer pleasing to the eye and has in fact shrunk and lost its shape, so that it is bound to pinch and scratch and make sores on the skin of the foot. Still, what is all that compared to the satisfaction she gets from such a victory over waste. Let it rub and draw blood, the discomfort is all the sweeter. She is willing to put up with much more than that.

As for beauty, she could not care less. Beauty is an expensive thing—madly expensive, yet worthless and deceptive. There is no greater prodigal, no greater mirage than beauty. Miss Raika never cared for it, she always shied away from it, and her experience so far has only confirmed her in this attitude. She never could quite understand why people make such a distinction between something that is beautiful and something that is not, and what it is that enthuses and enraptures them to a point where what they call beauty causes them to lose their health and spend their money, sacred and mighty Money that is above all things and against which no beauty of any kind can ever be adequately measured. And now that she is getting on in years, now that the vast and unimagined loveliness and joy of thrift grows more apparent and clearer to her, she is beginning to feel a stronger and more decisive hatred for Beauty—that heresy, as it were, which is like an evil heathen idol that leads people into lamentable ways and turns their faces from the one and only true deity, thrift. "A stitch in time"—this is the silent, fitting way to worship the deity. Stitching and darning means fighting against decay, means helping eternity perpetuate itself. That is why her petty and humble chore is actually holy and momentous, why it fills her soul with peace and contentment. It is something worth slaving over, it justifies all kinds of hardships and sufferings.

"Drudgery!" This, too, is a form of delight. She knows it very well, for she has endured many things in her life for its sake, and has got much satisfaction out of it. And why shouldn't a person suffer here and there when he knows that by virtue of it he is sparing himself much greater evil and paying for something infinitely more worthwhile? Man would not be a rational being if he could not see that this course is advantageous and safe. When all is said and done, how can we compare our small inconveniences and self-denials in the service of thrift with all that thrift gives us and all it can save us from? Thrift preserves life and stability around us, it constantly makes us richer and perpetuates, so to speak, what we already have; it protects us from expenses, losses, and chaos, from penury, from the misery that lies in wait for us at the end, which is darker and more infamous than death itself, indeed a true hell while we are still alive here on earth. If a person only remembered how everything around him steadily and imperceptibly dwindles and wanes, breaks, shrinks, and fritters away, how puny and ineffectual are the measures he can and does take in his struggle against it, he would willingly accept every hardship and privation only to ward off this evil, and he would feel ashamed for every moment of rest and inaction, and for every morsel of food he eats and for spending unwisely and indulging in luxuries. In this unequal fight, one must endure everything with the fanatical courage of a martyr.

Lost in these reveries, Miss Raika feels a chill coming on. She sticks her needle into the stocking and, feeling stiff and heavy all over, gets up and goes to the stove to look at the fire. It is a fire in name only; actually it is no more than a feeble little flame that can barely ever warm up the room, and yet Miss Raika seems to feel it is a flame that consumes wood and coal like Mt. Vesuvius and Mt. Etna combined, or like that American volcano whose name she can no longer remember but whose flame is known to devour and burn up more than all of the European volcanoes put together. She is about to toss in a few lumps of coal, but flinches back at the same instant, almost as if she were on the verge of committing a great and irreparable sin, then grits her teeth and resolutely goes back to her seat. Here she continues to darn her stockings. She is pleased with herself and content with the world, in which evidently there is always room and always another opportunity for extra thrift. (She remembers having read in a newspaper at one time that the regulation temperature in the military barracks during the winter months is fifty-eight degrees Fahrenheit.) Thinking about it she feels the cold much less. She is warmed by the thought of the shovelful of coal she had denied herself. At the same time, her hands are blue from cold, her lips gray, her nose red. Now and then her whole body is racked by a deep inner shudder of cold. And yet Miss Raika refuses to give in and does not leave her chair. She is like one of those trained and seasoned soldiers who can't help a brief shiver in moments of danger, but manage to overcome it and march forward undaunted.

And so Miss Raika goes on mending and suffering but does not surrender or complain. Cramped and stiff with cold, she darns the threadbare spot on the stocking, carefully weaving the cotton through the yarn filaments that have slackened and pulled apart, looping the needle under one thread and skipping the next, securing one and omitting the other, back and forth, one after another, until at last the worn patch is mended and secured.

And afterwards, as she looks at it, her whole being expands in the knowledge that one more housekeeping item has been set down in the asset column of her consolidated balance sheet of losses and gains. And even more: that in the formidable and unceasing battle against waste, spoilage, and costs, another victory has been won against odds, that on the great galleon of the universe, constantly threatened from every quarter, one more insidious leak has been plugged up. Frequently, in her moments of happiness, that knowledge swells to a sense of victorious exhilaration.

Then it is time for another hole, on the same stocking or perhaps a different one. And each one seems hopeless and beyond repair at the outset. Yet each, in the end, yields to victory. Hour after hour goes by in this seemingly monotonous and dreary task. But the monotony is deceptive. For as she guides her needle and thread through the warp and woof of the stocking, Miss Raika lets her mind wander between daydreams and memories, dwelling now on one, now on the other, from stitch to stitch, from memory to memory, as if the needle were rethreading the whole fabric of her life.

Childhood, those early years of which the poets and philosophers speak as the happiest time in the life of man, that guileless period in which one knows nothing of money or the effort of making it, or, for that matter, the strain of keeping it, that time had never existed for Miss Raika. Those years were an empty colorless blank in her consciousness. Her life really began somewhere in her fifteenth year. It began at a dark point, and with a bitter experience.

This happened over thirty years ago. Her father, Master Obren Radakovich, was then one of the most respected Serbian merchants of Sarajevo. He was not a native of Sarajevo but hailed from one of the frontier districts. He had come to Sarajevo as a young man immediately after the Austrian occupation of the 1880's and had quickly, by dint of acumen and a few lucky breaks, established himself as one of the more solid businessmen. He married Radoyka, a gentle good-looking blond girl from the old and reputable Sarajevo family of Hadzi-Vasich. With this marriage he consolidated his position in the bazaar. Master Obren's store was at the head of the great Churchiluk Street, or Furrier's District. He was a wholesale furrier, but as time went on he managed to expand his activities in other directions as well. He became one of the leading stockholders in the first brewery at Kovachichi and a member of the board of various other companies.

Miss Raika's recollections of her father were among her oldest and most vivid memories. As far back as she could remember, he had always been the main and most important figure in her life. Yet whenever she thought of him, she saw him as he had been in the last year of his life. They were living at the time in a spacious new house on the very bank of the Milyacka River, below the Protestant church. She had then just started fourth grade at the girls' high school. She could see him quite clearly, and would do so till the moment of her death. He was tall, straight, slim, without an ounce of excess flesh; with graying mustaches and white hair at his temples. On his head he wore a black bowler. His suit was dove-gray, his starched shirt and high collar were impeccably white, and he wore silk ties with blue and black stripes. On his chest a gold chain, on his fingers two heavy gold rings, one a wedding ring and the other a symbol of his guild; on his hard round cuffs two globular links made of solid gold. When he walked down the street he carried himself well and proudly, so that he resembled a statue which could neither bend nor sit down. His face was grave, like a saint's. He hardly ever laughed or chatted, and confined himself to brief instructions and curt orders. And this man, great and magnificent in her eyes, was her father, who took her on his lap after lunch and supper, just as he used to do when she was five or six, and stroked her hair and asked in a warm voice: "And what did you do today?"

And while she babbled about the events and her childish errands of that day, he would gaze out the window, hearing, as it were, only the surface buzz of her excited chatter. But even that, for her, was part of the mysterious greatness of her daddy; his way of not really listening when spoken to, and his manner of gazing pensively out the window and into the distance. Besides, this was also his manner with grownups! He never said anything about himself, but only put questions to people and absently listened to the answers, like someone to whom anything people might say was known well in advance and who used the interval of their speech to guess and consider the answer which other people would later give to his future questions.

This great and towering daddy of hers was always the same, or so at any rate it seemed to her, a man free of human foibles and baser needs, free of the pain and cares which are the lot of everyone; while the deep lines of his face and his gray hair appeared to her as marks of a special dignity and extraordinary greatness. Only the godlike creatures on Mt. Olympus, about whom she had begun to hear at school that autumn, might bear some resemblance to him, although they could never be the same.

Just then, in the fall of that year, suddenly and without any warning, her father toppled from his pedestal. At that moment her destiny was broken off and changed. Like the first onset of gloom on a clear day, her father's features grew ashen. He took to staying at home more often, and people came to see him instead; they closeted themselves in his room and held whispered, hour-long conversations.

Her mother, Radoyka, a blond and artless woman of timid spirit and a soft frail body, was unable to offer a satisfactory explanation. And yet, the mystery was revealed to Miss Raika in all its ineffable gravity. At school she happened to get into a senseless argument with a classmate, a strong aggressive

little girl who, like all children of the *nouveau riche*, had no
compunction about speaking her mind. This girl, who was
unusually hefty and clumsy for her years, fell down as they
were playing, and Raika giggled out loud. At that the girl
flushed furiously, picked herself up and said in front of everybody: "What are you laughing at? Laugh at your father!
He really took a tumble!"

"My father doesn't tumble," she said.

The little fat girl laughed spitefully. "Your father is
broke. Everyone knows that. He didn't just tumble, he pulled
the others down with him too. Ask anybody!"

It is these brief and vicious flare-ups in a schoolyard, these
first astounding and wounding human words, which one can
never forget afterwards, for those that come later in life
merely twist the knife in the original wound.

Broke! Her father had failed and they were all talking
about it; she was the only one who knew nothing and had not
guessed it. What sort of failure was it, where did it stop?
What happened to those who failed? Especially if they tum-
bled from the same great height her father must have fallen
from.

That day she came home with a deep frown on her brow,
took a better look at her mother, whom even then she regarded as a weak and helpless child, and approached her
father as a "fallen man" for the first time. She could not understand how, where, and why this thing had happened, but
now her terrible and unbelievable knowledge seemed to find
fresh confirmation at every step. Her father stopped going
out altogether and the doctor became a daily visitor. Father
never left his room; he drew up papers and reports with his
bookkeeper Veso and held quiet conversations with merchants

who were his associates. Then even that stopped. Except for the doctor and the nearest relatives, there were no more visitors. Her mother wept all day long. And when they built the first fire in the big tile oven, her father took to his bed. As soon as she came home from school, she would sit down beside him. He had lost weight and had grown dark in the face, strange, unshaven like that, his neck bare, his Adam's apple jutting out, his eyes burning. He said nothing, and she dared not ask him anything. She only felt the need to sit next to him, perfectly still, her lips parched and drawn, with a thin dark wrinkle between her brows which showed no signs of vanishing.

It was during one of those winter days that she took the strange and fateful vow which was to influence her life. Her father beckoned her to the bed, then propped himself on his elbows with a great effort, passed his hand over her head as once he used to do, and told her in a quiet voice: "Daughter, it's time that you and I had a talk. I always thought that I'd go on and on . . . that nothing could touch me. I'd no idea I would have to leave you like this. And now . . . well, here we are! You are a sensible little girl and ought to know how things are, and pretty soon a time will come when you'll have a better understanding of everything. No, don't cry. Listen well and remember what Daddy is telling you. From now on you'll have to be your own father and mother, because your mother . . . well, you know what she's like, a good woman but soft. I will not leave you in disgrace. I've coped with my obligations, and even those that were not my responsibility. I want you to remember that. But I can't leave you anything except this house in which we live and the store in Churchiluk and your insurance with Adria which will mature in three years, when you're eighteen. You can use it as dowry or money to live on, whichever you wish and decide. No, please don't cry. You're my big girl, you'll arrange everything nicely and sensibly, I know. Master Mihailo, your godfather, will be your guardian. Obey him and respect him. And you'd better start getting used to thinking with your own head and making your own decisions and looking after your affairs by yourself."

At that point her father pulled himself more upright, put his face close to her ear, and began to tell her, in a calm and solemn voice, strange things which she had not heard before. Only his pain, which he carefully concealed from her, interrupted his speech now and then. His long talk was one of those monologues which men speak in times of great stress or at the moment of death, when mankind and the world at large are seen in a warped and singular light. And she heard him with dry eyes, holding back her sobs and whimpers, absolutely numbed by the magnitude of the moment—a moment in which the as yet obscure but all-encompassing secret of human existence in society was opened up before her.

"You are going to be alone, because your mother won't look after you; if anything, you'll be looking after her. That's why you've got to understand and remember well what I'm going to say to you. You must understand once and for all, and don't ever forget it, that a person who doesn't know how to strike a balance between his income and his expenses according to the demands of his life is headed for certain ruin. If you're unable to do this, no legacies or money-making or possessions will do you any good. Your income doesn't depend on you alone, but on various other people and circumstances as well, but your thrift is entirely up to you. To it you should devote all your attention and all your strength. When it comes to thrift, you must be merciless with yourself and others. It is not enough to skimp oneself and one's needs, because that's only a minute part of thrift. Above all, and at all times, you must suppress those so-called higher considerations, those lordly habits of inner gentility, delicacy, and high-mindedness. People who are about to deceive us put some rather fancy names on these weaknesses of ours, and they count with them when they approach us, but they consume all the fruits of our ability and endeavor and they are most often the reason for our lifelong slavery to poverty and sometimes our total ruin. These are the things you must ruthlessly pluck out of your heart, for the habit of thrift should be ruthless, like life itself. In my own life I used to think differently and do the opposite, and that's why I ruined myself. But now that I can see it with my own eyes, I want my failure to be an example and a warning to you. I know that everything inside you and around you will prod and urge you to do otherwise, but you must not give in to it. Work as much as you can and want to, but try to save, and keep saving always, in everything, and pay no attention to anything or anyone. Our life here is such that people can't improve their lot with work but with thrift.

"And you'd better learn that people are decent and conscientious only toward those who don't depend on them or ask anything of them; because the moment you bind yourself and put yourself in a position of dependence, it's the end of everything, friendship and kinship, reputation and respect. The one thing that stops them is what you hold firmly in your hands, and only insofar as it represents a value, and depending on how well and skillfully you can guard and protect it.

Remember this well. All our emotional responses are at bottom weaknesses, and make us the target and prey of everything around us. Train yourself not to feel the least bit flattered when people praise you, and don't let it bother you when they call you a tightwad, a heartless and selfish creature. The first is a sign for you to be on the alert, the second that you are on the right road. The successful person is not one who is good and unsparing, but the man who can manage to be neither one nor the other and still hold his own against the rest. Actually, the reason why the crowd applauds good and generous men is that they and their ruin are the crowd's means of sustenance. Learn early never to let yourself be confused or seduced by words. Look only at the thing in question; as for the name people have given it, leave that to those who have dreamed it up in order to distract your attention. He who respects himself and looks after his own, is respected and looked after by everybody; you can put your trust in nothing else. Therefore, look after your own, so that, as far as possible, nothing of what you possess should ever, even for a single minute, come to depend on the good will of other people. . . . It breaks my heart to have to leave you so young and inexperienced in this world, which only now, at the end of my life, I have truly got to know, but you can ease my pain by showing that you have understood my advice, and by giving me your word that you will remember it and follow it always, come what may."

Here the patient began to gasp and the little girl, unable to hold back her tears any longer, burst out crying. He pulled her abruptly into his arms; huddling in his embrace, and quite terrified, she swore to him that she would save hard and mercilessly, whether she still lived with her mother, or married, or remained alone, and that she would keep a tight grip on her life and not allow herself to become a victim of her own weakness or other people's greed.

Two days later her father died. It happened at noon. He simply turned to the wall, not saying a word to anyone, not even making a sound. And no one ever learned exactly what had taken place between the dying man and the little girl whose life was only just beginning, or about the fateful pledge he had exacted from his daughter.

And so a new life began. The girl, who had just turned fifteen, and had so far led a sheltered life, grew even more serious and withdrawn. At the end of the year she dropped out of the *lycée*, where she had finished the fifth form. A year later, having attended the usual memorial services, she came out of mourning. She altered and lengthened her old dresses and, before she had a chance to become a real adolescent, began to resemble a hard, self-contained grown girl who knew what she wanted and was concerned only with that, regardless of what the world had to offer or wished to force on her.

Her relatives tried to intervene, to cheer her up and make her change her ways. They invited her over, took her to family gatherings and holiday parties in other people's homes. She went willingly enough for a time. She visited young girls and boys of her own age, and listened unsmiling to their songs, as if they were something alien and incomprehensible, and to their laughter, that infectious, unwarranted, easy laughter which is the precious essence of youth and whose true worth can only be compared with health. She even laughed herself, but the laughter involved only the surface of her face; her laugh was not rueful or anxious but rather absent-minded and insincere, and the short deep wrinkle above the hollow of her nose remained untouched. By the same token, no one could persuade her to learn dancing or to invite her school friends to her place for entertainment, or to buy herself some new dresses that would be a little more in fashion. Even though still very young, she already stood out among the girls of her own age as a complete and distinct female type. By the strange logic of social life and feminine nature, she seemed to exert a fascination on her girl friends, rather than the opposite. As her clothes became more drab and outdated and as her manner grew less feminine and attractive, the sympathy of her pretty, trim girl friends seemed to grow in proportion. With her hair brushed straight back, using no powder or make-up on her face, her hands never gloved, wearing the same old dress and shoes all the time, she was popular and well thought of, perhaps the only girl in Sarajevo for whom no one had a word of criticism or reproach.

But with all that, they soon fell out of the habit of regarding her as a young girl, and passed over her when it came to arranging a dance or a lovers' intrigue, or those changeable but important cabals concerning engagements and marriages. For when a person separates himself from society on his own accord, the latter is apt to exclude him from its affairs without too much regret or prompting; moreover, society will take care to prevent his return to the fold, even if he should change his mind.

For another year or two, her relatives and a few friends tried to make her change her ways and to talk her into abandoning her eccentric behavior, so that she might keep in step with her contemporaries while there was still time. But she only shrugged and smiled noncommittally, then quietly went on as before.

Among those who tried their utmost to bring her into society and get her accustomed to entertainment and the social whirl was her maternal uncle, Vladimir Hadzi-Vasich, "Uncle Vlado."

Her mother had four brothers. The oldest, George, had gone to Belgrade when still a very young man; he had done well there, opened his own shop and married. The two younger brothers, Vaso and Risto, jointly took over the old family firm in Sarajevo and were living in much the same style and circumstances as their parents had. The youngest brother, Vladimir, who had graduated from the business school, had no thoughts of joining his older brothers' establishment; he preferred to live as a gentleman of independent means and was fond of expensive entertainments and good things. He was barely four years older than Miss Raika, for he had been born three years before his sister, Miss Raika's mother, was married. Cases like this were not uncommon at one time, when women bore many children and girls married very young. Miss Raika remembered him as a child, though her most durable recollection of him was as a young man in his nineteenth year, tall, fair-haired, handsome, easily given to laughter, amiable, and full of life. That was in the years immediately following her father's death.

They were close friends, she and Vlado. He was good and attentive to her, his attitude a blend of brotherly affection and fatherly concern. With him she went out to dinners and entertainments in the homes of relatives and friends, and from him she received her finest presents. Never before or afterwards had she known a man who so passionately loved to give presents and was so deft in choosing exactly the gift that best accorded with the wishes of the recipient, one that was bound to give him the most pleasure. He was indeed a marvelous person but cursed by God; a friend to everyone except himself. Even to this day, more than thirty years hence, she could still tremble at the memory of that gay young man, and her heart would grow heavy at the thought of his morbid and irresistible passion for giving things away, for scattering his strength, his health, money, fortune, the fatal speed with which he distributed his largesse, his incomprehensible desire to rid himself of everything, to strip himself absolutely bare, as if each object he possessed attained full value in his eyes only when he gave it away and saw it in someone else's hands. Even today she could feel that motherly tenderness she had once had toward him; she could still experience the slight dizziness that used to overcome her at the sight of that living whirlpool of prodigality, that mad squandering and frivolous throwing away. For although he had been her uncle and her senior by a few years, he had always seemed to her like a small and weak child, incapable of finding his bearings and helping himself, who only needed to be offered a hand to pull himself out of the whirlpool; and yet there was no one who could do it, or knew how to, not even she. It was pathetic and a sin to watch him ruin himself.

He lived on like this for several years, a young man with unbridled ways and an angelic face, and in that time he managed to spend and give away all he had, including himself. In his twenty-third year, he died of tuberculosis, which was providential and fortunate for him, for it was hard to imagine what his life would have been without the possibility of further spending and giving. And that had been pretty nearly exhausted.

In the family, his memory remained as a frightening example to young men who were growing up. For Miss Raika, he was to this day a tender and terrifying memory, a question destined never to be answered. How was it possible to find in a person, inseparably bound, the most contradictory qualities of mind and body: generosity, good looks, and goodness side by side with indolence, dissipation, and an extravagance bordering on the pathological? The person who had been dearest to her in life was afflicted to an unnatural degree with a vice which to her was graver than any sin and blacker than death itself: the lust to squander! How could a man be so richly endowed with all manner of things, and at the same time such a senseless and lavish spendthrift? If there was anything bright and lofty in this life of hers, which consisted of petty worries, work, saving, and a determined solitude, it was the recollection of her uncle. And preserved in that memory, too, was some of that selfless pain and pure womanly tenderness of which, despite her peculiar, coarse way of life and her eccentric nature, she still felt herself capable.

In her daily and relentless struggle against expense and waste over the years, his countenance kept reappearing in her mind, enigmatic and frightening, yet also near and dear, like her own flesh and blood. This evening, too, when in the first onset of dusk her darning thread had started to blur and soften in her fingers, Uncle Vlado rose up before her as he always did, neither sad nor unhappy, as he should have been, but radiant, full of joy, and with a warm smile on his lips, selfless, forlorn, and culpable. She gave him a searching look full of heartfelt sorrow and utter perplexity, in which, however, there was no fear. He was as he had always been—a disarming sinner! And he would remain like that forever. His blue eyes, with their restless glint, looked on as if they were about to melt and offer themselves as a gift; and the shock of fair hair above his forehead shimmered and shone as if bent on spilling and lavishing itself on space.

As in a strange dream, she saw him quite clearly, there in front of her. She felt the need to cry out to him, to call him, to arrest his headlong rush to self-destruction, but he passed on with a smile, buoyant, adamant in his mad suicidal resolve to hand out all he possessed in the worst and most undignified way, regardless of whether anyone needed it or not.

Miss Raika did in fact give a little cry, for, trying to loop a stitch on the stocking, she had pricked the index finger of her left hand with the needle. This dispelled the phantoms of her youth and brought her for a moment to the reality of the present.

The room was sunk in twilight, cold and desolate after the bright visions. Wan and helpless, it seemed to her, were the efforts to save and conserve in the face of general extravagance, cheating, and chiseling. Depressing and futile to have to struggle against them, yet impossible to give up the struggle and capitulate. She went back to her darning. The fire in the stove was dying out, darkness reigned in the room. Miss Raika edged closer and closer to the window, feeling colder and colder as she did so. She thought of switching on the light, but changed her mind, took herself in hand, and went on working and tiring her eyes in the growing dark. Five minutes passed in this way. The clock ticked off the saved seconds, and she reflected with satisfaction: There, had I given in to my first impulse and put on the light, it would now have burned needlessly for five minutes! But with a little strain, I can still see and distinguish every thread. How well she knew this! There was always room for more economies, one could stint a little on everything, one's time, warmth, light, food, and rest. Always—even when it seemed truly impossible.

Occupied with these thoughts, Miss Raika cheerfully consumed her eyesight in place of the electric current, until her eyes began to water and darkness raveled her thread. At that point it was really hard to see. Still, before she put on the light, she sat like this for some minutes, her hands folded above her work, in the painful but exalting knowledge that the ultimate frontiers of thrift are nevertheless beyond reach. The thought made her wistful but failed to dishearten her. No matter how distant and inaccessible those frontiers were, they were still more deserving of effort, self-denial, and sacrifice than any other goal she might have set herself.

In the first gloom of the evening this seemed to her crystal clear and self-evident—more so than in daytime when the sun was shining, or at night when the lights were on.

In her present life, which was unruffled by outside events and visible changes, all was plain and clear as a clear day, all distances seemed close at hand. And in this near-darkness beside the guttering stove, with the finished work in her lap, all phenomena seemed to become even more lucid and vivid. The past was close at hand, memories flocked back of themselves. She loved to remember her beginnings. They were, so to speak, a time of poetry in her life.

CHAPTER TWO

THE FIRST MONTHS AFTER HER FATHER'S DEATH HAD BEEN grievous but majestic, like the chords of a funeral march which are sad and at the same time uplifting, for they seem to say that it is in the nature of life to go on living even while plunged in mortal sorrow.

Already in those days Miss Raika's life was beginning to take on its unmistakable direction, and did so swiftly and apparently for good.

It was then still an unusual thing for a woman, especially one of her age, to take care of her own affairs and to go around personally to various offices to discuss things with business people. But her case was looked upon as exceptional, and was accepted as such. They were all quite familiar with this slender young girl with intense dark eyes and pale cheeks, poorly dressed, totally unaware of fashion and free of the woman's need for adornment and beautification. They all knew that her father, Master Obren, had gone bankrupt and died a victim of his own goodness and his strict, old-fashioned ideas of a merchant's honor. So they received her accordingly; and she, in turn, made good and prudent use of it. She went to see them with her modest requests or specific demands—unsmiling, never saying a word too many. The majority went out of their way to help this melancholy girl who seemed to be the victim of particularly bad luck. In this way, she managed to accomplish many a useful transaction and to bypass many legal strictures. Her problems were solved in the smoothest and most favorable way, and she received the sort of valuable advice which ordinarily was denied to a businessman. As a result, she succeeded after a while in settling, very favorably, the obligations she had inherited from her father and she cleared up many doubtful points in his bookkeeping, paid several debts that had been given up as bad, and cashed some papers which, had they been lying in someone else's safe, might have been considered useless.

In these transactions, she was greatly helped by her tutor and godfather, Master Mihailo, and by the director of the Union Bank, Dragutin Paier.

Master Mihailo was a sickly and tired man, descendant of an old merchant family of Sarajevo, in which tuberculosis exacted a steady toll without ever wiping out the family. There was hardly a year when one or another member of the family was not a patient in a sanatorium somewhere in the Austrian Alps or down on the Adriatic coast, and this included their sons and daughters and lately their grandchildren as well. From the business point of view, also, the position of their house was shaky and complicated. But Master Mihailo's greatest cross—one he never spoke about—was his oldest son. This quiet and unusually talented young man, endowed with a restless mind and the handsome frail body of a saint, had been for six years the most brilliant student at the Sarajevo Gymnasium, a highly precocious youngster, before he took to writing poetry and neglecting his studies, after which he finally ran away to Serbia without completing his baccalaureate. Now he lived in Belgrade, as a poet and a Bohemian. For many long months father and son had corresponded copiously and to no avail, but now even this contact had been broken off. Illness, sorrow over his son, and business worries had sapped and exhausted Master Mihailo, but they had given his visage a certain pained dignity; his face, with its large brown eyes which were constantly inflamed with all that hurts and oppresses man but that decency and one's position require to be borne in silence, resembled the faces in the Spanish paintings of the "Golden Age."

Master Mihailo did all he could to insure that Master Obren's widow and daughter had a roof over their heads and food to eat and that they felt their tragic loss as little as possible. In this he was abetted by virtually all the Serbian merchants in the Sarajevo bazaar, by all relations, friends, and admirers of the unfortunate Master Obren. Particularly conspicuous among the last was a foreigner, director Paier of the Union Bank of Budapest. This man with a German name was a person of indeterminate race and without a real nationality. His father had been a German from the province of Banat, domiciled at Osiek, his mother a Croat from a noble family which set much store by its noble title. Her father's mother had been a Rumanian, her maternal grandmother a Hungarian. Usually in people such as these different and irreconcilable kinds of blood are apt to clash and fight one another, but in this man they seemed to flow quietly side by side to create an unusual and harmonious whole.

He was a tall, striking man, with thinning gray hair, large blue-gray eyes, soft and ample in his movements, both in his walk and speech. He was married to a Hungarian, a wealthy eccentric woman who lived away from his home, on her paternal estate somewhere in Hungary. They had an only son, a good-looking boy who also was away at school in Hungary. Considering his ability and connections, Paier could long have occupied a more important post than his present one, he might perhaps have been a member of the board at the bank's head office in Budapest, yet he not only was cool to the idea but insisted on remaining at Sarajevo, where he had grown roots and become part of local life. He had a richly and tastefully furnished apartment in Logavina Street. He was a passionate hunter and excellent tennis player, had a fine collection of old arms and folk embroidery, and a good library in several languages. He bought old pictures and helped young Bosnian painters, though never expressing an opinion about their work. As for the bank, which was one of the biggest in Sarajevo and located in its own handsome building on the river quay, he ran it as though it were a relaxing hobby, quietly, yet competently and well.

Besides his business dealings with the late Master Obren, Paier had also been his good friend for many years. After Obren's death, he thought it his duty to help the man's widow and daughter and make it easier for them to find their way. And he went about it simply, without commotion or many words, as was his habit in all things.

Thanks to these people, and to the almost masculine perseverance of Miss Raika herself, the legacy of Master Obren Radakovich was settled in due course in the best possible manner and the problem of his family's security and maintenance was favorably resolved.

All of Master Obren's business outside Sarajevo was liquidated, while in Sarajevo itself the firm of Obren Radakovich was taken over by his manager of many years, Veso Ruzich, on the understanding that he would work for the successors at a reduced salary. Business, naturally, fell off, but the small store at the entrance to Churchiluk Street remained —cramped, clean, badly lighted, and empty, with its large old sign above the entrance: *Obren Radakovich, broker and agency representative. Founded 1885.* Underneath, in modest small letters: *Veselin Ruzich, owner.*

This man, who had always been known in the bazaar as "Master Obren's Veso" and whom even now no one thought of calling Master Veso, had spent his life in the shadow of his employer and found it perfectly natural now to continue working in the shadow of his name, to preserve what was left and to serve the dead man's family. Veso was an orphan of uncertain origins, born somewhere in a village, stunted and short of figure, but pudgy and round-cheeked, virtually beardless, with a thin voice and a pink, prematurely lined face. This small man, who alongside his late employer had seemed to have no will of his own and no independent initiative, was in fact a hard-working, soft-spoken little peasant. He dressed simply, but was neat and trim in appearance. He was married to a woman called Soka, who was as small, blond, and pudgy as he. They lived in the residential quarter of Sarajevo, in a modest little white house that "sang" with order and cleanliness and had flower boxes in the windows and flowering perennials in its miniature courtyard. They were childless and led a quiet harmonious life, like a couple of turtledoves.

Now, following the death of his employer, Veso sat in the store all day long, alone and worried like a foundling. Missing the support of Master Obren, he felt abandoned and inadequate, although his mind did the best it could and his small eyes and delicate red hands were constantly on the move. In this adversity, he proved himself not only loyal but, in his own way, smart and judicious too.

Soon after the death of her father, Miss Raika began to drop in almost daily at the store. There, together with Veso, she went over the books and accounts and talked about this and that. With a frown furrowing her forehead, calm and laconic, she familiarized herself with bookkeeping, correspondence, and with the whole system of business. In vain did her friends point out that this was no occupation for a woman, much less for one of her years. Every day she spent an hour or two in the store with Veso, not so much because she had no confidence in him—no one would ever entertain such thoughts about Veso—and not because business required it (there was precious little of it just then), but because she wanted to learn, to know, to see also this side of the mechanism that had claimed her father's life, a mechanism she was getting to know better and better as she visited the various banks and authorities while settling her small insecure estate. And the very act of sitting in the drafty half-lit store, next to this man Veso who himself was like a living memory of Master Obren, gave her the feeling that she was carrying out the promise she had made to her father.

In addition to the store and her dealings with the business

people and visits to the authorities, Miss Raika never for a moment forgot the house itself. Here, too, as time went on, she set about imposing her will.

The house is now in my hands, she told herself after the memorial service at the end of the first six months of mourning. The words seemed to find an echo in her chest, almost as if something bittersweet and aching had fluttered aloud and swelled into the beat of a second, more powerful heart.

Some days later, she talked to her mother about changing their system of housekeeping. She did not reveal her entire plan—only the parts that concerned Mrs. Obren and which she had to know.

"Father wanted us to economize and so make up for at least some of the harm people have done us. I promised it to him. We had better start doing it right away. From now on, we won't heat the large sitting room or the tile stove in the foyer. We'll heat your bedroom, because that's where you sit and spend most of your time. I'll look after the servants, the food, and everything else from now on. You'll be able to take it easy and do your embroidery."

Widow Radoyka burst into tears. These days she burst into tears no matter what one said to her. And anyway, she could hardly yet grasp the full significance of the words.

The following month Miss Raika called in Simo, the boy who took care of the horses and cattle, cut firewood, brought water, and did all the menial jobs. He had joined the household at the time of Master Obren's marriage. He was single, without wife or family, a husky, unassuming, good-natured man, the kind of whom one says he was made to be a servant and to lead the life of his masters. He stood before her, rubbing his fierce brown mustaches with the back of his left hand.

"I asked to see you, Simo, because I want to tell you that father's death has changed a good many things in our house. People took away not only what was theirs, but ours as well. So we have to do the best we can to get along."

"Oh, we'll manage somehow, Miss Raika."

The girl went on as if she hadn't heard him: "We'll have to sell the horses and the cows, and so we won't need a stable boy."

"What? How do you mean?"

"What I am driving at is this. You can stay on here till January first and in the meantime start looking for another place."

Simo turned and glanced around, as if looking for someone grown up and sensible rather than this young girl who didn't know what she was saying. "But I thought now's the time you need a man around the house. I'm not asking for wages. Week before last it was seventeen years since I joined the late master, bless him. Why, for his sake, I wouldn't dream of leaving you and Madam alone, even if I had to live on bread and water." His voice thickened and a shadow fell across his eyes.

Again the girl felt an odd flutter in her breast, a sweet and dangerous tug, like someone teetering over a great height. This made her hesitate, but immediately afterwards she remembered that this was one of those moments of weakness about which her father had talked on his deathbed; she drew her head higher and said in a colder and sharper voice than she intended: "I know that you were always good, Simo, and that father was fond of you, but I'm afraid the times are getting to be such that it's better for you to look for a job as soon as possible."

The burly man left confused and downcast, and the girl next called Theresa, the cook. She too had been part of the household for six years: an energetic woman, a little peremptory and sharp of tongue, like all good cooks the world over. Raika braced herself and stiffened even more, as if for a big test.

"Theresa, you know that we lost everything when father died. So we've got to change our entire way of living. There'll be no more guests, no more big cooking in our house. Your work from now on will be much less, and moreover I'm going to work with you. We can no longer afford expensive help. I've already given notice to Simo. We are quite willing to keep you on at a salary of twenty kronen a month, instead of twenty-four as up to now. If this suits you, you can stay on. Think about it till tomorrow and then tell me. From now on I'll be in charge of the money for the house needs. For the next few weeks you and I will go to the market together every morning."

This caused shock and genuine consternation not only in the household but also among neighbors and even distant relatives and acquaintances. Several relatives warned Miss Raika's mother not to allow the immature and capricious slip of a girl to throw her weight around the house. But all the mother could do was either cry or smile. Master Mihailo also arrived and counseled the girl not to do things rashly, for although their situation was serious, the trouble was not so great as to warrant the shutting up of the entire household. The girl replied calmly that she knew best what her father had told her at the moment of his death, and even though she was not old enough to make some decisions, in her own home she could act and do as she pleased.

After the New Year, Simo indeed left the house. Theresa remained another two months, at the reduced wage, but could not hold out much longer. Miss Raika went to the market with her, paring the expenses a little more every day, steadily whittling away at the quantity and quality of the purchased groceries. In the end, Theresa's cup overflowed. She took tearful leave of Mrs. Obren, the mother, and afterwards spread word in the neighbors' sculleries that she would rather serve a regiment of hussars than that monster of a child, who was sure to end up as the witch in a harrowing children's tale if she didn't mend her ways.

Miss Raika engaged a young country girl to do all the housework. She and her mother took over the cooking. Relatives and friends of Miss Raika's who at first volunteered advice, soon grew tired of her obstinacy and let her do as she wanted. And what she wanted she did methodically and with patience. She carried out each one of her decisions swiftly and implacably, although she fretted over it for a long time before making it, and in the intervals between these single decisions she sometimes allowed much time to elapse; time, in fact, helped her not only to put her decisions into effect, but helped her to shape new ones as well.

While her uncle Vlado was still alive, he managed to talk her out of some exaggerated economies and to force her to keep up her connection with the world, however tenuous. He brought gifts to her mother—his sister—so that she would feel as little as possible the tight fist and austere moods of her daughter. When he was around, one could still laugh and banter, for he was one of those people to whom it was hard to deny what they asked and easy to forgive when they were in error. And even the constant wrangling between him and Miss

Raika, occasioned by her passion for thrift and by his spend-thrift ways, was gay and good-humored.

When they least expected him, he would breeze into the house and find Raika hard at work, her hair in a wrap, dusty, and covered with soot up to her elbows.

"Come on, get ready. I'm going to take you to the park for ice cream. There's a whole crowd of friends over there."

"My God, look at me. The weather was good, so I thought I'd clean out the attic."

"The attic won't run away. Go on and get dressed. The carriage is waiting."

"Carriage! Dear God, you really are going to end up in the madhouse!"

She shot a glance through the window and saw the spanking-new fiacre and the driver with his red fez and a flower tied to the tip of his whip. The very thought that the coachman was hired by the hour, and that each moment's waiting increased the expense, gave her a stab of unbearable pain, almost as if blood were draining out of her drop by drop. She put her hands over her face, so as not to look at him or the carriage, and cried shrilly, to drown out his laughter: "No, I don't want to see you or him, Vlado, I'm really very angry!"

"That's the way I am. Take me or leave me."

"I'd just as soon leave you." But who could remain angry for long or keep a straight face in his presence?

They began to chase each other and laugh and scuffle around the room. At last they made a bargain: he would dismiss the carriage (for she could not bear the thought of the expensive wait), and she would go to bathe and change. Afterwards, they set out on foot through the city. He smiling and handsome in a white suit of Japanese silk, with a rose in his buttonhole, and she sullen, tense, her hair combed back in a fashion for which there was no name, her skirt longer in the back than in front.

And, sometimes, much stranger and crazier things happened, because where he was concerned no marvel was ever out of the question or truly impossible. One early morning he suddenly appeared in their house, bleary-eyed, covered with dust, with a grin on his face and a kid lamb in his arms.

"You're always telling me I moon around doing nothing for a living," he told them with a grin. "Here, I've gone into business and agriculture. I bring you the first fruit of my work."

And as he sat down and told them the story, they could see what he meant.

With a couple of cronies, who were like himself, he had gone to Bosnia Springs. They had spent the night there over drink and music. ("What's a summer's night? Nothing. Before you've turned around, it's gone!") At dawn they had piled into a carriage and started back for Sarajevo. On the way they came across a large flock of sheep, some of which had just been weaned. Their fiacre pushed with difficulty through the thick and swaying pack that was reeking of wool, milk, and dust. At first they were infuriated, but then the spectacle began to interest them.

Young men who had spent the night in drink and song are apt to feel expansive in the first blush of a summer dawn. They have a powerful craving for adventure. At those moments, there is no notion that will not occur to them, or one that they are not prepared to carry out. One of the companions suggested that they jointly buy up the entire flock of sheep, drive it to Sarajevo and sell it there, then divide the proceeds.

The idea was greeted with enthusiasm by all three. The driver in charge of the sheep was a hired hand, and he told them that the owner lived at Alipasha's Bridge. When they got there, the latter turned out to be a cunning peasant speculator, who at first turned down the offer of the young gentlemen revelers. But when they earnestly and stubbornly insisted that the "deal be consummated," he began to raise the price. The haggling ended in a ridiculous sale, at least 300 per cent over the prevailing bazaar price. The young men emptied their pockets of all cash to purchase sixty-one rams and eleven lambs, then drove their flock in the direction of Sarajevo. Along the road they sobered up and began to regret their folly even before they reached the town. As it was market day, they dropped in at the cattle market. There they learned that it was not easy to dispose of so large a flock all at once. When they grew bored with the whole thing, they picked a stranger and left him in charge of the sale. The upshot, naturally, was a tremendous loss.

Miss Raika laughed at the foolishness, yet she also felt like crying at the frivolous wanton carousing of these young men who certainly were old enough to be heads of families and households. At the same time she wanted to know how much they had paid for each head of sheep and what the total loss amounted to. But Vlado laughed it off and, by way of answer, thrust his quiet white lambkin in her face.

The lamb remained in their house, grew quite tame, and lived with them like a puppy. They became so fond of it that they could not face the thought of slaughtering it, and eventually they sold it to a butcher.

Not long afterwards, Uncle Vlado began the last year of his life, his twenty-third, a hard year, ugly with debts, litigations, bailiffs, with things going from bad to worse and culminating in illness. He died in Dubrovnik, all alone in a hotel; on the second day of his arrival, he choked on his own blood. The hotel valets carried off the few valuable things he still possessed. Even his deathbed was the most expensive he could have chosen!

After that, Miss Raika grew more and more solitary. She herself could not say how this happened, or when, or for what reason. Her closest friends saw her less frequently. Friends of her mother's still kept dropping in for a while. But when she realized how much coffee and sugar went into these idle chitchats, Miss Raika took to locking the pantry shelf and carrying the key with her. So these visits, too, became less frequent.

Now only the cousins and relatives, from both the father's and mother's side, still came in occasionally, obeying the powerful laws of blood which go on even when everything else comes undone, in keeping with the old tenet of middleclass families: "He may be what he is, but he is ours." They came reluctantly and filled with all kinds of fears, wondering every time what unpleasant surprise might be in store for them. For this house, which once was hospitable and sparkling with the sort of warm opulence that was less a matter of money than an expression of the big heart and innate nobility of its owner, was now growing colder and more forbidding by the year.

While nothing had been removed from the house, all items of furnishing that were likely to wear out through use, or those that could be put away, were placed out of reach of human hands, human feet, and, as far as possible, human eyes as well. Miss Raika felt that if these objects were safely under lock and key in the various chests and closets, they so to speak became partners in her economy drive, while those that were left in use were bound to diminish a bit every day, since every touch and every gaze of strange eyes wore away another little particle. She looked upon the first group of objects as an investment that multiplied itself in secret, and upon the second as a principal which, exposed to light and undefended, kept crumbling and melting away and spending itself, creating in the process new expenses of its own.

Yet even the house effects that remained in use underwent a strange kind of transformation. Objects stood around as if quarreling among themselves. While one couldn't say that the house was unclean or neglected, it was a far cry, just the same, from that bright healthy cleanliness that had been the gleaming hallmark of a happy home, for excessive parsimony is one of those obsessions that in time bring physical squalor in their wake. For the moment, the house was still "living off" its earlier cleanliness. But the first omens were not wanting. In all the rooms and around every object there was an unmistakable air of morose listlessness, a cold and stony brooding that seemed to thicken by the day. Gradually, but relentlessly, the objects seemed to shed, with each day and hour, something of their luster and warmth; they filmed over with a gray tarnish, the first harbinger of grime. One could see at a glance that the things were kept clean only to an extent to which no one could say that they were dirty; all that was asked of them was the bare function for which they were made, without which life would not be possible. Their appearance reminded one of the furnishings in the rooms of Moslem religious schools, or some Christian convent, or the household of a solitary eccentric who lived only for an idea

for the sake of God, the rest of the world gave them generously.

Operating on a fixed order of movement and timetable, they appeared in certain houses on certain days, even sometimes at a certain hour; they received *their* coin or *their* piece of bread, as if this were a share of that homestead to which they had an unwritten but sacred right; then continued on their way, heaping their blessings on the inmates, blessings that were more than empty words, and leaving behind a more acute sense of happiness for all that God had given, which neither men nor bad fortune could take away and which charity and compassion were certain to protect and preserve.

The meaning and purposes of this beggary are not the same as those in the countries of western Europe. There beggars are often reprobates, parasites, and cheats, who prey on their victims, while our variety (in our oriental understanding anyway) are themselves victimized, creatures who heft on their backs the inescapable load of human misery and by dint of it have a claim on the rest of mankind, on the happiness of the happy and the riches of the rich. Our kind of beggary has its own rationale, and is intimately bound up with the concept of human destiny among our middle and trading classes, and with our way of life and worldly acquisition. It represents a sort of necessary, ancient and established exchange between those who have and can give and those who are unfortunate and needy, a natural and recognized method of supplementing and correcting a state of affairs which otherwise no one would know how to try to improve. For that reason, and by a tacit hoary convention, beggary is looked upon as justified and beneficial, indispensable alike to those who give and those who receive.

In this house, over the last eighteen years, beggars had been received magnanimously and given ample gifts. That was well known. But this, too, now began to change. Still, Miss Raika was quick to see that here she could not be as brusque and thorough as she had been in the matter of hired help. Her mother, who gave way in everything, balked long and obstinately over this one point. Giving alms to mendicants was to her a profound and sacred ritual; she had learned the habit in her father's home, and continued it in her husband's. She could not conceive of any tampering with the sacred custom as long as there was a crumb of bread in the house. So Miss Raika dared not break the tradition all at once; but she took the job of almsgiving into her own hands, like everything else.

The beggars felt the change right away. She now received them in her own way: cool and stern, eying them sharply to see which of them deserved help and which didn't, studying their rags for signs of cunningly hidden possessions and their bodily disfigurements for insincerity and dissimulation. The majority of these tramps, having known her since childhood, greeted her with waving hands, with mumbling, or with a pauper's obsequious grin, expecting in vain that she would smile back.

When she made sure that the wretch was really old and helpless and that there was no excuse with which she might turn him away, she shut the house door and went to the kitchen. There she took a piece of old bread and dried-out cheese and went back to give it to him. However, as she was still unsure of herself and a mere apprentice in the difficult art of thrift and parsimony, she suddenly remembered, while still in the corridor, that the next beggar might be in much greater need, and she returned to the kitchen and deposited the cheese on the pantry shelf. Then, taking the bread alone and looking at it on the way, she decided that the piece was too large and again went back to the kitchen; she broke the loaf in two and left one half in the bread basket. And as she was on the point of going, having decided that the piece was the right size for the beggar, she changed her mind again, reached for the knife once more and cut a thin slice from this piece also. As she dropped it in the beggar's hands, she still kept her eyes both on the bread and on the man's expression, trying in this way to convince herself that she had not made a mistake and given him too much.

To her, any pretext was good and sufficient to deny and turn away a beggar. One of them might forget to close the yard gates, another would bring in mud on his bare feet and soil the fine white gravel that was the pride of merchant court-yards of Sarajevo. Then again, one day she happened to read in the newspapers how a poor woman had died in Paris in rags and penury and afterwards they had found a hoard of 250,000 francs in her straw mattress. For a whole week after-wards that gave her an excuse to turn the beggars from the door and accuse them of hypocrisy and of "sleeping on money."

So it went day after day, month after month. Finally the unspeakable came to pass, a thing that had not happened in living memory in a merchant's house that was still inhabited: beggars began to drop out and in the end stayed away alto-gether. Mrs. Obren complained bitterly: "The poor and the needy don't come to my door any more." She often stood by the window and watched the street in some fear and bewilder-ment; she could then see with her own eyes how familiar beggarly figures slunk past and made a detour of their house, as though it had been struck by plague and abandoned. And as if that were a grievous and irreversible curse, she wept and ate her heart out worse than she could have done over a personal hardship.

Thus Miss Raika freed herself, methodically, one after another, of all the things she considered to be obstacles in her path, a path whose ultimate goal she confided to no one, since she herself could not see it clearly or fully. At last came the day when her insurance policy matured. She was to receive twenty thousand kronen after the first of the year, from an insurance company in Trieste.

And, in fact, at the end of January, Master Mihailo, her guardian, came to see them. He was quiet and unassuming as always, only this time a little more solemn, as if deeply moved by the news he was about to impart. His breath was labored on account of asthma, which interfered with his work and was the bane of his life. He came to tell Raika that the company had paid her insurance and that the money had been deposited in her name in the Union Bank.

Miss Raika took the news without any visible excitement. Only the wrinkle between her eyes seemed to thicken, indicating her strenuous concentration.

The guardian gave her the papers, which showed that the company had paid the whole amount, less taxes and a sum of seventy-six kronen for handling. He told her at the same time that the company, which had been most accommodating throughout the transaction, expected her to give her permission to the Sarajevo newspapers to publish the usual notice commending it on the prompt liquidation and meticulous payment of the policy.

"All right, I'll give my permission. Provided they refund those seventy-six kronen and absorb the expenses themselves. Not otherwise."

Master Mihailo gave the girl a look of surprise, like someone who can't believe his ears and wishes to corroborate with his eyes what he has heard. Patiently he explained to her that it was perfectly in order to have a public commendation appear in the press, and how one couldn't tie that to expenses, which, as the regulations clearly state, were for the account of the insured party. All companies operated on that principle and their fees were well earned; in any case, such a notice would not cost her a penny.

"Perhaps not, but it would be useful to them, and for that they should pay me."

Master Mihailo departed, coughing and shaking his head.

The notice did not appear. And Master Mihailo was in for more and bigger surprises from his goddaughter.

One day soon afterwards Miss Raika dropped in at Master Mihailo's store and, finding him alone, informed him briefly and simply that she intended to take advantage of the law that would enable her, in view of the exceptional circumstances, to obtain majority at the end of her eighteenth year, instead of the usual twentieth. She set out all the arguments she would present to the court: the business of the shop, which had bogged down after her father's death, her guardian's illness and preoccupation with his own affairs, her responsibilities toward her aging mother, her readiness and willingness to conduct her own affairs, which would then certainly proceed more briskly and advantageously. And so she had come to request his approval.

Master Mihailo peered at her with his tired and prematurely aged eyes, in which wonder and a pained surprise were reflected. He began to roll a cigarette. Gazing at his fingers, he said: "Very well, child. Do you find any fault with the way I have handled your affairs?"

"Oh no, Godfather, none whatever. Dear God, no. But you can see for yourself the position we're in. And besides, why should you be saddled with our worries when I'm young and healthy enough to take care of them? I'll always come to you for advice, of course, but it would be better if I looked after our business myself. Anyway, that's what father would have wanted too."

Master Mihailo stared at the girl as if he were seeing her for the first time—as if straining to find in that face an outline of the child he had once known.

In the end he gave his approval. Miss Raika took care of all the rest. Six weeks after that conversation, the lawyer brought her the court's paper officially declaring her to be of age.

On being informed about it, Master Mihailo accepted it with all decency, not showing his displeasure, and hiding his anxiety. "You are now," he told her gravely, "legally free to manage what is yours. Still, you're like my own flesh and blood. I make no distinction between my children and you. Whatever you might need, you can always count on my help and advice. Remember that."

Raika thanked him; she did not, however, volunteer any information on how she intended to manage and use the money she had got from the insurance. Lately she had hardly ever discussed business matters with her guardian; now she avoided such talk altogether. She preferred to talk directly to the person she needed, and only about things she wanted to discuss. She scarcely ever said "Good day" to anyone unless it was necessary. That had been true even earlier, but was especially true now that she had come into her own money.

Master Mihailo was not the only one to wonder. Director Paier and some of the oldest and most experienced merchants could not get over the way she presently took charge of her insurance money, and how swiftly, shrewdly and discreetly she put it to work, in the best tradition of hallowed bazaar economics. She went her own determined way and could not be budged or deflected from it either by flattery or by criticism, and she allowed no consideration to stop her. Her money was beginning to work for her.

Indeed, her money had been working for her for some time.

People could not help noticing that she had long given up the work of liquidating her father's inheritance and was increasingly occupied with new business which she herself had initiated and was directing. And still they all continued to assist her and to receive her as often as she came to them, treating her with exceptional kindness, as Master Obren's orphan.

Now, however, that her resources had suddenly expanded, she had fewer occasions to knock on strange doors. In the course of the next few years she would learn to know people, institutions, and business; she would be able to follow, all by herself, the news and fluctuations of the Sarajevo money market—not the big public one, but the small, clandestine, lively money market which was invisible to most people but all too familiar to the unfortunates, to victims of their own aberrations, to slaves of usurious interest rates and implacable maturity dates.

And, in any case, people were beginning to knock on *her* door.

Sᴀʀᴀᴊᴇᴠᴏ ɪɴ ᴛʜᴇ ʏᴇᴀʀ 1906! ᴀ ᴄɪᴛʏ ᴛʜᴀᴛ ᴡᴀs ᴛʜᴇ ᴄᴏɴ-
tending ground of influences and overlapping cultures, one
in which diverse modes of life and conflicting ideas clashed
head-on! Yet all these various and distinctive classes, faiths,
ethnic and social groups had one thing in common: all
needed money, all needed more of it than they had.

First there was the great mass of little people who did not
possess even the most necessary things. Their existence was
one long desolate craving for, and endless pursuit of, money.
But even among those who had a little, or at least appeared
to, each one desired more than he had. Sarajevo had always
been a city devoted to money, one that needed money, and
now it was more so than ever. The people of Sarajevo, already
burdened with the Turkish legacy of habitual indolence and
with the Slavic hankering for excesses, had lately adopted
the formal Austrian notions of society and social obligations,
according to which one's personal prestige and the dignity of

one's class were measured by a rising scale of senseless and nonproductive spending, often by an empty and ludicrous extravagance that was devoid of all sense and good taste.

It would be hard to imagine a town with less money and shakier sources of income and yet with a greater thirst for money and with less will to work, one with fewer economic skills and with greater appetites and demands. Here the mixture of oriental customs and Central European culture had produced a mode of social life in which the indigenous folk vied with the newcomers in creating new excuses and outlets for spending. The old traditions of self-denial among the poor and of thrift among the well-to-do had long ceased to bind. If there were any people left with the old bazaar habits of moderation and with strict principles of a modest wage and regular thrift, they found themselves outside the social pale, comical remnants of times long gone by.

In this community, then, in which a great and pressing need for money had spun a densely tangled web of debts and usury in all conceivable forms and amounts, Miss Raika set about creating her fortune. People of her kind, who needed less than they had, were so few that they could be counted on the fingers of one hand, while those who had the need of money, either because they were destitute or because they lived above their income, ran into the thousands. Uninterested in social relations and incurious about the organic interplay of causes and consequences, she took her cue from what was visible on the surface, as people dominated by a great passion usually do. It didn't take her long to begin to look upon the whole city and the life around her as her hunting ground, and to lose sight of everything except her craving for prey.

Some years earlier, in her father's store, Miss Raika had

started receiving people who were urgently in need of loans. Beginning modestly and harmlessly enough, the enterprise had grown by leaps and bounds, especially later on, when she came into the insurance money and attained her legal majority. And while her bookkeeper, Veso, paying no attention to her activities, carried on the petty business of the store, haggling with peasants over a few fox pelts, Miss Raika began to experience that joy which "breeding money" gave to people of her bent, that cold intoxication which secretly warmed and illumined the usurers in their musty holes-in-the-wall, better than sunshine, more beautiful than spring. And when the business of loaning money began to grow and the number of callers mounted, she took to seeing them not only in the store but at home too. Naturally this applied only to the selected, important, and distinguished clients.

The mute and joyless house, empty of laughter and conversation, of warmth and ornament, avoided even by beggars, now began to receive new, unusual visitors. One could observe then how different were the types of people whom money, or the need of it, drew together as if by an unseen thread.

For the young girl, in the beginning, each visit was an event for which she carefully prepared herself, and which she remembered long afterwards. But as time went on and the number of those who came because of their urgent needs grew larger, she received them more listlessly, with waning respect and a growing caution and bluntness. (She gained a new insight into the people who, driven by an extreme need or by some overmastering passion, desperately sought loans of money, and learned how weak and helpless they were, ready to do anything, and how one need not treat them with respect and consideration. This was revealed to her right at the start of her activity, by itself as it were, and she made ample and unscrupulous use of the knowledge.)

Winters and summers, Miss Raika sat in her sparsely furnished foyer, at a small table on which there was not a single book, not a single slip of paper, only an ancient inkwell with a cheap pen that harked back to her school days. She sat on a plain hard stool, next to which there was one other, still smaller and harder, for the visitors. The room was not heated even during periods of biting frost.

"Don't take your coat off," Miss Raika would usually say to her visitor, adding in a voice that had something vindictive in it, "because the place is not heated." And having made him thoroughly uncomfortable and placed him at a disadvantage, she would ask him what he wanted, tersely and with a faint air of astonishment, as if he had made a mistake in the house door and the identity of the person he was addressing.

In a great many cases the talk ended with the caller walking out empty-handed, after he had first bared all of his misery and anguish to Miss Raika. With those who, on rare occasions, managed to accomplish something, the matter was usually put off till the following day; and on her desk next morning there would be a sheet of paper with the written conditions for a short-term loan. Depending on the term of maturity, the note was invariably for a figure 10 to 30 per cent higher than the amount which the lender actually received in hand. The remaining stipulations were entirely in accordance with the law—that is, with its extreme provisions. Money was never paid out in the house itself, but in Veso's store, and even through intermediaries; often in a very roundabout fashion, in the office of a money-changer, in front of Imaret Street, or through some petty shopkeeper squatting in a half-empty and to all appearances drab and poor hole-in-the-wall. For deep down beneath the visible and clamorous surface of the society which lived, spent, enjoyed itself, and squandered, there also existed an unseen, unobtrusive, sturdy, and durable network of usury, a mute, nameless, and hardy fraternity of those who had pruned their lives of all that was superfluous and secondary and had discovered a way to something which to their way of thinking was basic and indispensable to society, those who gratified their only passion at the expense of countless little and big passions and lusts of the rest of the world.

With most of these visitors, however, the point of serious, factual negotiations was never reached. Obeying some mysterious but infallible instinct, Miss Raika would interrupt the person in the middle of his explanation, in a firm and ringing voice, and inform him that he had been misdirected, that, indeed, she had had a little money at one time but had loaned it to friends. At that point, usually, the "party" would leave the room (which was icy in the winter and unbearably stuffy in the summer), disappointed at his lack of success but also relieved to have freed himself of the presence of this stern girl with piercing eyes and an athlete's handshake.

It was only on rare occasions that the interview took a different turn, and they were the ones she remembered much longer.

One day in February, the visitor happened to be a tall handsome woman, dressed in a long coat of black silk trimmed with an expensive brown fur around the collar and cuffs. On her head she wore a matching fur cap. Her face was pale and delicate, slightly flushed from the cold and moistened by the humid air, and her eyes were blue. She was a foreigner, a Pole by origin, but had grown up in Bosnia. Her husband was a Croat, a government official, a dandy of proud and haughty bearing, known as a lover of dice and good wine and gay women. Miss Raika knew them by sight and by name.

The young woman opened the conversation awkwardly and in obvious confusion, and then, brushing aside all circumspection and pretense of business experience, began to come out with the truth. Her husband had lost a sizable amount of money in a card game at the officers' casino and had given his word of honor that he would pay it within twenty-four hours. She had telegraphed her parents and her brother, who was a manufacturer in Poland. She had another brother in America, who had sometimes helped them in similar circumstances, but here the problem was time. The sum in question was not too high either: one thousand two hundred kronen, and she was sure to receive it within the week, but it was imperative that the debt be settled by the next morning. Her husband had sunk into some kind of dark apathy and threatened to commit suicide. She had to save him and was willing to agree to any conditions and interest on the loan.

"The person who sent you to me made a mistake, madam," Raika informed her. "I have no money to loan. Whatever I had, I've lent to friends, and I'm now waiting to get it back."

The woman half-rose in her chair. "I beg of you, miss. They told me you could."

"They misinformed you."

"Miss, you are my only hope. Only you can save us."

At that, Miss Raika turned away, hoping by this act to

terminate an unpleasant and futile discussion. As though she had been waiting only for that, the woman burst into tears, flung out her arms, and then clasped her hands almost into the face of the astonished Miss Raika.

"Look, miss, I'm begging you on my knees. In the name of God, I beg of you."

To escape her, the girl shrank back as far as she could on her stool, while the young woman fell to her knees and thrust her whole upper body into her lap. Her words were smothered by her sobbing.

"We'll pay back every penny! For the love of God, don't let us drown! I implore you!"

After her first consternation, Miss Raika managed to pull her knees away, but the woman slumped face down on her shoes, as if someone had cut her in two, and clutched her legs above the ankles. Miss Raika jumped up, pushing the stool behind her.

From that height, she stared down at the woman at her feet, doubled and shaking in a spasm of uncontrollable weeping. For a moment she felt something sweet and warm tugging at her breast, almost like a second, bigger heart. She bent over a little as if to help her up and calm her, but then changed her mind, drew back the outstretched hand, and spoke in a thin unnatural voice: "Don't, madam . . . please! They advised you wrongly, believe me. You don't have a minute to lose, so you'd better hurry and look for money where you'll be sure to find it."

Some time passed before the poor woman got to her feet, still muttering: "Miss, I beg you . . . I implore you, save us! He will kill himself!" She kept repeating it all the way to the front door, but there, all of a sudden, she drew herself up, wiped her face, adjusted her hair, and, without a greeting or another glance, went out.

Miss Raika was left in confusion, almost with a pang of shame, but the sensation was somehow remote and it failed to coalesce. Soon after the incident, however, she was swamped with work and had no time to think about the beautiful unhappy young woman, or to be concerned with her future fate. All she knew was that the young woman's husband did not shoot himself, because some two weeks after the visit she saw them promenading along the Milyacka Quay, arm in arm, snuggled close together. They were of the same height and build, like two siblings, and as impeccably dressed as if someone had clipped them out of a fashion magazine.

And there were other kinds of visitors too.

One day—it happened to be a dry scorching summer day —the narrow stool in the foyer was occupied by a lieutenant of the gendarmery, a Sudeten German by the name of Karasek. He was posted in a small town not far from Sarajevo and was known as a *bon vivant* in the city's night clubs frequented by officers. He had often been disciplined and transferred on account of his messy private life and still messier finances, and now he had been asked to resign.

He was a burly man with large brown eyes and a strong neck encased in fat. He seemed to be bursting out of his uniform. Waftings of barrack soap, mingled with a smell of brandy, exuded from his person. In his right hand he held a pair of new yellow gloves made of deerskin. Speaking German, he opened the conversation in a voice of studied self-assurance typical of alcoholics: "I need money, Miss Radakovich. A biggish amount. I should like to know what your terms are. Two thousand kronen for three months. I believe my pledge would be acceptable."

But Miss Raika never let him explain the details of his pledge, so as not to have him think that her refusal was based on the poor quality of that pledge, and because there was no point in prolonging the conversation unnecessarily. "You'll have to excuse me, but I have no money to lend."

"You don't?"

"No, I don't. I never had. A long time ago there was a modest sum of money, from an insurance policy, and this I have invested. That is all I possess."

The officer's confidence melted visibly. "All?"

"All, Lieutenant."

"All . . ." He repeated the word and transferred the gloves from one hand to the other, clutching them more tightly. "As for the terms—whatever they are—I'm prepared to accept them."

"I'm terribly sorry, Lieutenant, but I have no terms or money to give you."

The officer did not answer; he kept crushing the gloves in his right hand. On his forehead, where the hair had begun to thin noticeably, there appeared tiny beads of sweat, like dew. He stared hard in front of him, past Miss Raika, as if looking for someone behind her. To break the embarrassing silence and his stare, she got up first. (It is easier to bear even the most unpleasant look than a pair of eyes that obstinately ignore us.) The lieutenant started too, almost blushing, cleared his throat, reached for his cap on the desk, then lightly and soundlessly brought his heels together. "So . . . it's nothing. Thank you, miss. Good-bye."

The following Sunday, the *Bosnische Post* carried a brief

notice in small print to the effect that Lieutenant Karasek "passed away suddenly during a tour of duty at Tarchin."

Without having to make any inquiries, Miss Raika learned that the officer had taken poison and that two Sarajevo moneylenders had been left with worthless promissory notes, each to the tune of several hundred kronen. She felt content about having refused him, for he would probably have used the money to pay off his smaller debts and would have spent the rest, and two or three months later the outcome would have been the same, with the difference that she would have remained his biggest creditor. And yet, it was not pleasant to remember the lieutenant, his vacuous, lifeless words, curt and hollow like an echo, and his blind unseeing stare. In the months that followed she often thought about him. This usually happened at the moment when, facing some stranger who needed money, she gave her customary reply that she had no money to lend. The alarming thought would come to her that the person was about to rise, bring his heels together, and say: "So . . . it's nothing. Thank you, miss. Good-bye."

However, the visitor in question would get up in an altogether different fashion, muttering different words, and the sense of foreboding would leave her.

These things angered her and she usually forgot them afterwards, but still, she could never quite free herself of the haunting and senseless fears, nor escape the sense of trepidation, when some "party" or other was taking his leave, that the lieutenant's gestures and words were about to be repeated there in front of her. Quite some time had to pass before she forgot it all completely.

In those early days a few individual callers still stood out like separate phenomena in their own right, exceptional and interesting because of their problems; but after a while all of them began to fuse into a long blurred procession, a gray mass without a face or name that needed money.

Besides, Miss Raika soon realized that she could not go on in this manner, receiving every client in person, and in her own home. Her activity was fast becoming the talk of the neighborhood (it was not loud as yet but the kind that spreads around in whispers among the initiated). Old friends of her father's admonished her several times. Presently these visitors stopped coming to the house and, instead of going to the store where Veso was in attendance, began to drop in at a small shop in Ferhadya Street, kept by a Sarajevo Jew called Rafo Konforti. To this place now came all those who were "temporarily in trouble" and those who sought small loans "for a week"—that is to say, people who were willing to pay back twenty kronen for every ten borrowed after a week, or, failing that, to pay a "late charge" of one krone for every ten per week until they could retire the whole debt together with the over-all interest. Such were the lethal traps that wore the appearance of timely help and relief to the deluded victims.

Visitors were received by Rafo at his little shop, but to those in the know it was no secret that the money obtained here on such terms was in reality Miss Raika's. Indeed, they knew perfectly well that it could never have been Rafo's.

This Rafo Konforti was a ruddy-faced, heavy, excessively fat man, though still very young. Reared in poverty, for his father had been a little tailor with a large brood of children, he had, while still an apprentice in a haberdashery, begun to trade independently on the side, and to wear good clothes and daydream about bold schemes and big "killings."

Among the Sephardic Jews of Sarajevo he had the reputation of an enterprising but erratic young man with too much spirit and too wild an imagination. As soon as he finished his apprenticeship, he opened his own shop in Ferhadya Street. This was a small, nearly empty cubbyhole, in which he sold everything and anything he could lay his hands on. Usually he bought up lots of faded or out-of-fashion haberdasheries and sold them with the help of loud advertising, both printed and spoken—a novel procedure at that time. He would display the merchandise on two wide counters in front of the shop. The walls and windows of the shop would be plastered with red and green posters: "Bargains! Price war! Bargains! Today only!" "Must liquidate at a loss!" "Take advantage of this opportunity!" The greatest advertising attraction was Rafo himself, with that rotund body of his, laughing and red-faced, gyrating like a motor and sending up a whirlwind of talk and merriment all around him. And as he talked, he constantly clapped his fat outstretched hand to his chest and repeated over and over: "Honor of my name!" "By all that's dear and sacred to me!"

Everything that happened in and around the town, every word uttered by the passers-by, merely gave Rafo fresh material for his jokes, chatter, shouting, and self-promotion.

"Stop cheating the poor people, Rafo," some wag would say in passing, just as Konforti was singing the praises of some old neckties to a couple of undecided customers.

"What? What's that you're saying?"

There and then Rafo abandoned his customers, rushed out to the middle of the street, clapping his hands, placed himself squarely in front of the man and barred his way. His dark Spanish eyes glistened wetly, his excitement was more overwhelming than real. "What? I should cheat these good people! Me? By my honor and fortune, we are liquidating at a 10 per cent loss," yelled Rafo, who always used the first person plural.

"All right, Rafo. If you say so," replied the man, wishing to continue on his way.

But Rafo clutched both his hands. "What do you mean, if I say so? Well, I do say so. Come into the shop and let me show you the invoice. Let the invoice speak for itself, my dear sir! Do you want to take a bet on it? I'll put down fifty kronen—a poor man's fifty kronen—against five of your rich ones, and I'll bet you we're selling at a loss."

Rushing up to the counter display, Rafo snatched the necktie with a histrionic flourish, pulled it out straight from end to end, and held it up before the man's eyes. "You see this? Let it rot and stink if we make a single penny on it. Come on in and let's look at the invoice, and if it turns out I'm lying, I'm going to give it all away for nothing."

A crowd began to collect around them. They guffawed and enjoyed the scene; they never tired of it, even though it was a daily occurrence. And there were always a few men among them who were seeing it for the first time, and always some who bought something.

Such had been Rafo Konforti's beginnings. As the years went by, he had grown more serious, more hefty, less mobile; especially when, some three years before, he had married a girl from a rather wealthy and very reputable family from Travnik. And even his marriage had been highly unusual. The girl, who was lovely and an only daughter, had fallen in love with the spirited young man at some Jewish celebration in Travnik. When the parents refused to consider Rafo as a son-in-law, the girl eloped with Rafo, without trousseau or dowry. It was a real honest to goodness elopement, with revolvers coming off (in the dark, wide off the mark), with a loud hue and cry and police intervention. The young couple somehow managed to reach Sarajevo. The parents had no alternative but to give their blessing. Now Rafo and his wife already had two children. However, the bridegroom still nursed a grudge against the parents. He would help them when needed but reluctantly and always through a third party.

Konforti had been one of Miss Raika's original clients, at the time when he first opened his own shop. In the beginning she had loaned him small sums of money, with a good deal of misgiving, under multiple guarantees. But after a while it turned out that, with all his joking and bounciness, he was really less eccentric and more capable than he appeared.

As early as two years before, Rafo had proved himself a useful and farsighted man in her eyes.

One early evening in October 1908, he came to her house and requested an extension of the payment date on one of his notes.

The weather was unusually warm and pleasant. From the balmy night outside, a strange noise came in through the window and mingled with the monotonous sound of their counting. The air vibrated with a solemn and awesome sound. All the bells of Roman Catholic churches seemed to be ringing. The waves of their booming sound were like a counterpoint to the rich and stately voices of a hymn which an invisible throng of celebrants was singing somewhere in the main streets of the town, in the tepid, almost summery dark.

Miss Raika lifted her head and listened.

"Do you hear? Do you know what it is?" Rafo asked quietly, with a note of excitement in his voice, leaning in the direction from which the sounds were coming.

"Yes, I know . . . the Annexation," Miss Raika answered without much enthusiasm.

"That's right; now it's official. Austria-Hungary has annexed Bosnia and Herzegovina. And they've ordered mobilization at the same time. Partial mobilization they call it. Troops are marching to the Serbian frontier—and all the way to the Russian frontier too. Don't you see, now's the time to put your money in gold ducats."

"Everyone knows that. They'll all be doing it."

"Well, not quite," said Rafo quickly. "It's not like that at all. Who says everyone knows about it? And even supposing some people know about it, that doesn't mean they'll be doing it. People are not smart, Miss Raika. They take their sweet time and they're careless. Besides, not all of them have the ready cash. Look, I know about it and I'm telling you, but I'm not buying because I have nothing to buy with. But you, miss, you have. Buy as much gold as you can, I implore you. Invest all the liquid capital you have and you won't be sorry. In a month or two we'll see whether there's going to be a war or not. If yes, you'll be holding gold instead of paper money, and if not, there'll still be time to sell and at a profit. Listen to me, I'm talking to you as a friend, you'll not regret it. If you want me to, I'll buy the ducats for your account. I'm not asking a penny's commission; you can decide about that later, depending on how much you make."

Konforti flipped his hands excitedly as he spoke and his eyes flashed so that they appeared to be almost squinting. He had the distressed air of a man who had no ready money to carry out a sure and profitable operation.

Slowly and cautiously Miss Raika began to buy ducats—chiefly from local Moslem women. (Afterwards she regretted her caution and tardiness.) Rafo, too, obtained them for her account. And sometime during January of the following year, when the international crisis over the Annexation was at its peak, Rafo, like a hunting dog, suddenly gave the signal to sell. Miss Raika balked and argued with him, for the price of gold was still rocketing, but Rafo urged her patiently and insistently to get rid of it as soon as possible, while it was still on the upswing, because in a week or two it was bound to dawn on everybody that war had been avoided and the ducat was sure to tumble just as rapidly. Miss Raika took the middle way, the fainthearted woman's solution: she sold half her ducats at a profit of 30 to 45 per cent, and with the other half she waited to see what would happen. A fortnight later gold indeed began to slump and she just managed to dispose of it in a hurry and still show a gain of 10 to 15 per cent. This reduced the over-all profit on the transaction, but it demonstrated to her at the same time that Konforti was a man on whose opinions one could rely. She gave him a commission of 1 per cent.

It was this Rafo, then, who at the beginning of 1910 took over the visible portion of Miss Raika's business. By that time, there were no more jostling crowds in front of his little shop, no more shouting, no loud and colorful posters, for he no longer dealt in noisy "bargains" but made his living on whispered transactions which were neither seen nor heard. The store carried a modest stock of merchandise, it was true, and there was a young assistant to look after it, but the main business was done by Konforti himself behind a glass partition, where he had a desk, a small iron stove, and a large safe. Here came people who urgently needed a loan, they held whispered conversations with Master Rafo, laid down the jewelry they had brought as collateral, or some other acceptable security, and then took their money and walked out of the shop with a conspicuous air of relief. It was the way of all spendthrifts: whenever, under the pressure of some emergency or passion, they obtained what they needed for the moment, they invariably fell under the illusion that they had shrewdly and forever solved all the problems that harassed them.

Once a month, heavy and short-legged as he was, Rafo would walk all the way to the other end of town to visit Miss Raika. It was the longest walk he ever took, almost an expedition—just as balancing his accounts with Miss Raika was the most difficult part of his business. And as they pored over their account sheets in the front room, Rafo would call heaven to witness that his figures were correct, while Miss Raika would wear her clairvoyant "I can see through it" air; and all Rafo's oaths on his honor and good name, all his heartfelt exclamations and spirited hand-waving, availed him nothing in the end—what counted was the final tally, based on sober reality.

The year 1912, with its Balkan war, brought another crisis and another one of those upheavals in which money was lost and made with equal ease. This time, again, Miss Raika was on the side that gained. Abetted by Rafo Konforti, she again carried out a simple but effective operation with gold ducats, which they purchased from widows or young men of aristocratic families who lived above their income and spurned work and refused to earn their keep. But now the profits were much smaller, since the recurrent crises were no longer acute or clearly defined—they no longer had a beginning that was plain to see and an outcome that was possible to guess; instead they had become tangled and obscure, they crept into every branch of life, and they seemed to peter out at one moment, only to crop up suddenly the next.

And so time fled for Miss Raika, quickly and insensibly. For time only lies heavy and wearying on people who live preoccupied with trivial worries about their own person and enjoyment, but is fleeting and imperceptible to those who submerge themselves in a work that transcends them; measured by the grandeur of a bold and perhaps unrealizable dream, time is all but nonexistent. And Miss Raika had been living for years with a great dream that overshadowed and blotted out everything else. Her dream was always one and the same: to avenge and atone for her father's death. Because she had been unable to save him, she would at least carry out, without mercy and consideration for herself or others, the vow she had made to him—the way she understood it. Over the years this dream of hers had expanded and changed, depending on the goals it set itself and the means it used, without her even becoming aware of it. At present the dream even had a name. It was called "Million."

She had once read somewhere about an American multimillionaire who had started out as a newspaper boy and who was supposed to have said: "The first million is the hardest, afterwards everything comes easy. It's only the man who doesn't want to be a millionaire who doesn't become one. You have to want to be. That's the secret!" This glib and perhaps tongue-in-cheek journalistic blurb struck her as a splendid inspiration. It gave her courage. At that moment, all her confused old longings suddenly had a clear name: million! From then on, the word twinkled before her like a star that never guttered—not by day, not by night, not even in dreams. Bewitched by the distant golden objective, she kept working and saving, daydreaming and plotting in her desolate house, which was beginning to look more and more like a tomb. The road to the goal was long, very long, but this made her thrift all the sweeter, the money she earned all the more sacred. Pitifully few were those who found enough strength in themselves to follow that goal, but the number of those destined to reach it was even more infinitesimal. She knew it only too well. By the same token, she also knew what it meant to be one of those who took the road.

Not one of the people who stared her up and down on the street, or gossiped about her in the various homes, was ever likely to guess the name of her dream. In her turn, living only for and with this dream, Miss Raika walked past them as if they were dead. In all that happened around her and in the world, in all things that animated people, including those nearest to her, indeed in everything that created motion and events between nations and countries, she could hear and grasp only the part connected with her dream: the endless, intricate, and perpetual talk of income and outgo.

To her, the world at large was really two worlds, completely distinct though not entirely separate. One was the ordinary, everyday world, regarded by most people as such, the whole noisy vast land with its inhabitants and their overlapping lives, their longings, drives, thoughts, and beliefs, their everlasting urge to build and destroy, their unfathomable games of mutual attraction and antagonism. And the other, the other was the world of money, a realm of acquisition and capital husbandry, low-voiced and discreet, familiar only to a narrow circle, but with all that a vast region of silent struggle and constant scheming, ruled by the mute twin gods of percentage and bookkeeping. Soundless and unseen, this other realm was not a bit smaller or less diverse than the first. It had its own sun and planets, its dawns and dusks, zeniths and nadirs, its own fallow and fruitful seasons; this world, too, had its inner meaning and derived its great mysterious power from it, it had its own life principle, on which everything was based and around which everything revolved, something that feeble and mortal men could only guess at. This shadowy, antipodal side she regarded as the true face of the world; the other side, the dark reverse of it.

It was a world in which Miss Raika belonged with her whole being and in which, indeed, she wholly existed. Her presence in the other, workaday world was in many ways like that of an ascetic who has long achieved mystical union with the Infinite and found in it his new center of gravity, and who now, in a purely transient and temporary fashion, keeps wandering here among us simply because he has to; wandering lightly and freely with a smile on his lips, for, as far as he is concerned, anything that is outside his real world deserves no more than the kind of smile which grownups bestow on children's games and toys.

Her days, months, and years went by like a dull sound or a distant mist. Her contacts with people and the community were now whittled down to the barest minimum compatible with the demands of her business and income. She had long since turned down the last proposal of marriage; for, in spite of her solitude and the eccentric plainness of her appearance, she had had several young suitors, at least in the beginning. They had ranged from an assistant lecturer in mathematics, a modest and shy man, to a storekeeper, a young widower with two children. All had received the same treatment: she turned them down to a man, curtly and without a second thought, paying not the slightest attention to her mother's or her guardian's objections.

In much the same way, she had long before broken off not only with idle young people but with her married friends as well. Her behavior and activities had further estranged her from her relations. They stopped inviting her over, or coming to visit her; and if it hadn't been for her mother, they wouldn't have set foot in the house at all. Raika didn't bother to conceal her utter indifference toward them or, for that matter, toward anything they said or thought. In their turn, they spoke and thought very badly of her, of her way of life, her morbid parsimony and shameful usury. Aunt Gospava, a small, sharp-tongued, overbearing woman, arbiter and mouthpiece of all Hadzi-Vasiches and a dozen related families, used to complain at the gatherings of the clan: "I don't know what's become of the girl. She's like a wild pear tree—so far from the road she's no earthly use to anyone. I don't know, I honestly don't know. How is it possible *those* parents produced *this*—thing?"

At those gatherings they never stopped wondering after whom Raika had taken. And like as not, they would bring up the name of her great-grandfather on her mother's side, the late Master Ristan.

There were still some people living who remembered the tall solemn old man with steel-gray eyes and tight fists, who had lived only for money and his good name, even though the name he in the end managed to make for himself was that of a tightwad. When someone asked him for a favor in the name of friendship, he was apt to answer: "What sort of friend are you? A friend is a man who doesn't ask for anything." He used to go to the market every day and do his own shopping. And he was less proud of his large well-established business than of his knack for discovering good but cheap merchandise on the market stalls, or of the fact that there was no peasant or city tradesman who could get the better of him in a deal. When he went shopping for eggs, he brought along an iron ring to measure the diameter of an egg; the egg that went clear through the ring was not for him. While he thus rummaged through the eggs in the farmer's basket, the merchants behind their counters would nudge their sons and assistants and admiringly point to the sturdy and imperturbable old man. "Look well! This is the way to make money and wind up with a lot of houses."

However, with all his heartless pinching and avarice, Master Ristan was also known to loosen up the purse strings and spend money to entertain and be a host, when this could not be avoided or when the prestige of his house demanded it; and he did it with so much dignity and real style that the pennies he spent were often more impressive than another man's gold pieces. This girl Raika, on the other hand, trimmed and scrimped to such an extent that she no longer knew what was fitting and decent, she was no longer like a girl from a comfortable home but more like a creature out of a medieval ghetto. In all the history of Sarajevo, no one could ever remember a woman's going into business and working with money and bills of exchange, and certainly not a female usurer and money-grubber. Never had this been seen in any community, Christian, Moslem, or Jewish. And this sorry freak and disgrace had to happen in their family!

This was how the worried relatives talked among themselves. They took particular exception to the way in which Raika treated her mother. Several of them invited Mrs. Obren to leave her daughter and move in with them, but she declined. Alone and cowed, aged before her time, she kept close to her room and withered like a captive without a will or voice. When, during the holidays, one of the older ladies, relatives or friends, came to visit her, she cried a few quiet tears but did not complain to anyone about anything.

Among the people of the town, Miss Raika already had a set reputation—an unlovely and unusual one in every respect—first for being a queer and revolting child-freak, and then for being Miss Moneygrub and a person without pride or feeling, a monster among womenfolk, a kind of modern-day witch.

As early as the period of mourning after her father's death, when she had gone over the accounts of the store with Veso, Miss Raika had cut down all charitable contributions, which in Master Obren's time had been quite substantial. In later years she had reduced them still further, until one day she decided to wipe them out altogether. Veso, who on this subject, as on many others, did not see eye to eye with her, put up a stubborn fight.

"Don't do it, Raika. A person is not alone in this world. You can't ignore the living."

"You can, if you have to. I can't give what I don't have."

"Easy now! I'm not saying you should throw it away, but a time comes when you have to give."

"Give your own, then."

"I will. But you ought to give too. I'm telling you for your own good."

"Thank you for the advice. I know best what I can or cannot do."

Her cold harshness made the little man angry. "It seems to me you don't know what you're saying."

"I know perfectly well."

"Then you don't know what people are saying about you."

"I'm not the least bit interested."

"See, that only shows you don't have as much of a brain as you think you have. If the late master were alive . . ."

"You know perfectly well why he is not."

"Hold it. Of course I know, but you, my fine little miss, you're going much too far. You keep hiding behind that vow you say you made to your father when he was near his death, but all you've done so far is more like a curse, not a vow. The late master would never have allowed you to do what you're doing. This could not have been his wish or intention. You just like the smell of money, that's all. It's got you panting and frothing at the mouth, and you're simply using his words and his advice to cover up your own wicked itch. Only remember what I'm telling you. Money's not everything. Make money at the cost of your good name, and you're a poor businesswoman. I don't care if you make a million, the price is not worth it."

Haughtily and with bitter disdain, Miss Raika gazed at this dwarf who had the temerity to speak to *her* of *a million*. Veso went on sputtering in that metallic voice which spineless and ineffectual men take on in moments of anger.

"You can think what you want, and do things the wrong way around, that's your privilege, but I'm telling you it's no good and you'll be sorry for what you're doing. Only it'll be too late then, I'm afraid. You think you're the first person to find out how one penny makes two. That kind's been around since the world was made and their money's never lasted long. Sooner or later the devil claims his own."

They had many such quarrels, but no wrangling could convince Miss Raika or persuade her to abandon her attitude. The people who visited the town stores and collected donations for humane or patriotic purposes usually came out of her store and her house empty-handed. She made it a rule not to donate anything to anyone. This prompted several local newspapers to criticize her and make open references to her methods of business. *Serbian Word* published a column about some "descendants of those who founded and maintained Serbian institutions in Sarajevo, who now neglect this fine tradition and, sunk in materialism and ugly self-interest, forget their duty toward the people and people's institutions." The Social Democratic newspaper *Freedom* openly attacked Miss Raika for her refusal to contribute to the fund for sick workers' children, and called her "Shylock in petticoats!"

Her erstwhile guardian, Master Mihailo, and director Paier, too, warned her not to overdo it, to contribute at least something, the way every other citizen did, so as not to alienate herself from the community and cut her ties with the world. But Miss Raika stuck to her guns and went her own way, utterly indifferent to the popular verdict; she had neither the time nor the inclination to brood over it.

More and more, as the years went by, Miss Raika took on the appearance of a peaked and quaint old maid, while her life revolved around the shop and home; she was entirely occupied with money and financial transactions and devoid of any leisure or human company or the need for either. Her only regular activity not immediately concerned with business were the visits to her father's grave. Every Sunday morning, in fair or in nasty weather, she took a walk to the cemetery at Koshevo. She never allowed her mother to come along.

People in the street were used to her strange appearance, which was even more incongruous when the weather was sunny and fine and the streets were alive with gay, festive crowds. Tall, with a scowl on her face, and walking like a man, she presented an image which contrasted sharply, both in dress and in bearing, with the leisurely and elegantly decked womenfolk who were strolling and chattering on their way to church or to the promenade. She always wore the same charcoal-gray suit of mannish cut and an ancient black hat that was much too small and sadly out of date, and a pair of well-worn shoes with flat heels. People gave her quizzical looks out of the corners of their eyes or else stared at her with unabashed curiosity, and this happened not only on the street but also at the cemetery; but she paid them as much attention as she paid to the unknown dead who filled the graveyard.

As soon as she sat down on the simple bench beside her father's grave, the last link between her and the multitude was cut. Here she was detached and sheltered from everything. Silence was all-encompassing. The view was enclosed since the cemetery lay low between the green slopes of the Koshevo Valley. From time to time the stillness would be accompanied by the slow ripple of sound from the church bells in town, and the landscape would be ruffled very gently by the grazing shadows of summer clouds which sailed through the sky, white, stately, and slow. But none of this was noticed by Miss Raika. All she saw was the grave.

The plot was green and well kept, lined along the edges with white flint gravel; at the head was a low marble tombstone with a cross, beside it there grew a night rose, set into the soil together with its pot. Between its green branches one caught sight of the graven and gilded letters on the tablet: *Here rests Obren Radakovich, merchant, died in the 45th year of his life.*

Miss Raika would gaze at those lines for a long time, without flinching, until her eyes gave out and the letters grew lopsided and became golden sparks, mingled with tears. Then she closed her eyes. She shrank back into herself. All her senses grew numb and deaf to outside impressions; she was lost to the world. She communed with the grave. Out of that bent and cramped body there came welling, in wave after unstoppable wave, a great outpouring of womanly tenderness—that remarkable force which, unseen and yet allpowerful, dwells in these frail beings and radiates out of them in so many different ways, creating and undoing lives and destinies all around itself.

Choking with emotion, Raika gasped and whispered into her clenched fists: "You! You! You!" As she expelled this single simple word through her lips, her changing voice contained all the nuances of tenderness, pain, and sorrow of which a woman is capable at the various stages and in various circumstances of her life. But after this initial unburdening of her long-suppressed and unused feelings, she would regain her reason—strong, true, and relentless like an icy angel with a flaming sword in her hand.

The man who had been the sole and steadfast object of her tenderness no longer existed. He had gone under, because he had not been able to protect and preserve what was his, because his weak ailing heart had distracted his attention, because he had allowed his vision to become clouded by human thoughts of honor and pride, because, like the generous and brave man that he was, he had passionately wanted to share everyone's trouble, to place himself in other people's position, until one day, retracing his steps, he found himself without a position of his own. This had been his lot, and was now the content of her life; and the two of them were bound inseparably by his death and by her life.

At this point the girl usually sat up, collected herself, checked and smothered all emotion, and then, her dry eyes resting on the gilded letters of the marble slab, began to give a wordless accounting to the grave. She recapitulated mentally all that she had accomplished in the course of that week, and explained and outlined everything she planned to do in the following, asking his endorsement of the former and his approval of the latter.

She would get up around noon and turn back to town. At that hour of the day, when the streets were thronged, her curious appearance was even more noticeable, but she looked neither to the left nor right. She told herself that these were the very same people who destroyed helpless and honorable citizens but deferred and kowtowed to the harsh and pitiless ones. Braced by her "dialogue" of a moment before, she felt calm and purposeful once more, filled with a lofty disdain toward the crowd, which even now could not touch her and was sure to grovel at her feet as soon as she gained her battlement—the one called "Million." Her step grew lighter and she felt as if she were soaring, not only in her thoughts but with her body as well, above this wretched milling throng, stepping over them as over an anthill.

THAT SUNDAY OF JUNE 18, 1914, WAS NOT DIFFERENT FROM
any of the earlier Sundays, save that Miss Raika felt
strangely dreamy and listless as she got ready for her usual
visit to the cemetery. Lingering a little longer than usual by
the open window, she gazed at the opposite embankment of
the Milyacka and at the steep hillside covered with greenery.
The sky was still full of the pink light of sunrise and the
town lay under a bank of freshness, but the other side of the
river, with its quay, had already come to life. Pedestrians
were rushing to and fro, carriages clattered, automobiles
drove by with a loud din, and here and there was a glimpse
of men in parade uniforms, bright-hued, looking as if they
had burst into bloom on a summer day.

Miss Raika watched it all, but none of it grazed her consciousness any more than a vague dream. The part of her
mind that was awake was filled with another, more vivid

content, the reality of her night's dream. And, loafing thus by the window and watching the bustling city in the stark light of the summer day, she still lived and relished the uncertain joy of that dream, which had neither a constant form nor a name. She could not recount it or fully explain it even to herself, but while she dreamt it she was totally immersed in it, and this feeling persisted all through the next day and was especially real in the morning, while the dream's memory was still vivid and the events of the day had not yet displaced and blotted it out.

It was not the first time she had dreamt about her dream of a million. In the last few years she had dreamt it several times, in different forms and in varying detail, and it was always the same: that the first million had been reached and topped at the same moment. Each time, as this occurred, she experienced a delicious radiance that suffused her inwardly and at the same time bathed her from the outside. The unquenchable source of this rapturous, intoxicating shimmer was there in her breast, just beneath her throat; if she laid a hand on her chest and then raised it to her eyes, she could see that the hand was dipped in the shimmer, which was a mixture of gold and silver, though neither a liquid nor an airy substance but rather something between the two, which seemed to lift her up from the ground like a benign elemental force, detaching her from the world, shielding and protecting her from every evil and humiliation that might overtake a person. Filled with this radiance and washed by it, she moved in a way that was neither walk nor flight but a kind of air-borne sensation halfway between a proud step and a miraculous soaring. It was a moment of exquisite happiness, when from the height of her attained million she realized that she no longer shared the fate of the rest of mankind and was not bound by the laws of competition in which the common mass was writhing and choking. And she would spend all the next day under the influence of this dream; and it would seem to her that everywhere in her thoughts and calculations, in the objects around her and even on her own person, there appeared from time to time a faint shimmer of that radiance, mysterious and splendid, yet more fleeting than a distant crack of lightning, more to be guessed at than seen.

This morning was one of those—when Miss Raika hovered uncertainly by the open window and, though awake and already dressed, roused herself with difficulty and took unconscionably long to begin her working day, just as some other woman or girl of her age might have tarried by the window lost in thoughts of love's ecstasy or love's torment.

Watching the brisk human traffic on the opposite bank of the river, she recalled having read in the newspapers some days before about the visit to Bosnia of the heir apparent to the throne, Franz Ferdinand, and about the preparations being made for his arrival in Sarajevo. In fact, she had not actually read it, but had seen the big headlines of the articles on the front page. Unlike most people, she usually skipped lightly over the front page and gave all her attention to the back page, which carried the notices of auctions, sales, public loans, and news of economic developments and of the money market. The pleasant memory of her night's dream, which held her spellbound, here by the window, was now marred by the thought of those headlines. She had never been fond of newspapers, and shrank from them as from something repugnant and dangerous; lately she even hated them, and not without reason.

With this uncomfortable thought she at last wrenched herself from the window and made ready to leave.

As she walked out of the house and toward the bridge, she saw a line of automobiles on the other bank, brightly dappled with military uniforms and moving smartly along the quay in the direction of the center of town. By the time she had crossed the bridge, the cars had disappeared. But as she was passing a narrow street between two large government buildings on her way to the Koshevo Road, there was a sudden loud sound of an explosion somewhere in the town. Miss Raika thought that the Archduke might have been in the procession and that the noise came from a cannon fired in his honor.

She remained at the cemetery as usual until midday. On her way back home she had a vague impression that the streets were more animated and the people were anxious to get home. She wondered about it briefly and then forgot it. Absorbed in her own thoughts, eyes on the ground, paying no attention to anyone or anything, she took the same way back to the house. Thus she never saw that on the palace of the Land Government, on both balconies, two large black flags were fluttering in the wind; they had not been there in the morning when she went out to the cemetery.

She and her mother were finishing their modest Sunday lunch when there was a knock at the front door. It was Rafo Konforti. Astonished at the unexpected visit, and even more at Rafo's strange appearance and behavior, she let him into the house without a word of greeting.

"Did you see, miss, did you see what happened?" stammered Rafo, his eyes wheeling around the room from object to object.

"What happened?"

"Well, don't you know? Don't you know? Oh, Miss Raika, it's a calamity, a terrible calamity for the whole world. Assassination! They've killed the Archduke and the Countess, his wife, and some other people."

He said this excitedly, while his hands shook and his eyes shone with the horror of his own words.

"But who killed them? What for? When?"

"Oh, some young man from Serbia. Schoolboys, miss! Students . . . right here on the quay by the Latin Bridge . . . they killed both of them. May the good Lord have mercy on us!" sighed Rafo.

A moment of silence followed.

"Anyway, miss, I came to tell you to watch out. Don't go near the bazaar, miss. Keep out of sight, you and your mother, because there's going to be trouble."

"My God, there's no one here but us two women, Master Rafo. Why should anyone want to harm us? We have nothing to do with those things, you know that."

Rafo shook his head impatiently. "I know you don't, but anything can happen. It's a big thing . . . heir apparent! You should hear what they're saying in town. May God protect us!" Rafo leaned closer, adding in a terrified whisper: "There's a mob in the streets, they're after plunder and arson. A Catholic priest made a speech. There's talk about looting and destroying all Serbian shops in the bazaar. They might even break into Serbian homes. God save us! That's what they're saying. I thought of you and Mrs. Obren, so I came to tell you. The best thing, miss, is to sit tight here. And we'd better not see each other until the commotion's over. You understand? Sit here and keep quiet. Qu-i-e-t! I'll send my boy now and then in case you need anything."

Presently Rafo took his leave, with fear in his eyes and a finger on his lips.

It was only after she was alone that Miss Raika began to feel a certain queasiness. Without saying anything to her mother, she went to the window and stared at the opposite bank of the river. Everything seemed to be in its place as always, the crowd was neither smaller nor bigger than on any other Sunday at this time of the day, and yet the entire view seemed somehow different and new; it had an air of uncertainty and fear, although she would not be able to say why and in what way.

All holiday afternoons are longer than those of a weekday, but this one seemed to drag interminably.

And when the sun went down, melting in its own fire behind the woods on Hum, Miss Raika forbade the lighting of lamps in the house. She sat with her mother by the open window. The hot breath of day, mixed with a fine dust, still filled the air. Church bells were tolling with a dull funeral sound; they were dominated by the deep and booming voice of the Roman Catholic cathedral. Presently she had to come out and tell her mother what had happened and explain the imminent danger to the Serbian homes and stores. An easy crier, old Mrs. Obren promptly burst into tears, just as she might have done for some other, less important cause. Her daughter comforted her briefly and absent-mindedly, but she continued to weep. The bells kept tolling in the distance, from the Residence and Banjski Mount, and in the short intervals between their sound waves one could hear a strange, drawn-out echo reverberating against the steep mountains around the town, like an expected answer to this metallic music of death and rioting. All of it was punctuated now and then by the composite monotone voice of the mob which was yelling and shouting somewhere in the center of the town, alternately hailing the dead and calling for revenge. Finally the darkness closed in, sultry with heat and strange sounds and awesome premonitions of great and fateful events. The lights fluttered on throughout the town, while the two women brooded uneasily by the window, sitting closer together than usual, as if waiting for something.

The mother sighed heavily a few times, which among women is always a preamble to a lugubrious conversation. Her daughter wanted to head it off. To her, the mere thought of a conversation was enough to make her uncomfortable.

"Go lie down," she told her mother flatly. "It'll be all right. You don't have to be afraid of anything."

"I don't know what's going to happen, daughter, but it won't be anything good when these important people of theirs start losing their lives."

"Lie down and go to sleep, Mama. It's none of our business."

But even while she was saying it, she listened to the voices in the dark distance as if to check the accuracy of her words.

"It is, daughter. More than you think. They'll take it out on the poor Serbs again, you'll see."

Miss Raika said nothing and the conversation faltered.

The two women sat for a long time and listened to the night outside, which, once the tolling of bells died away and the demonstrations quieted down, sank into a more ominous silence than usual, for nowhere could one hear the faintest sound of music or singing which ordinarily went on and on during the summer nights. The world was plunged in that stillness which the high and mighty impose when dying, at least for a while, on a narrower or wider circle of those who remain alive. Finally the two women went to sleep. The mother lay in her dark room and pondered her helpless, widow's worries, fearful not only about her "poor Serbs" but about the world in general; she made no sound or movement and lay absolutely quiet, for that was the way she had done and endured everything in life. The daughter, in her own room, read a German travel book for a time. (Travel books were the only kind she bought and read regularly. In them she sought and found something that seemed to have a vague but fascinating pertinence to her own life, especially if such writing was about unfamiliar continents and discoveries of hidden treasures and new markets.) Then she put out the light and went to sleep.

She woke up before dawn, fresh, cool, and rested, yet alert as if she had never gone to sleep. As she lay in her bed, with pressed lips and knitted eyebrows, she peered intently through the darkness which was beginning to thin and pale around the window.

Waking up at dawn! For years she had been used to solving her problems at that hour of the morning—problems for which neither the daylight nor the dark of the night could find a solution. Now was the moment to come to grips with this anxiety which Rafo had brought into their house. Now, at the first crash of dawn, a person was as reborn, his mind was razor keen, as if new yet rich with experience. The world outside, insofar as she could perceive and understand it, as much of it, anyway, as her bondage to her dream allowed her to see, spread out before her and determined her attitude toward all things. She felt instinctively that a crisis was near at hand, a time in which it would be hard to make money and easy to stumble, and she rebelled against it with all the strength of her being—a strength which, from the earliest days of her youth, had tended to flow in one direction alone.

What had happened? The Archduke had been killed. A great catastrophe, no doubt, one that would echo far beyond the confines of this town and would strike at all kinds of interests far more important than her own. That much was plain to her; but she could not resign herself to the fact that there were some things in the world which, through no fault of hers, could jeopardize her possessions and knock her plans awry. What did phrases like "general problems," "political events," and "national interests" mean to her anyway? Something alien and far off, which she had always been careful to shun. As far as she was concerned, all of it existed only insofar as it yielded a profit, or, in the contrary case, as something to be avoided with the least damage. What and who were those students? Shaggy young men she had sometimes seen promenading along the river, with time on their hands, conspiratorial and puffed up with their own importance, wearing threadbare winter overcoats with raised collars, their heads bowed under the wide-rimmed black hats.

What was all that to her? Where did it all come from? And when, suddenly, it all became knotted together like this —the heir apparent, politics, students—it likely portended some kind of loss to her, or danger, or, in the best case, a holdup of her work, which had nothing whatever to do with any of it. Really, none of it was any concern of hers! She resolutely turned her back on all of them and tried only to skirt them or step over them, as she would over any other obstacle on the road. She could not bear the thought that her business and her interests were connected to these things, predicated as it were on something that was utterly beyond her control, and that she was obliged to share the misfortune of some nebulous community. What have I to do with Serbian students? she asked impatiently of the fading cutout of sky on the window. Suddenly there rose in her a furious will to rid herself completely and forever of all ties and considerations, so that no one would ever have the right to ask anything of her, just as she herself had never been bound to anyone or demanded anything in the name of those ties.

Abruptly she sat up in bed. No, she must not let herself be found on the losing side, not at any price! She would do anything, but this she would not permit. "Not this!" she whispered aloud and beat the pillow with a clenched fist, as if to hammer her resolution home.

She had planned to go to the bank at nine o'clock, to call on director Paier and find out whether there was any truth in Rafo's fears, and to ask his advice on what to do and what position to take so as to avoid harm and trouble. Now she couldn't wait any longer but got up and was on the street before nine. Her mother looked askance but dared not make a sound; her frightened tear-filled eyes irritated Miss Raika, so that she felt impelled to shut the door behind her with a bang.

Shunning the quay along the river, she took one of the inside streets on the left bank, the long one that was normally quiet and somnolent, called Terezya. She observed the few pedestrians there but saw nothing unusual about them.

Even in the hottest weather, mornings in Sarajevo had a breath of crisp mountain air in them. One inhaled it with relish and stepped lightly. Thus she quickly came to the bridge at Chumuria. She could already see, from her side of the river, the big white building of the Union Bank, when from the direction of Chumuria there came the sound of a shouting mob, like the one of the night before. The vanguard of the crowd spilled out on the quay. Miss Raika took shelter behind a tree, ready to turn back home if the demonstrators crossed the bridge toward her, or else to continue on her way to the bank if they went up or down the quay.

One had to live through days like these to realize fully what kind of people lived in this town that lay scattered like a handful of grain partly along the ranges, partly in the narrow valley along the river. It took an event like that of the day before, or perhaps even much less, to bring to the surface the hidden temper of these people who ordinarily slaved for a wage, or else loafed, threw their money away, or vegetated in the steep and winding streets of the poor quarters—streets that resembled a gully after a spring torrent. Like all Eastern cities, Sarajevo had its own ragtag and bobtail, which for years on end led a secretive, scattered, and to all intents and purposes tame existence, but which in circumstances like these, whipped by the mysterious instincts of the herd process, fused together and erupted like a volcano, spewing the fire and lava of the vilest passions and appetites. This mob of *Lumpenproletariat* and petty hungry citizenry was made up of people who were different from one another in their faiths, habits, and style of dress but one of a kind in their innate and treacherous coarseness, in the passion and baseness of their instincts. Followers of three different faiths—Moslem, Roman Catholic, and Orthodox—they hated one another from the day of their birth to their death, deeply and blindly, transmitting this hatred even to those who were no longer alive, and looking upon it as something glorious and sacred, and at the same time a defeat and a shame for their infidel neighbors.

They were born, they grew up and died in this hate, this actual physical revulsion toward a neighbor of another faith, and often they spent their entire lives without finding an opportunity to express the hatred in all its intensity and horror; yet whenever due to some great or calamitous event the established order was shaken and law and reason were suspended for a few hours or for several days, this rabble, or some part of it, burst down upon this city which otherwise is well known for the polite friendliness of its social life and the honeyed words of its conversation. Then all the long-suppressed hatreds and secret hankerings for destruction and violence broke to the surface and, like a flame long smoldering and at last finding something to feed upon, dominated the streets, lapping, sputtering, and swallowing everything, until some force more powerful than themselves beat them back, or until they flagged and burned themselves out with their own rage. Then they would slink away like jackals with tails between their legs, back to their homes and alleys, to spend another few years in obscurity and confine their hatred to shifty looks, ugly snarls, and obscene gestures.

There might have been some two hundred noisemakers in the crowd, Moslems and Catholics, most of them poorly dressed and undernourished, with traces of misery or corruption in their appearance and manner. They shouted fitfully "Down!" and "Long live!" apparently at a signal from a slightly better dressed man who marched at the head of the procession and whose appearance strongly suggested that of a plainclothesman. They even attempted to sing the national anthem, but their coarse untrained voices made the song come out ragged and earsplitting. Two men in front carried a picture of the Emperor Franz Josef, one of those framed colored lithographs, obviously borrowed from a government office. The pair of them were dressed in rags and stunted, with bulging foreheads and glazed looks. Accustomed to living and working on the outskirts of the town, in the shadow of their poverty, they were now awed and at the same time aggressively proud at being allowed to carry the Emperor's picture through the main streets of the town. In their confused eagerness, they had turned the picture upside down, head to the pavement, but their huge fists, used to other work, held on to it firmly, as though they were tribesmen clinging to their fetishes. Marching slowly, as in a funeral cortege, they shot dark glances from under their crumpled hats, and their faces wore the brazen expressions of people who knew well what they were, but knew also that at this moment no one dared to touch a hair on their heads. And the framed image of the old man with white mutton chops and a bald pate that stretched his forehead almost to infinity, laced in a ceremonial uniform with gold buttons, red braid, and a row of stars and medals, solemn and resplendent, was in stark contrast with this pair of homeless Sarajevo citizens of tattered appearance and wretched demeanor, who clutched him in a tight embrace that enclosed him like a second, living frame.

After a moment's confusion and wavering, in which someone told them to turn the picture properly, the procession set off down the quay. Miss Raika waited till they rounded the corner of her old school and disappeared in the direction of the college, then turned across the bridge and walked toward the bank.

The tastefully designed white building of the Union Bank, at the corner of Chumuria, stretched for a whole block along the front of the quay. On the ground floor were the offices of the bank, and here all window shutters were lowered this morning; above were two more floors containing two large apartments, which were the most expensive in Sarajevo and had been tenanted for many years past by a doctor and a lawyer. The office of the bank director was at the far end of the main floor and had its own entrance from a narrow short street in the rear. Only strangers and newcomers approached the director's office through the bank's main door behind the tellers' windows; friends and acquaintances used the rear one. Here one entered through a narrow foyer and went straight into the spacious room of the director, which was dim and slightly humid and had to be lighted during the greater part of the day. To this large room Paier had managed to impart a special and agreeable look, as he did to every little thing he touched.

On the walls hung several bright watercolors of forest landscapes and hunting scenes; they were all of the same size and apparently by the same artist. The office was cool during the summer days, and in the winter huge logs of beechwood crackled in the big tile stove. The floor was covered with a padded gray fabric from wall to wall and on top of that, near the entrance, were handmade Bosnian scatter rugs and, under the desk in the rear, a Persian carpet. The desk was large and its top was neither littered with papers nor conspicuously bare in the manner of bankers' desks. There were photographs of Mrs. Paier, a dark-eyed woman with a feline figure, and their son, a handsome lad wearing the uniform of his boarding school; there was also a bronze statue of a deer, and beside that a vase of green glass in which there were flowers and green twigs almost the whole year round. Behind the desk, on wide shelves, there gleamed long rows of books with gilded bindings.

The office was dusky and fresh-smelling at this time, like a chapel. The flowers in the green vase were limp, they had not been changed yet. Today the bank was closed, like all the other institutions and offices, as a sign of mourning. The director had dropped in for only a moment, on his way to the cathedral to attend the requiem for the victims of yesterday's assassination. His stance was that of a man about to go out. He wore a black cutaway. A high starched collar and a black waistcoat gave him a somewhat formal and unusual look. With a familiar broad gesture of his arms, which contrasted strangely with his appearance, he offered a chair to Miss Raika; he himself remained leaning on the desk, with his arms crossed on his chest.

Miss Raika told him in a few words what she had heard from Rafo, and added her own fears about her house and her possessions. "You know that I've never had anything to do with these things and have always kept to myself. In fact, I have a bad name in Serbian circles for that reason. Even the newspapers have publicly attacked me."

Paier nibbled at his upper lip, which was the greatest sign of impatience one ever noticed in him.

"And so I came to ask you what I'm supposed to do. I'm willing to do anything. If you think a statement or something of that sort, or maybe a voluntary contribution . . . I really don't know myself."

At that Paier dropped his arms, came a step nearer and bent down to the chair in which she sat.

"Listen to me, Miss Obren."

There was a time when he used to call her by her first name; but lately, having been obliged to warn her about her eccentric behavior and shady business practices, he had gone back to the formal patronymic. Blinded by obsession, which did not allow her to see other, more important things, she had never even noticed that he called her anything else.

"Listen, Miss Obren," Paier went on. "I think that your Konforti alarmed you more than is necessary. I know that what's going on is grave and worrisome and likely to get more worrisome yet, for the whole country and especially for the Serbs, but there's no reason why you should anticipate things and make yourself conspicuous when no one's asking you to. And even if they should ask, you're Master Obren's daughter and you don't have to do it, any more than he would have done it if he were alive. You're a Serb and it's no shame to be a Serb. On the contrary. My advice to you is not to make yourself conspicuous, not even by showing your loyalty to the government. Don't let this mob scare and confuse you. Don't do anything you might later be ashamed of or sorry for. They won't be braying in the streets forever. Stay home for a few days, and if you need something, come and see me or call me and we'll put our heads together."

Paier said this in a lowered voice and his eyes batted in slight embarrassment.

Miss Raika left him dissatisfied and set off thoughtfully in the direction of her store. It was not her custom to watch the street and the people around her and to wonder about what she saw, but this time she observed everything very minutely. The shops were closed, but this did not give the streets a holiday air. Passers-by were fewer, the silence more pervading. The streets looked as if an unseasonable storm had swept and cleaned them overnight, leaving emptiness and a fear of new gales in its wake. The roofs and windows sprouted fresh flags of mourning. At the entrance to Great Churchiluk her store was untouched; its wide iron door was shut, like those of the other stores, with two crossed stanchions of heavy iron. She walked on in the direction of one of the suburbs, through streets that were all but deserted. She found Veso in the sloping narrow courtyard of his house, which smelled of flowers and glistened with clean cobblestones and white-washed house walls. At the end of the court, freshly made noodles had been spread out to dry on white sheets. Veso was dressed for the street, except for the white socks and house slippers on his feet. With a stick in one hand, he sat on a stone and kept the chickens from getting at the noodles. Miss Raika felt irritated by the idyllic peace of the scene, in which there was not a trace of the worries that oppressed her.

"Veso, I came to talk about our plans for the store."

"I was just getting ready to come and see you, find out how you were. I was ordered to shut the store, like all the others. So now we'd better wait and see what happens next."

"What do you mean, see what happens? Don't you know the mobs are running loose and looting Serbian property? We've got to do something."

"What can we do?"

"We can put out a black flag, that's what. I see the other shops are doing it."

"We could, I suppose," drawled Veso noncommittally.

"We could, and we'd better."

"Well, let's see first what the other Serb merchants do. We can always follow suit."

"I'm not interested in what they do. They can go break their necks for all I care. I'm not going to stand by and watch them burn my house and loot my store."

"Easy, Raika. Our store's not the only one in town. We're just one of many hundreds. The way they go, we'll go too."

"Who are they? What do I care about them? They're not my bread and butter. I have my own business. If anything happens to me, you think they'll come and ask me how I feel and how I'm managing?" She spoke fast and her voice quaked with suppressed rage.

"Well . . . see here . . . I wouldn't want to play it single-handed. You can't shut your eyes to your own people. Let them decide what they want to do, and I'll do the same."

Taken aback, she looked at him more closely. Frail and shriveled up as always, in his lounging slippers and with the stick in one hand, he was yet calm and unruffled and somehow bluntly masculine. He held himself straighter than usual, as if this tiny delicate body were mounted on a spine of steel.

She resented the unexpected self-possession and obstinate equanimity of this otherwise weakly man. Sharp angry words rose up in her throat and clotted momentarily on her tongue; and just as she was on the point of telling him flatly that she would do as she thought fit and as her interests demanded, that the attitude of the Serbian merchants did not concern her one way or another, they were interrupted by a brisk woman's voice from the house above: "Psh-h-ht, you vermin! Get away, go on! Veso, you poor clod, don't you see the chickens are gobbling up the noodles. Get away! Get away!"

Veso's wife Soka stood in the doorway of the house. She too was small, like himself, and wore a white apron tied at the waist. Her hands were dusty with flour, but otherwise she was neat and spotless. Flailing both her arms, she scattered the chickens, which indeed had taken advantage of Veso's absorbed conversation and were pecking away at the dough on the spread-out cloth. Veso promptly waved his stick a few times. The fowl scrambled away behind the house, and Soka came down to greet Miss Raika.

With this petty upset in the miniature household of the miniature couple, Miss Raika's talk with Veso came more or less to an end. She took her leave distractedly and left the courtyard, resolved not to expect any help from Veso in the present circumstances, her mind made up that she would carry on alone and rely on her own strength and judgment.

When a woman like Miss Raika decides to go her own blind willful way, nothing is either difficult or impossible for her. For although the shops were closed and the bewildered storekeepers had scattered to their homes, she succeeded in finding everything she needed even before midday; black flags of mourning were unfurled on both her house and store. She was not the first one to run them up, but she would be the last to take them down.

I N THE LIFE OF EVERY PERSON THERE ARE TURBID STRETCHES about which the memory prefers to keep silent, or speaks of in a muted voice. Such a time in Miss Raika's life were the four years of the war. They were four years of life that resembled a vivid and strange dream, accompanied by strong feelings of buoyancy and fear, and darkened toward the end by difficulties, suffering, and a great bitterness which would linger on forever.

The bodies of the assassinated Archduke and his wife were taken in a solemn cortege to the railway station. This was followed by mass arrests and all kinds of violence. The local press screamed itself hoarse with special editions and large headlines, aroused and fanatical street demonstrators spent themselves in shouting abuse which they barely understood. And after those several grave and extraordinary days a strange silence descended on all things, as after a great explosion. This was not the usual absence of noise, of loud and exciting incidents and clamorous movements of humanity. It was an active sort of silence, in which people listened with bated breath, expecting fresh upheavals, while the echo of the recent furor was still dying away in their ears. It was a manipulated silence, which was necessary to some but which no one really trusted, so that all men kept their ears to the ground and tried to divine from the inaudible, hidden vibrations "which way the thing would turn."

In this silence Miss Raika felt as in her own element. The thought that something might be lurking beneath this silence never crossed her mind, and she did not ask herself what might happen to the town, the people, or the world at large when the silence came to an end. The important thing was that the din, the chaos, the violent and erratic storming of the mobs had subsided. All that mattered was that a person could again look after his business, keep his accounts, check the transaction in progress, and plan for the future. The merchant community was perplexed, it was true; the people in the banks were reserved, stiff, and close-mouthed as in a church. In short, everyone was worried. Drawn faces and eyes reddened by crying were also in evidence; those belonged to the Serbs. But Miss Raika refused to concern herself with them. All she knew was that there was no more firing and shouting in the streets, no more breaking into people's homes and stores. Not one of her fears had materialized. Neither her house nor her shop had been broken into or damaged in any way. No one had criticized her. None of the rest was her problem. The only cloud in her life was the fact that she could find no one with whom to share her contentment and ease of mind and will to work. They all wore absent expressions and were tongue-tied. Even Rafo Konforti was slow to recover. Any time she asked him something, he would answer evasively; if she proposed something, he put it off with vague phrases.

"All right, miss, but let's wait till things settle down a bit. Then we'll see what's what."

And you could see his mind was a mile away.

Almost a month passed in this way, and then, as in a huge orchestra, the silence broke resoundingly and became a great deafening thunderclap. The first to erupt were the newspapers. Then massed peoples began to stir and events quickened in a way no one could remember, in unexpected forms, on a scale that had never been seen before. There was a tolling of bells, a loud din of army bands and cannon broadsides. The air kept trembling with one thing or another and the shock waves seemed to fuse with the anxiety that was beginning to take hold of the inhabitants of this ill-fated town. And again there was a rash of newspaper extras with headlines the size of a thumb.

The events refused to take place in a neat sequence, but came at a bound, helter-skelter. Ultimatum to Serbia, declaration of war, and afterwards entry into the war of all the great European powers, one after another. Now the shock waves became a quake and the general anxiety grew acute.

Dazed by all this, Miss Raika lost her bearings and assurance. She went to see Rafo Konforti and found him surprisingly alert, sprightly, and full of schemes. He was no longer waiting to see "which way the wind would blow." Whatever had to happen, had happened. He had only one piece of advice to offer, one single password: buy. Whoever bought quickly and took his time selling, understood the times rightly; he would do well for himself and no sudden change could touch him.

"What am I to buy?" she asked in a weak voice, looking timidly at Rafo, who seemed suddenly to have grown different and somehow stronger.

"Everything, miss. If you buy brick today and sit on it a couple of months, you're bound to sell it at a profit of 80 per cent."

Rafo was as good as his word. He did buy brick, among other things, at the Ilich brick factory in Koshevo, next to the cemetery. As he branched out, she began to sponsor him unobtrusively and on a modest scale. Little by little she grew bolder and more enterprising. Hatching these deals, making her slow and difficult decisions, selling and purchasing, feeling the tension which is an unavoidable part of all speculation, whether it results in losses or gains, all this filled her time and occupied all her attention. The important events and great changes that occurred throughout the world, and even here in front of her very eyes, made almost no impression on her; she saw them indistinctly, as through a veil.

The world was echoing to the footsteps of enormous multitudes in the first clashes of the war, to newspaper headlines that were like shrieks, to unbelievable threats that abruptly came true when least expected. And here in Sarajevo itself, next to her as it were, things came to pass which no one had ever seen or could remember. One lived fast and lustily, one suffered publicly and in secret. The town was full of new recruits. Some were still wearing their country clothes, while other perspired in blue and gray uniforms and new boots. There was a good deal of jostling and singing without any real joy, shouting and cursing; plum brandy and country tobacco were much in evidence, and so was the common desire for oblivion. Melon rinds and smeared fruit littered the pavement. All of it was marked by an unhealthy prodigality, in all directions. And, along with this, there were great distress and all kinds of suffering. Everywhere the Serb residents were being rounded up and led to improvised prisons; these were no longer just young people and students but respected merchants and peaceable government officials. There was no justice about it, or even a semblance of legality, which one might understand; it was simply a blind and arbitrary exercise of force, like an epidemic.

All these things which disturbed and frightened the public seeped down to Miss Raika eventually, bemused her for a moment, took her mind off business, then faded away again, pushed to the back of her consciousness by an effort of will. What to other people was the core and meaning of life, was to her a mere obstacle to orderly existence and gainful functioning. She was particularly irked by the rumors and talk of Serbian arrests and persecutions, which seemed never to stop. The topic was not to be shaken off even at home. Red-eyed, her lips swollen from crying, Mrs. Obren talked about it for hours on end; the homes of some of their closest relatives had not been spared, and in some every adult male had been taken away. Mrs. Obren visited them regularly, to offer her "condolences," and came back crushed, as from a funeral, and recounted every lugubrious detail: what the police were like when they came to search and arrest, some of them rude and insulting, others polite and considerate; what the arrested man took with him, or said before they led him away to the police station.

Miss Raika listened to these tales with displeasure and

boredom, privately hoping that her mother would shut up or at least change the subject, but an inner awkwardness, a kind of indignation, prevented her from interrupting. The old lady would go on talking, between tears, unable to cut short her tales which had become a sore and irresistible need for her. She would return, for instance, from a visit to their neighbor Lepsha, widow of Luka Pavlovich, and for a long time she would be unable to come to herself; she would sit down dressed as she was, and words and tears would come pouring out of her.

"Oh, poor Lepsha, that she should live to see this day! They took her only son, the fiends, and now she's left sorrowing in her old age. Oh, the poor woman! She told me all about it. 'I went to the courtyard door with him,' she said, 'and he turned around and said to me, "Don't cry, Mother," he said, "or you'll give the enemy a chance to gloat and take revenge. I don't want you to go knocking at people's doors and asking for help either. I know that right's on my side, so nothing can happen to me!" So then,' she said, 'I got a grip on myself and smiled right back at him, so he'd always remember me like that. I looked at him and could hardly see him. And after they took him away, I could swear he was still standing there at the gate, smiling at me and saying something.' "

Miss Raika got up impatiently and pretended to busy herself. With every day that passed, she found these tales of suffering and bravery more repulsive; it all seemed to her exaggerated, futile, and harmful, but she did not have the courage to come out and say so. This happened to her very rarely. In all other things she was quite blunt with her mother, but in this case, as with the subject of beggars some

time before, she dared not contradict her openly. She tried
not to be at home when these women, whose men had been
arrested, dropped in for a visit with Mrs. Obren, for then
there was no end to these plaintive reminiscences, full of
sighs and weeping, which she regarded as indecorous and a
waste of time and which evoked in her strange mixed feelings of contempt, boredom, and guilt. For she genuinely
hated what she called "idle chatter," hated even more the
brandy and coffee that were regularly served with it, and
hated most of all the passionate and ritualistic outpourings
of emotion in which she could not participate.

In these extraordinary times it was impossible to call off
such visitors and shut the house doors; not even Miss Raika
had the nerve to do it, especially if the women in question happened to belong to the inner family.

A frequent visitor was Divna, a close relative and classmate of Miss Raika's, wife of the well-known young doctor
Josifovich. The police had taken away her husband and her
brother-in-law. Divna had always been a thin woman, but in
the last few weeks she had all but dried up and withered.
Dressed in black, for she was still in mourning for her
mother, with her mass of dark and neglected hair above a
pair of large inflamed eyes, she moved like a character in a
tragedy. She would greet Raika in her distraught way, sit
down next to her mother, scarcely talking to either, and tears
would simply keep running down her cheeks; she would
make no attempt to wipe them, but would only avert her
head from time to time. Mrs. Obren would try to soothe and
calm her, in every conceivable way, while Miss Raika would
squirm inwardly at being unable to find a word or smile of
comfort.

Afterwards, when Divna had left, she would comment on it with a few dry words and try to change the topic. "I never saw anyone cry so much," she would say awkwardly, in a flat voice.

"Ah, daughter, she's crying for two of them. For her husband and her brother-in-law."

Discomfited, Raika would be at a loss for words, as if the conversation were in a foreign language.

The moment Divna went away, Aunt Gospava arrived. Again coffee was roasted and brewed, and there was fresh talk of arrests and sufferings; save that Aunt Gospava was the absolute opposite of Divna. Portly and bluff, she neither cried nor complained, but made up for it in talk, loud reckless talk. In the early days after the assassination, the police had arrested her son, who was a student of medicine at Prague and had taken a prominent part in the nationalistic movement of Bosnian youth. Soon afterwards her husband, a senior government official, had also been suspended, even though he was a perfectly peaceful, retiring, harmless man. Now he was moping around at home, more dead than alive, fretting despondently over the fact that such a thing could have happened to him—to him who "never allowed himself to be mixed up in anything."

Aunt Gospava was fearless to the point of incaution: proud of the fact that her son was in jail; and to anyone willing to listen she would say that the "Serbian people were not a piece of bread to be chewed up for breakfast by all and sundry." She complained about her husband, who was faint-hearted and spent all his waking time at home, or, if he did venture out in the street, walked with a bowed head like a criminal.

"Why, only this morning I said to him, 'Why do you sit

in your room like a woman? Get out among people. Only, I
beg of you, don't walk the streets with that face of yours. If
the mob sees you bloodless and slumping like this, they'll
know you're afraid of being a Serb and they'll go after you.
Lift up your head and show them your face. Walk right
through them as if they didn't exist.' "

Aunt Gospava would go on in this caustic vein indefinitely,
sparing neither the Austrian authorities nor the lukewarm
Serbs. She hardly turned to Miss Raika and would not give
her a glance or a word; one felt that any exchange between
them was bound to take an unpleasant turn. ("The Devil's
got her under his thumb," Aunt Gospava would comment
when the talk turned to the girl and her financial activities.)
So Miss Raika would usually find some pretext to leave them
and go to town.

But on the streets, too, there was embarrassment. No matter how absent-minded she might be, how preoccupied with
thoughts of business, or how firmly she kept her eyes riveted
to the ground, she could not help seeing a man going by here
and there, or, more accurately, a man being led down the
street. And if you didn't notice him, he was sure to notice
you. This happened to Miss Raika too. She had barely left
the house, crossed the bridge, and set off down the quay toward the center of town, when around a corner there appeared a group of some ten citizens; they were escorted by a
gendarme and a couple of army recruits in new uniforms.
Miss Raika quickened her step and averted her head for fear
of recognizing an acquaintance among the prisoners. As the
sparse column marched past, a cheerful young voice suddenly called out loudly from the last row: "Greetings,
Raika!"

She shot him a glance out of the corner of her eye. The

voice belonged to her relative, Konstantin Josifovich, a long-legged, fair-haired student of engineering, who was snub-nosed, bareheaded, his shirt unbuttoned at his sunburned neck. He was a cynical young man, whom she remembered quite well from the time he was in high school: an outstanding athlete and a wizard at mathematics. She looked at his laughing face and then looked away quickly. He called after her once more, still laughing, but now there was mockery in his voice: "Greetings! Greetings!"

It was this sort of thing that poisoned one's life and took one's attention away from business.

But even while she was thinking this, and quite independently of her reason, Miss Raika felt a cold slithering of fear down her spine—a fear of the authorities, of the possibility of being punished for taking part, accidentally and against her will, in some obscure deed that was punishable by law. And she thought with hatred about that Konstantin, "who really never did grow up," and all the other Josifovich kinfolk who, one and all, seemed hell-bent on going into penal servitude and dragging everyone else after them, and about all those arrests and sufferings around her, which elicited tears from some and laughter from others. She hung her head and stepped more briskly, turning left into the first street, determined not to watch, not to listen to anyone, not to answer any calls, not to allow her life to be ruined and her business obstructed by people and happenings with which she had nothing whatever in common.

But it was easier to make this decision than to carry it out. The arrests of her compatriots, acquaintances, and relations, the tears and talk that accompanied them, seemed to dog her every step; she tried to keep away from them and disclaim any connection. In the beginning she had done this by running away and ignoring them, by trying to avoid uncomfortable or dangerous meetings and talks, or by maintaining a neutral silence. And when that did not help, she dropped all pretenses and rudely discouraged all contacts and refused all assistance, even to those nearest to her.

When, in the fall of 1914, the Serbian army momentarily broke through the Austrian lines and advanced into Bosnia and toward Sarajevo, the authorities ordered the evacuation of this fortified town and sent most of the civilians into the interior of the province. Only persons employed in government offices or in work necessary to the army were permitted to stay on. Miss Raika managed to remain with her mother in Sarajevo.

And when the government issued war bonds, Miss Raika promptly bought a conspicuously large number. Local newspapers displayed her name prominently, as a good example to other citizens. The *Croatian Journal* took advantage of the occasion to point out how, the misguided and misinformed Serbian intelligentsia notwithstanding, there were also a great many "loyal citizens of the Greek Orthodox faith." No one, however, noted the fact that very soon afterwards Miss Raika smartly unloaded her commitments at a most favorable price.

In other ways, too, she used every opportunity to demonstrate her loyalty publicly. She obtained small flags and various emblems of the Central Powers and displayed them in the windows of her house; she also bought photographs of their sovereigns and commanders-in-chief, taking good care that the stuff cost as little as possible and that it was noticed.

At the same time, her business grew and prospered. The

first months of confusion and great upheaval, during which people lived from day to day and spent their money recklessly, were over. The year 1915 was well advanced and now it was clear to everyone that the war was not going to be short or easy, or as much fun as some people had seemed to think in the early days. All of economic life began to settle and adapt itself accordingly. Whoever grasped this ahead of other people, enjoyed a great advantage over them. One of these was Rafo Konforti. He gave up, one after another, all those businesses that were not directly related to the army or the war. And when his turn came to be conscripted into military service, he was classified as an "indispensable civilian" and permanently excused. Most of the Serbian merchants had already disappeared from the bazaar, and now conscription was beginning to swallow up the businessmen of other faiths and national origins. Konforti had little competition and his hands were free; these twin circumstances benefited his business enormously. And it was in his shadow that Miss Raika now operated and made money.

The onset of winter is ordinarily joyless and uncomfortable in this mountain town situated some fifteen hundred feet above sea level and at the foot of high ranges. Now, as the war dragged on, winter became even more of a problem. It was one of those hard wartime November months that gave everyone a sense of unease and made the poor shudder like wheat under a sickle. It was a cold and gloomy month, and night seemed to be by far the greater part of it; its darkness would merely thin and fade for a few hours to become a misty twilit kind of day, and there was enough dampness in it to fill a whole winter. Half the inhabitants had moved out of the city, but the streets were swarming with soldiers of all kinds of armed services and there were marching columns of Serbian and Russian prisoners of war and of local hostages and arrested men. The bayonet flashed overhead like a mute and eloquent symbol of the times.

Having permeated all homes, all human affairs and enterprises, the war threw away its mask and showed its true face during those slate-gray days. This was no longer a heady stirring of the masses, or that ecstasy of destruction which was so much like the ecstasy of creation, but misery and damnation for everything that was alive, even for dead objects, and most of all for man. Those who had once shouted at the top of their lungs, whipped by feelings of hate and fury, were now crestfallen and as if diminished bodily. With this winter, the war entered its second year and spread like an infection, the end of which could not be seen. Crop after crop of new recruits entered the army. The Galician and Ukrainian fronts consumed one Bosnian regiment after another. There were poverty and a dearth of supplies, and the public, not yet inured to shortage and incapable of sensible rationing, saw in them a harbinger of misery and hunger. Fear preyed alike on those who had and those who had not, on the ones who suffered as well as those whose turn was yet to come.

During the gray fleeting days of that month of November, Miss Raika hurried along the streets of Sarajevo, herself gray and numb. Her slim angular figure, in a black coat buttoned up to her throat, covered by a black hat of a mannish shape, looked as if it had been expressly molded for such weather and such times. Yet in this case the exterior appearance led to mistaken conclusions. Save for her exterior, which in any case had never been different, there was nothing about Miss Raika that was even remotely connected with those hard times or with the distressed town. Not even in her thoughts did she participate in the fate of her fellow citizens, not even those who, for reasons of their Serbian origin or their convictions, had been subjected to pogroms of all kinds from the first day, or those others who were openly or privately on the side of the Austrian government and were now beginning to realize that this loyalty exacted a price not only in noisy avowals and demonstrations but also in sacrifices of blood and money and possessions. By and large, everything that was going on around her and in the world outside was alien, distant, and unreal to Miss Raika. Political clashes and setbacks of universal meaning, great battles in the East and West of Europe, all these were to her merely big headlines on the front pages of newspapers. They were side issues—dark blurred patches among which she coolly and gingerly looked for clearings and charted pathways for her interests. And never had there been so many clearings, never had progress along these pathways been quicker and easier than now, when the great majority of people were occupied and swept along by the events, while she felt free and unencumbered, her road cut out before her, her connections good, the circumstances more favorable than ever.

Miss Raika pressed on with her big and small interests and deals, as sharply and resolutely as she marched the streets through the November days, glancing neither to the left nor right, never asking herself how it had all come about, or why, or how long it would last and how it would end. The widespread shortages, which were fast plunging ever more families into real poverty, hardly disturbed Miss Raika. With malice and secret gloating, she observed how there was less and less merrymaking in the cafés and streets, fewer and fewer pleasures, less pomp and laughter in the homes, how everything sank into poverty as though it were a kind of compulsory thrift, how the town and the people grew dumb and colorless, more and more to her liking and taste. If the word "happiness" had any meaning in her life, one might say that in those days she was completely happy; it was the happiness of a mole burrowing through the silence and darkness of the soft earth in which there is enough food and no obstacles or dangers.

In this leaden, drab atmosphere, in which no one rejoiced, no one spent or squandered, while she made money and practiced thrift as in a great universal enterprise without a visible or clearly definable end, Miss Raika lived and moved as in her own element. Anything that might tear her out of this deaf funeral silence she avoided like something loathsome and offensive. And yet this was not always possible.

One of those gloomy November days, she dropped in at the store in Churchiluk Street and found Veso not in his usual place but deep in a corner between the safe and an old chest of drawers. In the weak light, she saw that the little man was crying.

There were those tears again, where she least wanted to see them!

"What's up, Veso?" she demanded harshly.

He went on crying, making no sound or gesture.

"Well, what is it? What are you crying for?" she asked impatiently.

He only waved his hand at the evening newspaper in front of him. Across the page, large-size letters announced that the Serbian army had been destroyed and that, pressed from the north and southeast by the Germans, Austrians, and Bulgarians, it was falling back into impassable mountains, leaving behind all supplies, all its wounded and sick. "The armed force of Serbia no longer exists," proclaimed the large-type letters across the top of the front page.

"Come off it, Veso. You can't live on crying."

The little man, who until then had betrayed his emotion only by his clenched teeth and his short heavy breath, suddenly spoke out bitterly in that metallic voice of his: "Why shouldn't I cry! If only you'd cry too. We should all cry. Till the last eye is left, and it still wouldn't be enough."

She felt angry at the little peasant and at his weeping and mouthing of big dangerous words here in her own store, and suddenly all patience left her. She told him sharply and furiously: "If you feel like weeping, go home and weep, but not here in the store where people come in and everyone can see you."

"The way I feel, I could cry in the middle of the bazaar."

"Go ahead then, go and cry. I don't intend to attract suspicion and get mixed up with the police. I simply will not, understand?"

"Have no fear, have no fear," answered the little man with bitter disdain, giving her a sidelong glance, almost as if he were looking down on her. "There's no law against crying. And if there was, it's me who's crying, not you. Nothing is going to happen to you. They know you're not one to shed a tear for anybody."

"That's my business. And if you had any brain you wouldn't do it either."

"I weep because everything that's Serbian is weeping, and I'm not ashamed of it. And we'll see how far *your* brain will take you. And right now I'd prefer you to call me a weakling and a fool for crying here than to be an exception and a renegade like some."

And who knows how long this muffled bickering in the shadowy recesses of the store might have continued and what else they might have said to each other if a customer had not walked in from the street and interrupted them.

The strain that had existed between them up to that point grew even more outspoken now, but this attrition was so natural and unfeigned on both sides that they did not feel it was a particular burden, since each of them continued to do what he had to and in the only way he knew how.

Yet in the whole gallery of personalities and scenes of that period, which to this day remained clear in her mind in their details, although basically incomprehensible in their over-all meaning, the figure of Rafo Konforti stood out as something apart.

As early as the end of 1914, there had been a noticeable change in his work, speech, and manner; as time went on he changed more and more. She herself could not say when these changes had taken place or how they had developed, but she saw plainly and felt unmistakably that the man was changing. First, there came the rise. Konforti's climb was sudden, but, contrary to the laws of physics, and in conformity with the laws of society, he became not smaller but bigger in the eyes of his fellow citizens. The transformation was so swift and so profound that Miss Raika was unable to conjure up the Konforti of prewar years even in her memory. He became grave, calm, and self-possessed in his whole manner, stingy with words and sparse in his movements. There was no trace left of the fiery eyes and shaking hands, none of the rasping or those melodramatic oaths in his speech. Now he talked to her politely and attentively, yet was somewhat distant and strange and opaque, as though he were simultaneously watching, hearing, and thinking something else that was more important. He would grant a man anything but not his attention. He had left behind his old business connections and all his petty moneylending; his long narrow shop in Ferhadya had been turned into one of the many warehouses for his merchandise. Konforti himself sat in the brand-new well-lighted offices of the firm "Textile, A. G."— that is to say, he sat there when he wasn't traveling on business or to conferences in Vienna, Prague, or Budapest. And when he sometimes came back from these trips, he appeared even more distant and preoccupied to Miss Raika. In the summer of 1916, he went with his wife to Karlsbad and returned from there even quieter and more genteel, as if spruced up and somehow fairer.

With her own eyes, Miss Raika saw how that first million became a reality, and how quickly other millions came after it. And she wondered at how little resemblance all of it had to her own dream of a million—not even a vague resemblance. She observed it all, yet saw and understood very little. And before she could begin to grasp anything, there came the downfall. Just as she had not understood the dynamics of Rafo's climb, so now she failed to notice the first symptoms of his decline.

The spring of 1917 arrived, a long and difficult spring, when among a hundred houses in Bosnia there might perhaps have been one in which the inmates could eat their fill, and not a single one had all it needed. On a day in March, which remained pale and desolate from dawn to dusk, Konforti "received" Miss Raika in a short interview. She had come to ask his advice and request his help in connection with the fourth issue of war bonds, announced a short while before, for it was her plan to subscribe a large sum and then sell out as quickly as possible without a major loss, which now was becoming harder and harder to do.

She had not seen him for a whole month. He sat in an enormous upholstered chair, with his head lolling and his eyes shut; there were purple-yellow rings under them. He started and sat upright. With evident constraint, he listened to what she was saying about the petty business for which she had come. Not waiting for her to finish, he sprang from his chair.

"Good, good, Miss Raika, we'll arrange that easily. It'll be as you say." Then he spread out his arms and began to pace the room, talking loudly, on another subject altogether. "Ah, everything can be arranged, everything else is easy. But the people have to eat! Clothes are a simple matter. You can patch them up, you can turn them around. But you can't go without food! Look, Miss Raika, a hungry people, that's the worst thing there is. They can't make war, they can't live in peace. When there's no business, there's no life. A catastrophe!"

Miss Raika listened and followed him with her eyes, from one end of the room to the other. His wrought-up voice and quick movements contrasted with his appearance and bearing: as if under the dignified mask of a great captain of commerce there suddenly peered out the old Rafo Konforti from Ferhadya. She could not understand this unexpected outburst of indignation, or see what possible connection she, Raika, and her business had with the question of whether the people were hungry or full. It was something she simply never thought about. She asked herself now whether she ought to make some remark or other, but Konforti apparently did not expect her to contribute to the conversation, for he continued to pace the room and speak with bitterness, as if tossing words to someone in the distance.

"Your reason tells you that people have to eat first. Everything else comes afterwards. What can you ask of a hungry man? His soul? That's nonsense!"

He marched up and down a while longer, then halted abruptly, controlled himself, and said good-bye to Miss Raika, becoming quiet and vacuous once again. But from that day on Miss Raika began to look at him with different eyes.

From that day on she, too, began to watch and observe with more attention the signs of hunger, privation, dissatisfaction, and decline around her, in the people, in the authorities, and in the business district. And the signs were more numerous than she would have wanted. She did not have enough imagination to see them as different aspects of a whole, to penetrate down to their underlying causes, but she noticed them everywhere. They led her to think that war was nothing more than a large-scale undertaking, an enterprise whose ultimate scope could not be seen but which, like any other business, had its own bookkeeping and its final tallying, with the inexorable consequences of loss and gain. More and more often she thought about the end of the war and the effect which its outcome might have on her and her interests. It was beginning to dawn on her that her "good times" were coming to an end, that conditions around her were turning and changing, and that those stormy and difficult, yet for her quiet and fruitful, years would not and could not come back.

Veso was now visited in the store by young people who had managed to put off their military service; they talked to him quietly for hours on end, but the moment Miss Raika appeared in the doorway the conversation would falter completely or else take on a studied and insincere tone. As for Raika's mother, she still received visits from relatives whose next of kin had been arrested; however, the women no longer cried in that quiet helpless way of old but smiled pointedly and exchanged flashing looks. Divna was thinner and harder than ever. She was out of mourning. She cried no more. Her husband and brother-in-law were in Russia. Having served the first few months of the war in a camp at Arad, they had been made officers and sent to the Russian front. There they had taken the first opportunity and crossed over to the Russian lines. Now they were serving in the volunteer division of the South Slavs in the Russian army. The police and army authorities had harassed Divna and the rest of the family for a while with arrests and investigations, they confiscated the property of the two deserters, but none of it could shake Divna out of her stony calm. When they questioned her about the whereabouts of her husband and his brother, she would answer: "They are where they ought to be."

Aunt Gospava, who had been tactless and blunt even during the difficult initial years of the war, still talked quite boldly and openly. Her son had been sentenced to seven years in prison and was now in jail at Zenitsa, yet she told everyone that she was easy in her mind because she knew he would not serve more than half his sentence. As soon as she arrived at Mrs. Obren's, and before she ever sat down, she announced in her husky voice that she had been visited the day before by "some girls" who were making collections for the Red Cross, and that she had told them she would not give a penny, "seeing as I have my own cross up at Zenitsa."

Miss Raika shied away from these meetings and avoided

them as much as she could, but did so now with a sense of fear and discomfort, with a nagging unease she had not known earlier. And signs were multiplying, ever clearer and more explicit.

It happened that in the autumn of 1917 a large army assembled in Sarajevo, so that officers had to be billeted in private homes—as had been the case at the outbreak of the war in 1914. Thus an officer was assigned quarters in the Radakovich house, which so far had been spared. The officer in question was a young army doctor, a Croat, born somewhere in Slavonia, too fat for his years but a good-humored, sensible, and unassuming man. His name was Dr. Roknich. He was quiet and orderly, and demanded no privileges, which somewhat appeased Miss Raika's anger about the billet, but he had one uncomfortable quality: he loved to talk about everything under the sun, and especially about politics. To Miss Raika, any talk that did not concern her business was difficult and unpleasant at best; as for politics, she avoided them with a real aversion and superstitious fear. She listened now with dread as this man in the uniform of an Austrian lieutenant talked to her mother in his carefree, unctuous Slavonian accents.

"I am happy, madame, to be quartered in a Serbian house. I know what you people, the Serbs of Bosnia, have suffered and still have to put up with, and I want to ask you to ignore this uniform which I'm obliged to wear and not to look upon me as an Austrian officer."

The old lady gave him that faint little smile which most members of the Hadzi-Vasich family brought into the world at the moment when they first opened their eyes. Miss Raika was so surprised and appalled that she turned her back quickly and went into her room.

That was only the beginning, however. Whenever he was free, the doctor would join them on one pretext or another and casually and quietly begin to chat about this or that. As soon as the talk turned to war and politics, Miss Raika would squirm and look for a handy excuse to remove herself. Once or twice she tried to argue with him, maintaining that she and her house were in no way involved in the political fights, in the troubles of the Serbs and similar goings on, that she was content with the way things were and with her life.

The doctor would gaze at her out of his clear blue eyes behind large unrimmed glasses. "Look, Miss Raika, there's no need for you to say these things in front of me. I can't believe those are your feelings. If they are, you certainly are an exception and absolutely on the wrong track. Today anyone in his right mind will tell you that the Central Powers can't win this war, that they must lose. And it's good that it is so. It's good for all humanity, and a salvation and good fortune for all of us South Slavs, because otherwise we would disappear from the face of this earth."

And the young doctor told her some of the things he had seen on the Russian front, where he had spent the whole of 1915, and on the Italian front, from which he had just returned. He told her all he knew about conditions in the world, the activities of the Serbian government in exile on the island of Corfu, and the committee for the liberation of South Slavs. He spoke about the victory of the Entente and the defeat of Germany and Austria as an accomplished fact, and about the unification of all South Slavs as a natural outcome of that development. He quoted the speeches of the South Slav national delegates in the parliament at Vienna.

For Miss Raika all these were new and frightening things; she had never wanted to think about them, let alone discuss them. She was furious with the talkative doctor and cursed the day they had sent him to her house. She was forced now to think about them and had to admit to herself that she was afraid of the war's end and did not wish it to turn out the way the doctor had pictured it. Often these days, before she fell asleep, her usual fretting about money and business would suddenly be overshadowed by the awful thought that "things might go bad" after all, that the old turbulent times might return, with their newspaper attacks and long-haired students who boded no good for themselves or for others. And she only managed to fall asleep after she had warded off such thoughts by a most determined effort.

A fortnight later the pudgy and garrulous doctor left Sarajevo with his unit and by then Miss Raika could no longer shut her eyes to the prospect of the war's end and its outcome. It would be a terrible day, it seemed to her—a day when this bewitched stillness around her would be shattered, when all the men at the fronts, in prisoner camps and jails, would come back home, make their accusations, file their claims, and try to take up their old positions. She really could not imagine what it would look like, and knew only that life would be terribly dislocated and that everyone, herself not excluded, would be called upon to make extraordinary sacrifices and shoulder heavy responsibilities. And now, whatever she observed and heard around her only had the effect of multiplying such reflections and creating new anxieties, painful visions, and gnawing premonitions.

The year 1918 was indeed quite bleak. The people were tired and worn out by the long winter and near-starvation; the war seemed to be lost and endless at the same time. Business was no longer what it once had been. Trading had become a mad game of figures, a frantic hustle after hidden merchandise, leather or textiles, a headlong flight from paper money, and a blind rush for security and double security in the perpetual uncertainty. Anyone who needed money and had a predatory disposition, a pair of sound legs, and strong elbows, would get into the fray and grab his portion of a wagonload of goods that happened to be in demand at the moment, then withdraw with a profit and await the next opportunity. Suddenly everybody seemed to be in business— soldiers, priests, waiters, students who had not graduated—so that "real business people" didn't know where they were and could not keep up with the merry-go-round.

Rafo Konforti, whom Miss Raika scarcely let out of her sight these days, was the embodiment of all those changes for the worse. Like the war itself, he and his greatness were burning out. Invisibly, but fast, as once they had mushroomed, his business activities were ebbing and snarling; everything shook and disintegrated, as if by itself. And just as swiftly, though noticeably, Rafo's health, too, fell apart. Less and less did he resemble the Rafo Konforti of the "good" war years. When he received her, she would observe right away how much thinner and more preoccupied he was than the last time she had seen him. Nowadays it took quite an effort on her part to get him to concentrate enough for a realistic discussion of the serious business for which she would come to see him. It was plain that he had a compulsive need to talk of the hunger and destitution of the great mass of people and of the grave consequences this was bound to have for the state, the economy, and the individual. No matter how they opened the conversation, in the end he always concluded it with that. It was apparent that this idea obsessed him and pursued him, that it wore him out steadily and relentlessly. When he didn't talk about it, he fell into a gloomy silence and stared in front of him as if lost.

More and more often one read in the daily press that Rafo Konforti had donated a barrel of fat or a wagonload of cabbage to the People's Kitchen or the Poorhouse. Lately he had taken to buying various provisions in order to sell them to the people at an unusually low price. His old shop in Ferhadya came to life again. People collected in front of it in long queues and waited to lay their hands on a little food, "at Master Rafo's prices." As they distributed the food, his boys had trouble holding back the restless and hungry crowds, while Konforti telephoned now and then from his office in "Textiles, A. G." and demanded to know how big the crowd was and how the distribution was progressing. And sometimes, losing patience, he would leave his warm comfortable office and run like one pursued to verify everything in person and hand out the remaining food to the neediest without charge.

Miss Raika could not understand what was happening to Konforti, but one thing was plain: she could no longer expect anything of him, neither assistance nor advice, not even a simple sober conversation about business. She wouldn't have thought it possible that this man, so deft and full of energy, could become so utterly lost. And she felt abandoned and isolated—something that had never happened to her before. Instinctively and for the first time in her life, she cast about for a human being with whom she might talk and consult and in whom she would find understanding and support.

With Veso she was on bad terms. In reality he was the same man he had always been—modest and infinitely de-

voted to their house and store, but at the same time outspoken and firm in his disapproval of Raika, her attitude
and her behavior during the war. In any case, he had lately
become quite wrapped up in those whispered discussions with
the young men from the Serbian bazaar. She noted this with
misgiving and profound mistrust but dared not ask him
about it.

It was the first time since she had become an adult that she
felt herself weaker than and subordinated to the little man.
She had never had a high opinion of his ability or his convictions, but now she felt that there were some things in
which he was stronger than she, in which he surpassed her,
and she watched in awe how quietly and self-confidently he
went about the store, his eyes sparkling, while his blond and
usually limp hair curled up to a defiant mop on his forehead. This Veso, who had grown up in their house, stood before her now like a stranger without any sympathy or real
understanding, almost in judgment.

She had not seen her guardian Master Mihailo for some
years, except at Christmas and on his birthday. He was bedridden now—and had been for over six months—more dead
than alive, and unable to look after business or give advice.

She thought about director Paier. During the war years
she had not been in need of his favors, and she had seen him
rarely and talked very little with him, never even noticing
that a certain coolness and distance had crept into their relationship. Now she went to see him, ostensibly to discuss some
promissory notes she had deposited in the Union Bank but
actually hoping to talk about business and money in general,
and to hear from him what sort of change might be in the of-
fing and what one was supposed to do if "the thing" really

came about—the thing they were all whispering about and no one was willing to discuss with her clearly and openly.

Paier, too, was the same as he had always been. It was hard to say how much commotion was needed to make him change his manner or attitude toward people. Yet he either would not, or didn't know how to, tell her that which mainly concerned her, about which she had come. While one talked to Paier, all thing seemed to become transparently clear, easy, and well defined and all problems seemed to dissolve in mist, only to reappear once again the minute one came out of his office. Indeed, when Miss Raika left him, she was neither better informed nor quieter in her heart. On the contrary, she asked herself in wonder and puzzlement why Herr Paier, just like Veso, paused and deliberated between sentences, why the words of the two men revealed nothing, why their silences were heavy with unspoken distrust and mysterious reproaches. Why did the men she turned to flutter their eyes in that evasive fashion, gaze at her cryptically, and dwell on things that were not in the least important to her, and so coolly and aloofly that in the end she herself became confused and grew rigid and forgot to ask them what she needed? She searched her mind for an answer but couldn't find it—for after all these years she had still not learned to observe, examine, and look at herself with the eyes of another person. Instead, all she felt was the burden of loneliness and isolation which now lay twice as heavily upon her.

As for her mother, she never thought of her as someone she could talk to or consult with in anything.

What remained now was that grave in Koshevo. But even the grave had somehow lost its power of speech—nor was it easy for her to summon up her old words and impassioned whispers. But she went there all the same, rigid and scowling, every Sunday, punctual and conscientious as always, along the same path and at the same hour. She sat beside the grave but could not, as in the past, explain her clear plans and accounts; all she could offer him were muddled fears and vague but somber glimpses of the future. And when the usual time had elapsed, she would set off for home with her eyes to the ground, with that brisk step which was familiar to the whole town, more rigid than before and scowling fiercely, for she had not found the comfort she had sought. Miss Raika thought that the summer of 1918 would never come to an end. It didn't seem at all like a usual season of the year but more like a time of utter standstill, a time of bated breath in which one waited for something to happen.

People were restless, they behaved strangely. An early end of the war seemed almost certain, victories and upheavals came thick and fast, vague hopes and obscure fears nestled side by side in men's minds. Miss Raika was among those who were afraid.

As during that summer four years before when war was declared, she had trouble falling asleep with all her thoughts, calculations, and anxieties, except that then the object of her fear had been a clear and tangible danger, the war itself, whereas now every little thing made her jittery and this was much harder to live with, since those who quail before things they don't know quail twice over. But then as now, all her thoughts and energies tended in one direction: not to remain on the side that would suffer and lose. Never, never to be part of it! To stay clear of it at all costs!

But how was one to know which was the right, the winning side? How was one to hold fast in a world where everything was spinning, changing, moving in fits and starts? Was there such a thing as a quiet spot where a person might live and make money undisturbed, without having to share it with anyone? Was there anything worth depending on when even the power that had always seemed unassailable, the force which all of mankind regarded as supreme, in the end showed itself to be perishable and afforded very little protection?

Without the least understanding or even a dim appreciation of the world at large and the currents that now rent it with the noise and fury of conflict, Miss Raika indulged in the kind of reasoning that was a mixture of false premises and contradictory conclusions. At one moment she would tell herself that her life, her business, and her own person were in no way involved in all this, but a minute later she would be convinced that the events around her were closely and vitally bound up with her interests. She would wake up suddenly in the middle of the night with a stab of distress, aware of the loud erratic pounding of her heart, and would imagine herself foundering in the dark, helpless and ignorant as never before, wrenched forever from the kind of life and attitudes she had been accustomed to, so that she could no longer understand the world around her and herself in it. She trembled at the thought that a day might come when all that she had built and hoarded up would be jeopardized, when everything she considered solid and impregnable might come undone.

Indeed, seen from the private little niche in which she had watched the war from the very beginning, things did look peculiar and unbelievable. She had never paid much attention to what was going on and her ideas about the war were rather sketchy; yet here and now, in the place in which she lived and worked, something dreadful and inadmissible was about to happen: the side which represented authority, military power, and money, one that meant peace and order and thus also work and wages and an existence for those who desired only to live quietly and go after their own business, this side was about to be routed; and the side that preached and spread anarchy, the party of ferment, uncertainty, and stagnation, indeed the party of inevitable ruin, was to gain the upper hand. She could neither grasp such a horror nor become used to it as long as she lived.

It was during one of those nights that she had an appalling dream. She seemed to wake up suddenly, but it was a strange kind of awakening—from the depths of absolute unconsciousness straight into the white stark light of a day that knew neither dawn nor dusk but lay stonelike over the earth. She rose and wanted to do her little morning chores as usual, but immediately, after the first few steps, she was overcome by an odd sort of heaviness. Everything gave her trouble or went inexplicably wrong. She was nagged by the feeling that she had slept through some fateful appointed hour and missed an important piece of business, missed it and lost it forever. What kind of day is this? Miss Raika asked herself. It had been light for some time and she really ought to get going, yet her limbs felt weighted down and every movement was a strain, as if she were dragging herself through water. Her eyes drooped as if still filled with the dust of sleep. Was she in fact awake?

There are days of this kind that seem to begin on the wrong foot, with a sense of lateness and gloom, and all day long things go badly and mysteriously wrong. There are such days, but this was not one of them. This was a day on which something was bound to happen—if it hadn't happened already.

Yes, it must have. She herself could not name the moment when she first became aware of it, for it was not something she perceived all at once but rather gradually, bit by little bit, with each new step, each new word and glance.

The first person she met on leaving the house was the mail carrier. The only thing he had for her was a single letter, flimsy and unimportant-looking.

"No money orders?" she asked him mechanically.

"No, Miss Raika. There's no such thing any more."

She scanned his face slowly. It was the old, familiar, tired one, the face of a redhead. Yet today a canny smile played over it, and in his yellow-green eyes there was a sly and knowing twinkle. It was an air of gloating, such as a little man from the lower orders might allow himself when given a chance. She turned her back on him and went into town.

In the street, too, she came across more faces of the same kind. She could not say exactly what kind, but she could tell they were somehow changed. And as she passed from one to another, almost as if each face were a separate letter, she deciphered the meaning of this extraordinary day, until at last the whole unbelievable and electrifying truth lay naked before her: all money had vanished from the world! Money had ceased to exist. It had no meaning any more, from any viewpoint whatever.

Miss Raika felt as if someone had struck her on the top of her head, her eyes misted over and her mouth fell open. She stood rooted in the middle of the street. Then, remembering her cash box, her account books and notes, she darted forward.

She burst into her shop as if racing through fire, unlocked the safe-box with trembling hands, and rummaged blindly through the empty compartments, passing her fingers along the cool, bare, steel sides. She called out to Veso, the book-keeper—in vain, for he never was around when one needed him. Or could it be that when money ceased to exist the accountants and everything that had to do with money likewise vanished without a trace?

She rushed outside and began to call Veso, the police, someone, anyone at all, desperately anxious to find out what had happened to her and to the world around her. She screamed at the top of her lungs and beat her forehead and breast with her clenched fist, as if the flesh were not her own but someone else's. No one answered her or paid the slightest attention. She went on again, looking for people.

She peered into one shop after another. Everywhere it was the same thing—no one sold or bought anything for money. They all gave her the same sly glance and a leer, as if she were a dim-witted crank ignorant of something the whole world had known for some time. With each new step, with each question and reply, the truth grew clearer and more inescapable: money had ceased to exist. Money had indeed vanished from the face of the earth, as though it were a worthless and redundant thing. The planet had yielded up its last penny and no one seemed to miss it. People carried on, they worked and traded as before, but without currency.

"But how? What happened?" stammered Miss Raika.

"Well, you can see for yourself," a store-owner told her, impassive and distant behind his counter, just as once he might have said, "Our prices are fixed, Miss Raika."

"But what about the people whose business was money, who traded only in money?"

The minute she tried to find out more, tried to get to the bottom of this uncanny phenomenon that had all the earmarks of a freak grotesque dream, they all began to wink and grin, pretending to be busy with their things. Only one petty shopkeeper, fussing among the goods on the shelves, condescended to inform her over his shoulder: "All right, there used to be money. Now it's gone. Don't you have anything better to do than ask questions?"

And that was the end of the conversation.

She stopped at an intersection and asked herself through tears, like a lost child: What business can there be without money?

There now—she too had spoken the eerie, unspeakable truth out loud. There was no more money on earth! They had plundered the globe. No, that was not it. The truth was even more shattering, more monstrous: the people had given up the very idea of money. The world had lost all meaning. Gold coins had become like so many forgeries, paper bills were tossed on the garbage heap like those advertising throwaways which are handed out on the street corners and which promptly end up in the nearest litter basket. Stock shares were discarded like old magazines. Promissory notes were like letters from utter strangers who have long since passed away—incomprehensible, empty of meaning or value. Account books were frozen at the last entry and now lay useless and dead like some granite tablets riddled with obscure hieroglyphics.

Miss Raika continued on her way, staggering through the white metallic daylight from block to block, from one street corner to another. Now every little thing impressed her as merely fresh evidence of the fact that money had abandoned the earth and the world had become like a body without breath, without blood, too weak to stir. And most incredible of all, people seemed to be adjusting and taking it in their stride, as if in their infinite spite they had already made their peace with the idea of living without money.

What does it mean . . . ? Life has become a travesty and a wilderness, but still we have to live and go on. "Yes, we used to have it, but now it's gone!" No, it is simply a colossal fraud, a fantastic larceny! Or else the sick joke of some idle, good-for-nothing moron! In the name of God, what is it all about? Where is the government, where are the police? Why don't the courts and the Church do something?

She cried for help at the top of her lungs. Passers-by stared at her in cold astonishment. A policeman swaggered up and warned her to behave herself, otherwise he would have to take her to the station and lock her up.

So it's gone as far as that! The authorities have abdicated their responsibility and washed their hands of the whole thing. Appalled, Miss Raika hurried on. If it had come to that, where were the priests, the imams, and the rabbis? Wasn't there any law and justice left?

The priests were in their churches and vestries, doing more or less what they always did. Their gestures were the same as always: the same traditional rubbing of hands and the same tired old answers. There is but one currency in the world and its name is Grace. One must accept the will of Providence with a good heart. And in any case, their one abiding concern was Eternal Life; in the affairs of this world they merely bowed to the trends of the times.

Sickened and discouraged to the core, she ran from one to another and presently found herself in the square in front of the church. The clock in the tower struck nine. Thirteen chimes in all. There, the clock is still working and chiming! Hours are still counted, numbers still existed! But without money what was the point of it all? What was there to measure and count? Have they not robbed arithmetic of all reason for existence? Or had it, too, like everything else, adapted itself to the new order?

Miss Raika wished she could reach up to the tower and spit at the clock and all its numerals. In the fevered onset of this wish she felt as if an inner floodgate had suddenly burst open and swamped all of her with a rage she had never known. She yelled as loudly as she could, but the yelling was like a whisper compared to the overmastering rage she wanted to express: "Oh, you wretches! You cowards!"

Hurling the words in the face of Time and the whole world, she felt herself abandoned, defeated, all alone, but at the same time defiant and swept aloft by her indestructible love of money, her fierce last-ditch courage, her contempt for them all. Where are those now who are supposed to protect and save holy money? thought Miss Raika. Not one of them would lift his little finger! Yet they had all loved money; they had lusted after it so greatly, so passionately. She knew it better than anyone. Hadn't she watched them a thousand times in the most unbelievable, most ludicrous, most depressing plight and circumstances? For money they would have sold their all, they would have done anything. And now, overnight, they had betrayed it and turned their backs on it. Such is the true nature of the animal that calls itself man: he will shift with every wind and tag along with anything as long as he is allowed to continue here on earth, under the sun, in any condition and shape and at any price.

Now the wave of black thoughts and consuming rage, of bitterness, desolation, and futility, heaved up and broke over her, clouding her sight, smothering her voice, turning her knees to putty. She slid to the ground and lay motionless, a small puddle of clothing in the center of the cobblestone square.

At that point Miss Raika woke up and really opened her eyes. In the faintly opalescent light of the early dawn, filtering in through the window, her mad tortured dream melted away. And this real awakening was not less agonizing than the one she had dreamed. For some minutes her groping fingers felt and verified the warm pillow under her. Anger still coursed through her and all of her body still felt the cold touch of those stones in the church square. For a while yet the dream and wakefulness blended and lingered around her, until at last reality took hold and composed itself into the steady familiar shape of her room. By that time Miss Raika was on her feet.

Undressed as she was, she ran over to her writing table, unlocked the middle drawer, the one secured with an American lock, pulled out her leather handbag and shook the contents on the desk. There were six bills of twenty kronen each and some change. She examined them with bated breath, then stuffed them back in the purse.

There, everything was all right again! If these six bills were where they ought to be, then surely all the rest of the world's money must be in its proper place. Of course! It had only been a dream, an insane and hideous dream. Now it was over. How was it possible to dream such nonsense at all? And was there any connection between reality and dreams . . . ? The speculation left her with a faint sense of unease, like a shadow, and she resolved not to spend any more time brooding over it.

Feeling chilly, she went back to her warm bed. Her heart beat fast and irregularly, her breathing was still hard. The warmth of her bed and the cozy reassurance of reality soon calmed her. She closed her eyes firmly and dozed off again, even as a bubble of words, like a soft sound of chiding, burst and evaporated on her lips.

She rose as usual, a little before seven; then dressed, ate her breakfast, and walked to her shop. But even out on the street the sense of discomfort from the night's dream kept rankling in her and from time to time a doubt of the reality around her grazed her like a cloud.

Arriving at the shop, she ran into the postman in the doorway. This time he had actually brought some money orders. With some agitation she counted the bills, once, twice—and here again, a disbelief of reality shot through her mind. She hesitated a moment, then signed the receipts. Clasping the money to her chest, she lifted her head and studied the face of the man for a long searching moment. It was the old familiar face, harried and puffed from exertion (as though it were saying, "The work's not really hard, but the pay is low, the kids keep coming; trying to make ends meet is a job, I'm telling you"). There was no trace of that leer and the sly blinking she remembered from the dream. It was all right, then. Now at long last she felt completely reassured. She dropped both her hands on her little antique desk and, opening her palms, pressed them down hard on the green ink-stained baize. She gave a deep sigh.

Meanwhile the postman, having passed from the cold dusky shop into the sunlight of the winter morning, stopped for an instant and shuddered. All in one movement he seemed to shake off both his own gooseflesh and the memory of those piercing, frightened, and terrible eyes. Then, once more, he set off on his rounds, keeping to the sunny side of the street and muttering soundlessly to himself: "Brother, the way that woman looks. What good is all that money to her? She looks terrible, just terrible!"

So Miss Raika tormented herself in the sultry sleepless nights. The summer went by. The month of October was still full of warmth and greenery. Days and weeks seemed excruciatingly long, because events were piling up fast, overtaking one another like the final chords of a symphony; each one seemed to be the last, but after each one there would come, unexpectedly and inexorably, yet another. And then, at long last, the final one was sounded.

Miss Raika was taken unawares, as people of her sort usually are, by the very thing she had been dreading all this time—by the thing she had endlessly anticipated and pictured in her mind in the minutest detail.

(At this point her memory usually broke off; without quite fading or blacking out, it began to resemble a reel of film suddenly gone wild; it kept turning and working but showed and said nothing beyond a whirling streak of blurred spots and lines.)

One day in October, which was like all the other days— when she was neither less afraid nor more hopeful than usual —the houses of the town suddenly sprouted the first tricolors and the crowds in the streets began to embrace and kiss, weeping with joy. Tears once more! That day Veso didn't show up to open the store. Miss Raika walked through the city like a foreigner and one condemned. No one came forward to embrace her or stretch his hand out to her, and still she shrank back with loathing from all that public muzzling and squirmed at the sight of those perpetual tears, that great excitement, the loud gushing, and all those speeches and chatter.

She sat in her cold shop, feeling goosefleshy all over. Mentally she ticked off her far-flung investments and loans. It didn't seem likely that this time would pass without great damage. That was already quite plain. She wondered only how to cut her losses. She thought frantically, like a person who had to pluck from a blaze or storm that which was most precious to him and most immediately threatened, and who had only a minute or two in which to do it. She was startled out of her thoughts by loud steps and excited voices. Veso came in, accompanied by a group of young men. Some were armed. All were talking and gesturing with high animation. Her first thought was that they were drunk. She wanted to talk with Veso, but they wouldn't let her finish a sentence and seemed to look down at her with disdain, frowning and blinking their eyes as if they were unable to see her well or recognize her because she was so tiny. Nor did Veso behave any better. Never before had she seen him so wrought up. He waved his arms and kept talking incoherently.

"Oh, leave it alone, Raika! Who cares about that now! What counts is today, it's what we've waited for. If we die tomorrow, it won't matter! Go home. Oh, what a joy this is, don't you see!"

She saw nothing, except that his eyes were round and his unshaven good-natured face was high with color.

But things did not continue as innocently as they had

begun. In the store and in the streets, and even in her own home, acquaintances and strangers began to needle and taunt her with mocking remarks, and a few reviled her openly and rudely for her behavior during the war. She would rather not remember some of the things she was now obliged to put up with. It was all much worse and harder to bear than she could ever have foreseen. Judging by the words and attitude of the people who teased her maliciously or assailed her openly, her sin must have been particularly enormous in their eyes, but try as she might, she simply could not see what this sin of hers consisted of. All she saw was their inexplicable hatred and their urge to set her back, harm her, and foil her every undertaking. When she read newspaper articles and speeches describing the hardships and injustices suffered by some people during the years of war, she asked herself whether it was possible that this had actually happened in the same country and town in which she lived. At times it seemed to her that all these people had suddenly gone off their heads—all except her—and that that was the reason why they looked at her so crossly and persecuted her so mercilessly.

To people like Miss Raika, the world must very often appear to be hell. Insensible to most of the rules of the community and to the moral feelings and responses of an individual, incapable of perceiving their existence, let alone grasping their slow but inexorable effect, she really could not see the causal relation between what was happening to her and what she had done, watched, and heard during 1914 and 1915. And this was the most piteous aspect of her present torment. She did not know that violence and injustice led to revenge, that revenge itself was blind, and that those who were the target of it always felt it to be the blackest injustice. Just as she didn't know that even the most righteous punishment was invariably tainted with envy and deep-seated human malice. Utterly unaware of the fine points of violence and injustice, punishment and revenge, she yet realized perfectly clearly that she was now on the side that was being persecuted and harmed.

She did, in fact, suffer damage, and it threatened to get worse with each passing day. She dared not go to present her notes, and it would not have done her any good if she had. Business was at a standstill, the courts were empty, banks kept up a pretense of working, maturity dates came and went unenforced, bills of exchange lay inactive. People came from every quarter to take up collections, but no one paid his debts; men laughed at their creditors and borrowed more money, as if tomorrow were the end of the world. And newspapers wrote about taxes and war profits, about the expropriation of land estates, about big and small schemes under which the haves were to be deprived of many millions in favor of the have-nots. Often Miss Raika had the impression that whole countries and nations had made up their minds to commit wholesale suicide in one glorious spree, to eat and drink, celebrate and spend money, until every last person was rid of his last farthing.

Things in general seemed to go against her.

Right at the outset, during one of those October days, she witnessed the final downfall of Master Rafo with her own eyes. One morning she walked through Ferhadya, avoiding the main streets which were full of excited and enthusiastic crowds. There was a large throng of people in front of Rafo's old shop, and one could hear loud shouting and a wave of boisterous laughter. She approached the shop gingerly and saw Rafo Konforti behind his counter, turning over some limp vegetables with wet soiled hands. He had lost a lot of weight and looked quite sallow; he was bareheaded and without a tie. His clothes were soiled and disheveled. His eyes rolled timidly from side to side and he was saying something that was hard to understand because of the constant interruptions and loud guffawing from the crowd. It was only when he raised his voice that one could make out single words.

"There, not a penny left! People have to eat. I know it, even if the others don't. You've got to eat, so there!"

But the people, as if suddenly not hungry any more, laughed at the sick man and watched him with that heartless curiosity with which men watch even the most depressing spectacles as soon as they feel themselves part of a multitude.

Some were offensive and spiteful.

"Take it home, Master Rafo, and eat it yourself!"

"Is this what the late lamented Austria left you for safekeeping?"

"You put away all those millions and now you're giving us kale to eat!"

Others were more moderate and willing to treat the whole thing as a joke. They told him he was still the same old wizard and they could not believe that what he was doing now was not some kind of "bargain deal." Rafo clapped his hands to his chest, as he used to do years before, swore a solemn oath, praised his wares, and tried to answer every remark, asserting in a tearful voice that his only concern was that people should not go hungry. Except that when he had done this in the old days he had been hale, hearty, and live as a flea, whereas now he stammered awkwardly, slurring his words, and punctuated his speech with feeble, irrelevant gestures.

She turned her head and hurried away, to avoid looking at the misery and ruin of the man of whom it was possible to say that he was her friend, if such a thing at all existed in her consciousness.

That same day Rafo was taken to a mental institution.

And so days and weeks went by; but the excitement, rejoicing, and commotion in the town did not die down. Quite the contrary. It seemed as if all of life were about to be transformed from the ground up. First units of the Serbian army entered Sarajevo. This was followed by a round of celebrations and parades, banquets and thanksgiving; delegations began to arrive, new dailies saw the light of day, names of streets and institutions were changed. It was all too clear to Raika that this was no mere three-day wonder.

The New Year saw the appearance of a brand-new morning newspaper—*The Serbian Flag*. The main function of this ultranationalist daily seemed to be to judge and brand all those who during the war "had sinned against the honor of the people and its interests." In a special column, which opened with the words "In the name of order, justice, and peace, we demand . . ." certain individuals and institutions were sharply attacked. Here Miss Raika was also mentioned on one occasion—not by name, it is true, but the allusion was unmistakable. One of her relatives, who knew the editor quite well, went to see him and managed to stop further attacks.

However, what was effective with one newspaper didn't work with another. The newly founded *People's Voice* assailed, in its city columns, all war profiteers such as Rafo Konforti and the like, mentioning also the name of Raika Rada-kovich. That paper was presently joined by the Social Democratic *Freedom,* which had resumed publication. Here there were articles about "usurious interest rates," "transactions that wouldn't stand the light of day," "spiders that suck the blood of people and society." The writers demanded that the government appoint a special commission to scrutinize the activities and incomes of all war profiteers, and expressed the hope that "our society will, as far as possible, forever remove from our midsts such parasitic and harmful members, regardless of their positions and family connections."

The threats sounded serious and actually dangerous at the time; and the accusations were widely read, spread around, and interpreted throughout the city, in family circles, and reached all the way into Miss Raika's home.

Since she never saw anyone, she could not form an accurate idea of what the world thought and said about her. This was revealed to her piecemeal and by accident. One autumn night she woke up with a start, feeling as if someone were clutching her throat and as if her own heart were strangling her breath. (This had been happening to her quite often lately.) She rose quickly and threw open the window, trying to fill her lungs with the cool night air as quickly as possible. As she stood there, breathing hard and feeling goosefleshy all over, she heard on the street below her, somewhere along the river, a group of drunk men calling to one another. They came toward the house with much shouting, cursing, and laughter. Two of them stopped and leaned against the wall of her house. Hiccuping and cursing, they urinated right beneath her window. Stepping back from the window, she listened to their drunk and disconnected talk.

"I get cold easily," complained the first drunk, "and it's no wonder, my soles are worn clean through. Here it's almost winter and I still don't have a winter coat. And I don't see myself getting one."

"You can blame it on the brandy."

"Brandy nothing! I hardly see the stuff. If today weren't a holiday, I wouldn't have had a drop."

One of the drunks backed away and, as he fumbled long and awkwardly with his buttons, looked more closely around him. "What do you know! This is the house of Raika Radakovich."

The other man, still loafing by the wall, called her an ugly name and uttered a hideous oath, one that Raika had not only never heard but had never thought possible, one of those oaths in which heaven and earth were coupled in a single disgusting phrase.

"I hear she made a pile with the Germans. Now during the war . . ."

"During the war and before. She's been lending money at interest for I don't know how many years. I heard the men talking about it at the pothouse. There's no bigger usurer in all Bosnia, they said. She does it secretly, but all legal and proper like. A regular leech, I tell you! She's never been sorry for anybody. Has no idea what it means to be a Christian and have a soul. Counting her money, that's all she knows. There's no beggar ever got this much out of her. She'd grudge a pinch of incense to God himself."

"That kind, eh! Killing her would be a public service."

"Just killing her wouldn't be enough. I'd deal with that leech like they say in the old songs. Take her out on the road, pull a tarred shirt over her, and put a match to it. She'd burn like at torch. Like a torch!"

Lurching and cursing in unison, they went off after their companions, who were yelling for them in the darkness.

Miss Raika quickly shut the window and lay down. She had known more or less what her kinfolk and all the so-called better people were thinking about her; and now, with her own ears, she had heard the common folk, the ragtag and bobtail, who in all probability had never seen her in their lives. All put together, they comprised a hard impenetrable ring of hate, which was steadily tightening all around her. With a troubled heart, unable to sleep, she wondered desperately where she could flee to hide herself from this rabble that didn't have a winter coat to its name and had to keep itself warm with hatred and brandy, yet found time to check on other people's income and rave about tarred shirts and grisly kinds of death.

It was during those winter months that she stopped, for the first time in her life, her Sunday visits to her father's grave. She sat at home and thought about the grave but had no courage to go out into the street. Her fear of meeting people was stronger than everything else. She, who never in her life had bothered about people and had never really noticed them, trembled now at the very thought of coming face to face with a passer-by and being stared at and baited by him. She stopped going to the store. Carrying on any kind of gainful activity was now out of the question. All doors were closed to her. Veso, too, advised her to lie low for a while.

Long and ugly were those months during which she was forced to hide in her room even from her closest kinfolk, when the hue and cry against her was so great that she couldn't help feeling ashamed even though she had no idea of the reason for it, since no awareness of guilt ever so much as entered her mind.

As late as a few months before, she had not believed that there was anything in the world that could be stronger than her will or could put her out of action. Now she realized that she had indeed been discarded, that she was lost, defeated, without any notion of why and when, by a mysterious power that could not be expressed in figures or bribed with money and against which nothing could be done. In vain she asked herself what had become of her cool strength and sullen contempt of everything. Now the strength was gone, and the contempt was returning, three times as great. Moping at home, as if under house arrest, she realized that she would not be able to endure it much longer unless there was some kind of change, unless time and space removed her and blocked her off from this town of Sarajevo, the scene of her defeat. However, time drags on maddeningly and not even the wisest or the richest man has the power either to speed it or to prolong it by a single second. There remained space. To go away, not to be here any more, might mean a new lease on life, with new prospects and fresh energies. Pulling up stakes—it would almost be the same as forgetting and being forgotten, therefore saved. Going away would be hard and painful, but not impossible.

The relatives agreed that it would be best for her and for the good name of the whole family if she left Sarajevo, at least for a time. Some proposed a short stay in Dubrovnik, others that she move to Belgrade, in Serbia. For the first time in her life, Raika had to give in—there really was no other way. Had she been willing to sit around the house like this for another six months or a year, completely isolated, not working or doing anything, perhaps the commotion would have died down with time. But the very thought that, after all the upheavals and losses she had sustained in recent weeks, she would have to sit idle and live off her capital, earning no money and neglecting her interests, stopped her heart cold, sent blood to her head, and cut her breath. She could already see herself using up her reserves and drifting into penury and wretchedness. And the mere thought was enough to choke her. She'd sooner go, not to Belgrade, but to the wild and godforsaken ends of the earth—for this she could not endure.

Some time during the summer it was decided that she would move with her mother to Belgrade, where an uncle of hers, George Hadzi-Vasich, had been living for many years. The mother agreed, as she usually did to everything, with a tearful fluttering of her trusting eyes. And Veso took it upon himself to mind the store and look after their house, for which he would try to find a tenant.

Toward the end of 1919, miss raika and her mother left Sarajevo. They took with them several trunks and packing cases, while the most essential furniture was crated up and entrusted to Veso, who was to ship it by rail the moment they let him know they had found an apartment in Belgrade.

The trip was long, tiring, and unpleasant in every respect. Trains were slow and schedules were unreliable. There were no windowpanes in the coaches, the seats were broken, the leather and silk upholstery had been stripped off. The rush of travelers at the wayside stations was so great that some nimble and reckless individuals clambered in through the windows. And these people, who crushed one another in the entrance and huddled in one another's laps or stood tightly packed in the corridors, were for the most part unclean and badly dressed, reeking of onion and brandy; they behaved rudely and spoke profanely. The stations which they passed on the way looked as if they had just emerged from a terrible flood: their walls were battered, their fences twisted, their flower beds trampled. The red-capped station master, who saw the train in, wore the look of a guilty, unhappy man.

For the first time, war was revealed to Miss Raika in its true colors, with all the desolation it wreaked and the deep marks it left behind—marks that were made in a moment but took ages to erase. She saw now that she had barely known it during the four years in which she had worked and made money, shunning everything that was difficult and dangerous, not sharing in any way in the common suffering and distress, living among her own things in her own house, more or less as though it were peacetime. And having now dismantled her home and set off on this long and difficult journey, the end of which was shrouded in uncertainty, it seemed to her that the events of the last few months had not been as unbearable as she had thought, and that leaving Sarajevo had been a mistake. She quickly forgot the reasons for her flight and brooded only about the losses which her moving would cause her. She resented these train crowds and was offended by their every word and gesture, and still more by her own weakness and cowardice. Most of all she was irritated by the unshakable calm and placid little smile of her mother, by her unquestioning, angelic trust in everyone and everything. She felt as if she were going into exile, or running away to . . . she knew not where.

At Slavonski Brod they waited five whole hours in the cold rainy night for a connection. And despite their watchfulness, one of their suitcases was stolen. This was too much. On the badly lighted station platform, beside the shadowy hull of the train that was panting with white steam, Miss Raika began to bleat like a lost lamb. She called on God and the passengers to witness the foul robbery, but the people went by shoving and stumbling over her suitcases. There was no response, no one offered sympathy or help. They managed with the greatest difficulty to push their way into the Belgrade train, which was just as crammed as the Bosnian one had been. They had to stand in the corridor, in a strong draft. Miss Raika groped around with her hands and counted the valises by touch. She had the feeling that a piece of flesh had been torn from her body, that she would never reach her destination, that Belgrade, too, was only a mirage in that night in which unseen forces stole and pillaged from the defenseless with impunity.

They reached Zemun the next day before noon, in dull and chilly weather. The train went no farther, as the bridge across the Sava had been destroyed. Having had no sleep, thirsty, covered with soot, and sloshing after the porters through ankle-deep mud, they boarded the overcrowded ferry and crossed into Belgrade. It was dusk when they reached the house of Hadzi-Vasich in Smilyanich Street.

The reception which the two women got in that house contrasted so sharply with everything they had gone through on the journey that at first they stood bewildered and speechless beside their pile of luggage. The neat, spacious house shone with cleanliness, it smelled of order and plenty. The hostess, Mme Persa, known in the family and in the town by the nickname Seka, or little sister, and her two grown-up daughters, Danka and Darinka, received them warmly and cordially. They were offered sweets, water, and coffee, then taken to a smaller but warm room looking out on the courtyard, containing two beds with large, incredibly white pillows and comforters of yellow silk. By the time they had washed and changed, their host had also arrived. There were tears and embraces and the moment seemed to be one of those exceptional occasions when a person transcends the present and for a few hours lives another, more intense and richer life. Even Miss Raika could not help abandoning herself to that feeling of momentary relief and freedom from care.

During the evening meal in the brightly lit dining room, the relatives got to know one another better.

George Hadzi-Vasich had left Sarajevo as a boy some forty years before and had never gone back there. He had grown up in Belgrade in the house of his paternal uncle Peter Hadzi-Vasich, a reputable merchant and benefactor to many institutions; from him, too, he had inherited the store in Knez-Mihailo Street. He married late. Persa was then a young widow, having been married only a year to a merchant called Heraclides. She came from the well-to-do family of Stamenkovich, a hardware distributor whose shop was on the banks of the Sava River. In the first three years of their marriage, George and Persa had three children, first a son and afterwards two daughters. In 1915, Master George fled to France. Their son Misha was in the army, but on his discharge he also went to France and completed his law studies at Montpellier. His mother Seka remained in Belgrade with the two girls and, thanks to her family connections, her money and energy, kept the house together and brought up the children very well. Now Master George was trying to get his business started again. Misha had joined the National Bank, and Seka was beginning to look around for likely husbands for her girls, who had reached marriageable age.

Master George was now a robust, handsome, and neatly

turned out elderly gentleman in his late fifties. Like Raika's mother, he had the clear blue Hadzi-Vasich eyes, with their calm soft gaze. (That night the two of them couldn't look at each other enough; the moment their eyes met, they would start fluttering, and he would wipe a tear while she would cry.) Those blue eyes of his seemed to harmonize particularly well with his trim and completely white mustache and hair. Everything about him reminded one of an educated Belgrade businessman of the old school, whose bearing and manner with people was dignified and restrained; that cool and consummate professional cordiality had become part of his nature. He walked quietly and moved deliberately, spoke little and gave no sign of what was going on in his mind (not even the effort of thinking showed in his face); he looked one straight in the eye and, like all Hadzi-Vasiches, batted his eyes lightly and barely perceptibly, with so much patent friendliness that his interlocutor felt it to be a sign of special favor and trust toward him personally.

A relaxed and perfectly happy marriage bound Master George to his wife Seka. She was a strong and somewhat overripe woman with an ivory complexion and flashing black eyes, a lively talker. There was an air of brightness and venturesomeness about her face, and this impression was strengthened by the black down of a mustache and a crown of strong luxuriant hair. The strain of rearing her children wisely and honorably through the years of Austrian occupation had not sapped her vigor or her love of life.

Of the two daughters, the older resembled her mother, the younger her father. Danka was almost her mother's double; portents of a black down were on her upper lip, her roundness betokened future plumpness, while the as yet uncertain luster of her smiling eyes forecast the same energy and joy of living. Darinka was a chip off the Hadzi-Vasich block: slender, blue-eyed, with a calm thoughtful gaze that concealed neither mystery nor sadness.

Misha was a tall young man of twenty-five, blue-eyed like his father, well groomed, and carefully dressed, for his years perhaps a little too measured and serious in his talk and movements. He would certainly never invent a new system of government finances, but it was just as certain he would never make mistakes in applying the existing one. Everything about his person was orderly, everything glittered with the many golden ornaments he wore: a gold signet ring on his right hand, gold cigarette case, gold pencil on a gold chain, gold watch with a gold wristband on his left hand. Every time he moved, one of these golden things would flash briefly and unobtrusively.

Such was the family that took Miss Raika and her mother into its warm and affectionate midst. Mrs. Obren was perfectly happy. In that warmth of family life she lifted up her head for the first time in years and felt that she too existed as a free and separate personality; and she perked up and grew more cheerful each day, almost as if they had led her out of a dark moldy cellar and into sunlight.

During the first few days Miss Raika, too, felt good and at ease. No one questioned her about her life in Sarajevo. Everything seemed distant and forgotten. Belgrade was large, everything in it was nameless to her, and she was a stranger to everybody. But, after the pleasant interval of initial rest, she grew silent and constrained as she had always been and withdrew more and more into herself. This simple but open and cheerful life in a comfortable home with grown-up girls was not greatly to her liking. Their lavish openhandedness with everything, with laughter and words, with money and things, offended and repelled her. Their whole way of life seemed to be lacking in purpose and measure, to be improvident and insecure, so that it confused even her, deflecting her from familiar thoughts and throwing her plans into disorder. And realizing that she could not change it, or impose her own ideas on them, she desired to live in a house of her own as soon as possible, far from these gay young cousins and from the whole clamorous and lively company. She waited impatiently for the arrival of her household effects, which Veso had already forwarded, and in the meantime she tirelessly shopped around for a house in some quiet and distant street, where the cost of living would not be as high as in the center of town. Master George, with the help of his connections, managed to locate a small house in Stishka Street, and later obtained several more offers in the same price range, and now long and complex negotiations were in progress.

A special bane of Miss Raika's life were the visitors, who, due to Seka's reputation for hospitality, were quite frequent. To each female guest, Seka would want to present both "George's sister from Bosnia" and her daughter. Tuesday especially, Seka's day, was the most hateful day of the week for Miss Raika.

The house of Hadzi-Vasich belonged among the better antebellum houses in the area. It was one-storied and unassuming, but spacious, and had been carefully restored and painted after the war; it had a paved courtyard and a big garden full of choice fruit trees and low dense junipers. It was also different from most of the neighboring houses in that a separate wing had been built in the rear to contain the kitchen. Thus the entire building was given over to living quarters and the rooms had no kitchen odors and did not smell of winter stoves. The large foyer, from which one entered into other rooms, was furnished as a sitting room. The appointments were "stylish"—that is to say, the work of some foreign decorator and closest to the style of Louis XV. The chairs were covered with dark red velvet, while the tables and consoles, set on precariously thin legs, were loaded with vases, worthless porcelain bric-a-brac, and family photographs. The floor was covered with a Persian rug of the good old kind. The walls were hung with enlarged photographs of ancestors in fezes and their wives in embroidered vests and baggy, eastern pants, and next to them a reproduction of a Boecklin landscape with enormous cypresses and a dark forbidding lake.

It was in this room that Mrs. Hadzi-Vasich received every Tuesday, having "opened" her house like so many other reputable and well-to-do families in which there were grown-up daughters. For the young company on those occasions she also threw open the adjoining room, the biggest in the house, where they could dance to the music of a phonograph, while in the sitting room the older ladies of Mme Seka's age sat and talked, unable to get used to the Negro music of the new, postwar dances, wondering privately what these young people might think of yet before their daughters had a chance to get married, after which the worry would no longer be theirs.

Indeed, quite a number of Belgrade families at that time began to "open" their houses—to good things and bad, to every wind and casual visitor, but mostly to chance, that unreliable friend. The new community which was being forged of Belgrade residents and a swelling number of newcomers and which milled about on this narrow raised tongue of land between the Danube and the Sava rivers, did not as yet have any of the basic attributes of a real society; it had no common traditions or a common outlook on life, no kindred aptitudes or established forms of communication. It was simply a chance invasion of a motley multitude, which gathered here so that in partnership with the better people of Belgrade they might take advantage of a rare double opportunity: a great political and social upheaval, and one of the greatest military victories in the annals of the country.

It is certain that in the long history of Belgrade there had never been so vast a number of people in so narrow a space, thrown together by their interests and yet loosely knit and at bottom hardly congenial. These people, born and educated in the various regions of the Balkans and Central Europe, members of diverse faiths, ethnic groups, and professions, had been scattered wide by the four years of a world war and were now washed up here by the flood tide of victory, and they all sought to compensate themselves for the exertions and harm they had suffered in the armies of the world, under all sorts of duress, on the four continents. The old society of Belgrade, which was modest and small in numbers, became swamped in the flood of new humanity and neither could assimilate it nor wanted to be assimilated by it. Lulled by good fortune and success, the old society found itself now in a dangerous state of euphoria after the recent toils and anguish which had been beyond its strength, and was unable to regain its foothold or see its way in this new onslaught of people, customs, and ideas, or distinguish the good and the useful from the bad and the trivial, but was beginning to lose itself and its identity. It was natural in such circumstances that private ambitions were not clear or explicit; it was virtually impossible to make a true assessment of anyone's worth, or to see quickly through anyone's wiles, to completely deny anyone's claims, to affirm and staunchly uphold anyone's rights. There never was a better time or a more favorable soil for humbug and self-delusion!

Miss Raika fled from these receptions whenever she could. Tuesday afternoons she always found something to do in town or else withdrew to her room; for those playful young people seemed foolish to her, and the older women in the salon quite witless. Moreover, the receptions were no longer confined to Tuesdays. That frenzy for entertainment, which later would consume all of Belgrade, had already begun to infect the more comfortable homes. The irresistible urge to be seen at the noisiest and most diverse parties, in half-lit rooms clotted with swaying masses of bodies, had begun to take hold of everybody.

During the important holidays, and often on any pretext whatever, a party of friends would drop in at the Hadzi-Vasiches after dinner. There would be dancing to phonograph records, singing and banter, and also discussions about politics, art, and about the recent past which had all the earmarks of an exalted drama with a happy ending, and about the future which was a grateful and inexhaustible subject. Raika sat glumly during these conversations, a nuisance to herself and to others. If some of the older men happened to be present, fathers of these kids who danced and wrangled, she would be content. She would converse with them quietly, and question them indirectly about the measures being taken to overprint the Austrian kronen notes, or about the cost of houses and land plots. Everything about the young people repelled her: their style of playing and entertainment, their chatter and arguments. All she was able to hear and see of this youthful generation offended her and filled her with a distinctly uncomfortable feeling, in which there was contempt and anger as well as fear. It was all she could do to try to follow their "serious" discussions.

One evening the two sisters, Danka and Darinka, announced excitedly that among the young people expected after dinner there would be a couple of Bosnian poets, Stikovich and Peter Budimirovich, who had already made a name for themselves in the newest literature—one that was still awaiting its historian and its professional recognition but was the rage with young people and women of all ages. Moreover, both poets had been active in the revolutionary movement of Bosnian youth and had spent the four years of the war in an Austrian internment camp. Both as young poets and as fighters who had suffered for their nationalism they now enjoyed the undivided sympathy of both the society and the general public in the capital.

With those two new guests, the regulars also came. They included most of Misha's colleagues, many of whom had taken part in the war and lately completed their studies in France. They were a gay ambitious young lot. Some had already found positions in the government, and all seemed to share the feeling that a life of limitless opportunities was opening before them; the one point they could not agree on was how and to what purpose those opportunities should be used. In temperament, inclination, and outlook they were quite different, so that they often spent hours and whole nights in lively discussion, over coffee, cigarettes, and red wine. This did not prevent them from being boon companions; for if ideologies and opinions divided them, their arguments bound them together all the more firmly. All were of an age when such contention is the breath of life, and they loved it as children love their games. Life had not yet begun to wedge them apart and screen them from one another.

Among them were a few who kept aloof from all ideologies, and had no appreciation of the current conflicts and strife, but seemed already destined for practical work in economics or finance. They were sober, quiet young men, sedate before their time, who had already found their vocation and their path and who showed signs of indecision only when it was a question of choosing between the National Bank or some new economic institution that was still in the blueprint stage. By the same token, they were inclined to wait until all expatriate Belgrade families came back to the capital so that they might pick a wife from among the wealthiest and most influential. The host Misha belonged to that group. But this was more than offset by the flamboyant opinions of other young men, and by the manner in which they expressed them.

In the group were two young professors, Rankovich and Milenkovich. The former lectured on Serbian literature and was a leading light in a youthful democratic group which had a leftist orientation; he was a brilliant conversationalist and a fine dancer and singer. The latter was a socialist, a man of strong principles and a will all his own, who knew Marxist writings down to the finest detail; a polemical spirit and a passionate student of the subtle differences in doctrine. Those two were like a couple of leaders, and each one had his followers and sympathizers among the friends who gathered here.

The third and smallest group were conservatives and they were represented by Milo Adamovich, nicknamed Adamson, a graduate of law, who always wore some badge or other in the lapel of his coat. One day this might be a Red Cross button, the next an emblem of a choral society, for he was both a member of the Red Cross committee and committeeman of a great number of other—choral, cultural, and sporting—associations. He was a burly self-possessed young man with a bland and regular Roman face and big unflinching eyes, with a deep steady voice and measured movements. (Here, too, as elsewhere in the Balkans, this type of seemingly deliberate and forceful, but in reality nondescript and barren individual, was no exception.) Adamson was the kind who could put anyone on the defensive and always remain perfectly composed himself; who made others laugh but did not laugh himself, so that no one ever saw his teeth. Women were fond of him, but men were for the most part uncomfortable in his presence. His speech was larded with Turkish idioms, archaic phrases, and racy colloquialisms. He addressed everyone in the second person singular and could not bear the smallest joke at his own expense. His weapon was an irony that welled out of his powerful body like a natural force, in which there was something nihilistic and something a little patriarchal, an undertone of animal ruthlessness and also of fatherly good humor. To all the exuberant statements of his extremist companions he would answer jestingly, with a cool unsmiling expression. His stock rejoinder was: "That was well reasoned, friend, but who's going to finance it?"

In addition to these familiar regulars, there were newcomers from the newly created provinces, Croats, Slovenes, lively and likable Dalmatians. Each Tuesday one of them would bring a new guest, a person he scarcely knew himself, someone perhaps timid or aggressive, endowed with unknown qualities or with a reputation that was yet to be proved.

That evening, however, the two Bosnian poets over-shadowed everyone else, including Adamson. Stikovich talked about his prison years in Arad. With much skill he recounted several raw and depressing scenes, but his manner of telling was so detached and lofty that his audience was left with the impression that he had gone through it all like Dante through hell, remaining untouched by any of it. It was sickening and yet somehow pleasant to be hearing, from the vantage point of this free life which was growing richer and brisker every day, about sufferings that were past and gone. The girls begged him in vain to read some of his poems. He declined politely, with a proud disdainful smile that looked as though it were accorded from great rarefied heights, beyond all poetry and recitals. By contrast, the other poet, Budimirovich, did not let himself be asked a second time. As soon as they invited him, he pulled a rolled-up sheet of paper out of his pocket.

He was more frail and modest than Stikovich. With his tired bespectacled eyes, curved nose, and thin lips, his sharp profile had a stern, almost inquisitorial air, which his pained smile seemed to make more acute rather than softer. The girls watched his bony and finely chiseled hands while he read one of his prose poems, never once lifting his eyes. Free verse was a favorite mode of poetic expression in that period which was agog with bold ideas and turgid emotions, while as yet no one had had the time, the skill, or the patience to devise a more suitable and lasting form of expression.

He read in a hoarse voice, quietly and simply, yet with a kind of latent rigor that affected his listeners and spread silence around him. Even some of the elders in the salon felt compelled to get up from their chairs and come to the wide-open door to listen to the weak, almost prayerful voice.

Miss Raika, who sat alone, barely noticed in a corner next to the door, listened to the recital of the young poet as she did to all the youthful debates and phonograph music: with half an ear, glumly, and against her will. In the beginning she could make out neither the words nor the idea that connected them. It seemed to her there was something sad and impertinent in the spectacle of a grown man sitting down in the middle of a room, reading aloud and pompously what he had dreamed up in solitude, talking to himself as it were. She thought it inexplicable and rather embarrassing. But the general attention and silence around her, and the poet's voice, so quiet and incisive and threatening, forced her to collect herself and give it more attention. Only now did she hear what the poet was saying. Unable to grasp single words, and often losing track of whole sentences, she still managed to gather from the words she caught and understood that the thing was a terrible, bloodthirsty attack on wealth and rich people, on their money and their way of life.

> "Wherever I have wandered through the world,
>   my staff has grazed a rocky path, my eye
>   alighted on a rich house, my mind chilled
>   at a hardened heart.
> The sight of your proud and cruel bounty
> filled my soul with dismay and bitterness,
>   and later with rage and hate,
>   for I knew the infamy of being man
>   and saw the earth's face as a mockery
> of universe."

Miss Raika stared at the folded hands in her lap and, listening closely, asked herself over and over again whether

her ears did not deceive her and whether it was possible that this was spoken, as a poem, by a man who was supposed to be cleverer and more profound than other men. It was impossible, she thought, and stole a glance at the faces of the other listeners, but they only reflected a tense and devout concentration. No, it couldn't be possible; there was bound to be some witty twist at the end that would give the whole thing a different, a true and healthy meaning, and maybe turn it all into a joke. Meanwhile the poet went on reading and there was nothing in his tone or his words to justify her hope. On the contrary, the young man whom they called a poet was exhorting the poor of this world to cast away everything that divided them, to join forces against the rich, and rob them of their bounty. There could be no doubt about it; the words were unequivocal and their content crystal-clear. Then he addressed the rich:

> "You divided the world so well;
> everything for you and your children,
> for your children's children, and for your lackeys.
> What a clever division it is:
> everything light and beautiful for yourselves,
> everything dark and troublous for us.
> And now we all come into the world destined beforehand,
> you for a bright fate, we for a dark one.
> How well you allotted the world!
> But your allotment is only hideous, not eternal.
> Our anger shall ripen, an obstinate fruit at the
> height of summer: ashamed of their name,
> your scions shall renounce the bounty,
> for it shall be a burden to them and their undoing."

The poet continued to read, but Miss Raika did not hear him well, as blood had suddenly rushed to her head. She felt an irresistible urge to get up and leave the room but dared not do it while the silence around her was complete and the company frozen motionless. Every part of her rebelled at those blasphemous lies, clothed in the words of prayer, against that open call to plunder, that brazenness pretending to be a solemn recital, accompanied by a bland expression of the face and a head bent a little to one side. She twined her fingers convulsively and knew that she could not stand it if it went on much longer, that she would have to rise and leave the room no matter what anyone thought. At that moment she was interrupted by enthusiastic applause. The poet had finished. All the young people in the room were clapping their hands.

All of them, thought Miss Raika, male and female, without exception, were either rich or about to become rich through marriage, political connections, or work, and yet they seemed to approve this poetry with enthusiasm. She pulled herself up indignantly. Near the door stood the massive Adamson with a gray-haired, very fat gentleman. They had been attracted by the lively applause. Adamson was pointing out the poet, who was slowly and bashfully rolling up his sheet of paper, still in his reading posture.

"There, the one with the glasses, sitting in the middle."

"That one?" asked the elderly gentleman in some disappointment.

"That's right, him. Mr. Tapeworm himself, as you see. The little Bolshevik."

Miss Raika pushed resolutely past them and went to her room. She wanted to calm herself and collect her thoughts, to lie down and perhaps go to sleep and so wipe out the unpleasant impression of what she had seen and heard. But it was not so easy. Her mother was asleep in the other bed. Asleep? That was by no means certain, for she often pretended to sleep so as not to disturb her daughter with her presence. Besides, with her it was hard to tell whether she was quieter and stiller when she slept or when she was awake. Not being used to the presence of another person in her bedroom, Miss Raika felt irritated. She seemed to think that it was the reason why she could not concentrate. She felt as if in some kind of trap. No peace or solitude anywhere! Her mind kept reeling back to the poet's reading a short while before.

She lay down and switched off the light but felt even more cross and awake in the dark. Things get crazier and crazier in this house every day, Miss Raika told herself. What do those young people really want? (All at once there rose before her eyes those students on the quay at Sarajevo back in the year 1914. In their black capes, with their uncut hair, they sat around loafing on the white stone balustrade beside the river, whispering dangerous things to one another.) What was this aimless confusion she had been observing around her all these months? Who were these men who called themselves poets, journalists, nationalists, or communists, who were tampering with things that should not be tampered with? And how was it that no one stood up to them, to beat them back if need be, so as to remove this uncertainty and menace from the world? Was it all nothing more than the swagger and strut of idle youths in front of immature and foolish girls? Or was it a matter, as she seemed to think this evening, of a real conspiracy against money and thrift, order and common sense—in short, against everything that mankind respected, loved, worked for, and possessed? Who could explain it to her? Yet the very fact that such questions should be asked baffled and embittered her, prompting her to sit up in bed. From behind all walls and doors there seeped, like a distant simper in place of an answer, that wild African noise of the phonograph, to which they were all dancing once again regardless of their differences of opinion, and this forced her to thrust her face deeper into the pillow. And while she tossed about bitterly, she made up her mind firmly to move out as soon as possible, even if she had to pay the price they were asking for that house in Stishka Street, about which she had been haggling and wearing out her feet for three weeks.

However, what she lightly resolved in her sleepless indignation during the night was hard to carry out in the light of day when the bitterness had waned and the problem of cost reared its blunt and implacable head. She discussed several different houses and was confronted each time with a canny and unscrupulous seller whose real intentions were hard to see. She realized right away that these businessmen of Belgrade were of a different stuff than the soft easygoing men of Sarajevo. She learned to fear and respect those hard clever men who knew how to protect their interests and who rated another person by his ability to protect his own. And in their turn they, as well as Master George, who brought them in touch with his niece, were quick to sense how much strength, wariness, and cunning there was hidden in this old maid.

At last they reached an agreement on the house in Stishka Street, about which she had begun her negotiations. Raika managed to beat the owner down to the lowest acceptable price and arranged a most favorable mortgage. (The owner of the house, a wealthy Macedonian, remarked during the signing of the contract that he had never in his life seen a bargainer and a mathematician like this girl, and he had been buying and selling houses and property for more than twenty years.)

When the furniture arrived from Sarajevo, the two women moved out of the hospitable Hadzi-Vasich home—Mrs. Obren with regrets, her daughter with satisfaction, glad to have left behind her that immoderate life and to have broken off contact with that whole young crowd.

The building in Stishka Street, which was quite far from the center of town, neglected and quite damp, with its ancient Sarajevo furniture and old-fashioned trappings, became a true home to Miss Raika—one in which she could begin to find herself once more and rediscover her way of life and thinking. Here she again had the sense that she was wresting a little something from life. The house had two rooms in all suitable for living. The third was nothing more than a small cubicle, damp and gloomy, which served no useful purpose. Now the two women each had a room to themselves. House-keeping was resumed, frugal and thrifty as in the old days in Sarajevo. They cooked only once a day, heated only one room, and that only moderately. A maid came for a couple of hours every day and did the heaviest work. Life fell into the old routine. Raika again took control of their affairs and managed them in her own way. Slowly and cautiously she also resumed her business activities.

Life in Belgrade in the year 1920 was gaudy, lusty, unusually complex, and full of contrasts. Countless diverse and vital forces flowed parallel with obscure weaknesses and failings; old methods of work and the strict discipline of patriarchal life existed side by side with a motley jigsaw of new and still unformed habits and chaos of all kinds; apathy side by side with intensity, modesty and every kind of moral beauty with vices and ugliness. The panting and reckless bustle of various profiteers and speculators took place alongside games of intelligence and the dreaming of visionaries and bold ideologists.

Down the worn and partially destroyed streets came this foaming and swelling flood of people, for each day hundreds of newcomers dived into it head first, like pearl fishers into the deep sea. Here came the man who wanted to achieve distinction and the man bent on hiding himself. Here mingled those who had to defend their possessions and their status, threatened by the changing conditions. Here were many young people from all parts of a state that was still in the process of formation, who looked forward to the next day and expected great things of the changed circumstances, and also a number of older people who looked for a means of adjustment and for salvation in this very flood, hiding the fears and the loathing which it inspired in them. There were many of those whom war had thrown up to the surface and made successful, as well as those it had rocked to their foundations and changed, who now groped for some balance and for something to lean on. There was the hungry, badly dressed, unschooled kind; the kind whose spirit was broken and whose private shame would rankle forever; the aggressive sort that had enough to eat but whose appetites were ravenous and whose boldness knew no limit; dreamers and hotheads who had no thought of themselves, as well as cold designers and egoists; there were people of all religions and persuasions,

various races and nationalities, all professions and walks of
life; there were patriots with the old-fashioned kind of love
of country, naïve faith, and vague hopes for the near, perhaps better future; there were daring and perceptive inno-
vators, capable of seeing farther and better even at this early
stage; and there were agents of all nations, pursuing their
clearly defined goals. All of them, in short, were like some
rank and exuberant flora of the deep which wars and great
tidal waves had uprooted and peace tossed up to the surface.
For in this day of ours even the greatest wars and most perfect victories seldom, and then only incompletely, solve those
questions over which they have been fought and won, while
they invariably open up a great number of new and difficult
ones.

It was the solution of such questions that these people were
after. Like a school of fish looking for a better feeding
ground, this torrent streamed to the leeward side of the new
authority and new laws, determined either to adapt them to
their own ambitions and interests or else to become adapted
to them.

In this throng and in the air that surrounded it, there was a
morbid and deceptive, yet exciting and heady atmosphere of
limitless possibilities in every quarter and every direction.
At midday or toward evening, between Slavia Square and
Kalemegdan, you might unexpectedly meet some childhood
friend and, thanks to that accidental meeting, find yourself
the very next day in some fine position or even in possession
of sudden wealth, without anyone's demanding to know in
detail who or what kind of person you were. And by the same
token, you might spend many futile weeks knocking at the
doors of various authorities, with a briefcase full of the best

references and most emphatic credentials, and never get your rights recognized. There was something of the lusty chaos of the golden land of Eldorado in the life and appearance of this capital of a large new state, which so far had no clear frontiers, no internal order, not even a final name. In all things a rich and warm confusion prevailed—the first phase of a great spiritual and material flux, against which no one had rebelled as yet, since everyone found in it a little piece of something for himself and nursed the hope of finding a bigger one yet.

The life of that new Belgrade had not been recorded by anyone—for it is not easy to record it—but those who were alive then can recapture it in their memory to this day, and relive it with all their senses as though it were a special climate or a particular season of the year.

It was in this Belgrade that Miss Raika Radakovich trod the cobbled pavements, borne by the human flood. She walked quietly and warily, looking straight ahead of her and only rarely darting a quick glance full of mistrust around her. She could not say exactly what it was she was afraid of. One moment she would be startled by a cannon hole gaping from a deserted house, and in the next by a passer-by, one of the many demobilized soldiers in a greatcoat of a coarse gray fabric, without military markings. Flinching from the scars of war, she was just as afraid of the panting new life that was rushing and swirling blindly past the ruins and the homeless. And at every step she could see how much richer and more complex, and at the same time more dangerous, life was here than in Sarajevo; at first sight it looked easygoing and cheerful, like a game, but in reality it was tricky and merciless, like dice. She sensed this with the infallible instinct of people who are given over to a single passion.

Almost daily Miss Raika walked down Nyegosh Street, through snow and mud, in rain and east wind, and visited the various banks and especially the money-changers' shops that were sprouting every day in the block between the Hotel London and the Kolarats Café. Their eloquent, thrilling signs, consisting of two large-sized words, "Money-Changer," attracted Miss Raika's eyes from afar. In front of each a blackboard was set up, on which the rates of exchange for all currencies that day were marked in white chalk. In these "offices," which in fact were nothing more than narrow, half-empty, and hastily improvised holes-in-the-wall, there would usually stand, behind a new counter, beside a safe and a small iron stove, some Spanish Jew or other, Anaf or Medina, dressed in a winter coat, with a hat on his head, blue from cold, unfriendly and sullen. Miss Raika would not even notice his surliness. Indeed, not one of these money-changers was as curt, morose, and tactless in conversation as she herself.

She would lean on the counter and ask: "What are you paying for Serbian Tobacco shares?"

"How many have you?"

"Oh, quite a few. All depends on your price."

The man refused to commit himself, so Miss Raika promptly offered him other kinds of stock, questioned him about prices, and kept him busy, until she learned, or at least guessed, what she had wanted to know in the first place. Then she walked away, without a by-your-leave, having neither bought nor sold anything. The money-changers on the block soon got to know this dour woman and, seeing how their technique of moody haughtiness made no impression on her, began to talk to her as one of the fraternity.

Her actual transactions were infrequent, modest, and

extremely cautious; she found it harder and harder to summon up enough will and resolution to carry them out, while she spent more and more time on imaginary and unreal operations. She would make extensive and detailed inquiries in order to find out the most favorable price on one or another of her shareholdings; she would make a note of it and, a few weeks later, check to see how much she might have lost or gained had she sold it at the time. And she would enter the loss or profit in an account book, which she kept separately and daily read through and studied.

From this game, which was much more than a game to her, she derived much genuine excitement, both pleasant and unpleasant, and also gained new experience and knowledge. Burying herself like a mole in this petty and endless speculation, she thought less and less about her erstwhile dream of a million, and her need of it faded imperceptibly; and when she did remember it, it was almost as if another person had dreamed it and told her about it. Her memories of Sarajevo, too, began to pale rapidly. There was nothing to beckon her back there, not even that grave at Koshevo, which was now suspended somewhere outside of space, high aloft, without a name. And the shocks she had experienced there in the last few years began to seem milder, her losses more bearable. The only thing still left was the hidden fear that the newspaper attacks might be repeated and that some Belgrade newspaper might pick them up. That fear preyed on her even in her dreams. But nothing ever came of it. The fast and impetuous life of the capital swallowed up everything, good and evil, honor and shame, and, like a primeval forest or an ocean, smothered everything in oblivion.

She rarely visited the Hadzi-Vasiches and was beginning

to forget the acquaintances she had made in their house. And still, she did not quite manage to cut herself off from that world and to live as secluded a life as she would have wished. She kept up her connections, without quite knowing how or why, with two people she had met during the very last few days of her stay in Smilyanich Street—a girl and a young man.

The girl was Yovanka Tanaskovich, a distant relative of Mme Seka. Raika had often heard her discussed in the Hadzi-Vasich home as a girl with a mind of her own, until one day she had dropped by in person and met Raika and at once got on with her.

Yovanka! this ordinary everyday folk name, which was enough to bury a woman forever in a sea of country and city Yovankas, was pronounced by the men and women of the Belgrade society of that time in a particular tone of voice and with special meaning, as though it were some romantic, memorable name like Chlorinde, Armide, Oliviera, or Cassia. It was spoken without a surname or nickname, for it was understood by everyone that there was only one Yovanka in the world and in Belgrade.

She was an older girl, somewhere in her early thirties, small but well built, with strong legs, nimble and energetic in her movements, with shining brown eyes and a piercing look. Everything she put on and wore, be it a dress or an ornament, of whatever color, took on a gray nondescript tinge. She generally dressed carelessly and simply and gave the impression of a neglected, almost uncouth woman. Her hair was dark, strong, combed back, and ungroomed. Her hand-shake was like a man's, and she walked like a soldier; her voice was thick and hoarse from too much smoking, her speech quick and clipped. This girl of bohemian appearance and manner came from a respectable, wealthy Belgrade family, was a graduate of the faculty of philosophy, knew many people, and had numerous family connections throughout Belgrade society. An only daughter of parents who had died a long time before, she had been left a substantial legacy of property, land, and stock. She lived alone, like a frugal eccentric, giving no thought to marriage or the love of men, demanding nothing of life for herself.

Everything about her was chaotic, vague, and unpredictable. It would be hard to say what it was that powered and drove this restless and curious female, with such masculine energy and determination, through her fierce and tireless activities. All she wanted and craved was to participate in other people's destinies, schemes, passions, and ambitions. It was the only way she could exist, the only life that had a meaning for her. Numerous and tangled were her friendships with men and women of all ages and walks of life. At times it seemed as if she wanted to help the whole world and, having no cares of her own, desired to take everyone's upon herself. Inaudibly, inconspicuously, and selflessly, she would insinuate herself into the lives of the people she had taken under her wing, sharing in their successes, longings, and failures. In doing that she surpassed her protégés in zeal and pugnacity, convinced that she understood their intentions, and defended their interests better than they.

She would crisscross Belgrade from one end to the other in the deepest slush or a driving blizzard, visiting houses, shops, and government offices. Without an umbrella or galoshes, with frozen hands and a red nose, her lips blue from cold, wearing a long gray coat that resembled a military tunic—that was how one might glimpse her as she traipsed briskly around that unpaved and hole-pitted Belgrade in the year 1920. And if anyone stopped her and inquired where she was going, she might have answered, in a passionate whisper, edging past as it were, that she'd been running around since morning on account of a friend's baby who had diphtheria.

"You know Zagorka? She's liable to lose her head over the least thing. As for him, he's been on some kind of commission out in the field since yesterday; at least that's what they tell me. Anyway, he's not in town. The state hospital for contagious diseases is full up, not a bed to be had. Well, I managed to find a doctor, but now there's no vaccine. I'm on my way to the outpatients' emergency room at the city hospital. They're supposed to have it over there."

And she whipped on ahead through mud and fog, small and quaint, yet hard and wiry like a steel nib.

Or else one might come across her in front of the theater, walking patiently up and down, her hands deep in the pockets of her winter coat.

"What are you doing here, Yovanka?"

"Waiting for the director. Imagine, these tinhorns are cutting back and they let go young Kiriakovich, such a talented actor, while those other fossils are kept on and given fat parts and special testimonials. And he just got married a few months ago. His wife's from out of town. Now the baby's coming and there's not a piece of swaddling in the house, and not a farthing either! They were like a couple of turtledoves, but you know how it is—now they're starting to argue and go at each other. She's the daughter of a rich merchant from the interior, but the father cut her off when she eloped with Kiriakovich. Now she cries and threatens to go back to her father or jump into the river, and he's just about ready to chuck everything and go abroad with a traveling troupe. So I'm waiting for the director. He's my aunt's brother. I simply must talk to him, something's got to be done about it."

All in all, there was no errand she wouldn't undertake for someone she considered deserving of her protection. She sat up nights at the bedsides of the sick; she took into her apartment women who had run away from their husbands, she went to see lawyers on their behalf, and to seek the advice of clerics; she looked after jilted girls and modest young men who were facing college examinations or trying to get into government service; she watched over unhappy lovers, acted as a go-between in their quarrels, tried to find solutions for those who were in debt. Altogether, she played the role of Providence, for no visible reason or personal advantage. In this, it was true, she was quite selfless and good to the point of self-sacrifice, though moody and unpredictable, but she could as easily be aggressive and dangerous, capable of spite and revenge.

The tangled affairs of unsuccessful and unfortunate people were her true element. She would attach herself only to these, clinging to them obstinately, showering them with advice and favors, real and difficult ones, only to turn away from them suddenly, usually at the moment when their situation was mended, and from then on she would punish them, like a bad and offended fairy, with her mute hatred and slanderous whisperings. (Soon after meeting a person she would address him with the familiar *tu*, but after their first quarrel she would revert to the second person plural.) Discreet and well-ordered lives, successful people, or those who concealed their troubles and needs, did not interest her in the least. To them she accorded casual remarks and devastating irony, customary in the circles to which she belonged. Thus, for example, people might be talking about a certain Yovan Simich, a well-known geologist of Belgrade, who had been nominated doctor *honoris causa* at the University of Paris and was scheduled, in the next few days, to give a formal lecture at the Sorbonne. Yovanka's comment about it all would be: "I know him. He beats his wife. And besides, he eats with his fingers." To her, and to most of the people who were listening, this was all that it was necessary to know and hear about the famous geologist.

Such was Yovanka and her way of life and action.

No one ever knew about her personal life, no one ever asked whether she needed anything, wanted or loved anything. In reality, she existed only insofar as other people existed around her and to the extent to which she managed to batten on their lives. And for all the sacrifices and efforts she made on behalf of others, she found a twofold reward: the first was that in this way she never got around to looking at herself and thinking about herself; and second, that in the utter barrenness of her own personal life she could thus live tens of other lives and, like a freak and malevolent but powerful deity, ravel and unravel the threads of other destinies.

During the time when Miss Raika was moving and furnishing her house, Yovanka had managed to give her some unsolicited help. She knew where to find the cheapest moving vans, she telephoned the manager of the excise post at the railway warehouse, who happened to be the husband of a good friend of hers and could not refuse a favor, she personally accompanied Raika to the district court where, thanks to her connections, the remaining legalities of the house purchase were completed. Miss Raika accepted all favors, though she did not care overly for Yovanka's visits, which at times were frequent and long. And there was no way of preventing the visits either, for between these two unusual and in so many ways dissimilar women there was something that brought them closer and bound them together, albeit imperceptibly.

Two days before Miss Raika was supposed to leave the Hadzi-Vasich house, the family held one of those evening receptions for Misha's colleagues and Darinka's friends. Raika was still indignant over the last reception some ten days before, at which she had heard the young poet's reading and the still more mystifying accolade from the young and well-to-do crowd, but out of respect to her hosts she made up her mind to endure this one more evening, which luckily was to be her last.

Yovanka brought along one of her latest protégés, to introduce him to Mme Seka and her two nubile daughters. He was a certain Ratko Ratkovich. Even prior to that evening, Yovanka had spoken of him with enthusiasm. Judging by her description, in him were combined all the qualities which people esteemed most highly at that time. Born in Herzegovina, he had, while still serving as an Austrian soldier during the battles in the Carpathian Mountains, deserted over to the Russians in a most dramatic style, taking with him a whole company of Herzegovinian compatriots. From Russia, he had got himself transferred to Salonika, where he had fought as a volunteer in the crucial Allied breakthrough on the Salonika front. Demobilized, he was now engaged in trying to obtain the Belgrade representation of the American automobile company Ford, in which he was bound to be successful, since he spoke perfect English and had, during his stay in Salonika, made very good connections with some Ford representatives.

At the time, Miss Raika had given scant attention to Yovanka's gasping account of the young Herzegovinian of exceptional abilities and a great future, for she had been full of her own worries and never expected to meet him. And on that last evening her mind was perfectly blank even as she looked at the tall back of the man Yovanka was leading and introducing around the room as if he were an exemplary student. When he had done the first round, the man turned, came toward her, and, with a smile and a faint air of surprise in his whole manner, held out his strong ruddy hand. Only then, as Yovanka pronounced his name, did Raika look at his face. He said something, too, but Yovanka promptly led him away and introduced him to the rest of the company.

In reality, Miss Raika had neither seen nor heard him very well, because after her very first glance a single thought had flashed through her mind and frozen there: Uncle Vlado! It was not her habit to pay attention to the appearance of people or to scrutinize them long and minutely. As far as she was concerned, men and women did not exist by virtue of their dress, looks, or even the expression on their faces; for what had mattered to her about people since the earliest days of her youth were things that had no bearing or influence on her judgment and estimate of them. Even as a young girl, she had never known how to answer the question that was so common among her friends: "Whom does he remind you of?" Indifferent to begin with, she had in time become blind to the exterior appearance of people. And so at that moment she observed nothing unusual or different about this man, and yet all of him, as he forced himself on her consciousness and then abruptly turned away, indeed his whole bearing, carriage, and smile, immediately brought those two words to the forefront of her mind: Uncle Vlado!

It was so much more than a superficial likeness: it was her own memory, truly come to life and walking! And when later in the course of the evening, Ratkovich came and sat next to her, as he had done with each one of the girls and matrons, there was no longer any need to look at him. Everything was there: a wave of light hair spilling over the forehead, blue eyes whose darting seemed to disguise a deeper restiveness, and over everything that smile, glowing on and on. Except that this Uncle Vlado was better developed, broader in the shoulders, stronger and more incisive in everything. Moreover, he talked about things that alone were interesting and congenial to her, which her uncle had abhorred all his life: about work, business, and business prospects and plans. In short, there he was: an image of Uncle Vlado such as she might have dreamed in her sleep, yet changed somehow by the dream. And instead of making him stranger and more remote to her, the dream brought him closer.

That night and the next day she could not stop thinking about the remarkable likeness. However, since leaving Sarajevo and coming to Belgrade she had lived through many surprises and witnessed all kinds of unusual things, and so now she set down the exciting encounter with Uncle Vlado's double in her album of remarkable events brought about by change and travel. Having done so, she no longer thought about him as vividly as on that first evening. Gradually he receded to the back of her mind, for she was occupied with the business of moving and furnishing her new house. And she probably would not have remembered him again if Yovanka had not continued to visit her in her new house.

Miss Raika, who all her life had shrunk from unnecessary visits, also tried to discourage Yovanka's, or at least to curtail them as much as possible. But, it seemed, a man caught up in a snow avalanche in the mountains had a better chance of extricating himself than one under the onslaught of Yovanka's lively sympathy and protective fury. There were times when she didn't come by for two weeks, being occupied elsewhere with her numerous duties and errands, but then she would drop in three times in two days. She came early in the morning and late in the evening, at any time of day, only never twice at the same hour. Chilled to the bone, soaking wet, spattered with mud up to her neck, she burst into the house with her useful suggestions and violent advice, with endless enthusiasm or with bitter tales of unknown men and women whose destinies she happened to be cooking and stirring at that moment. To escape these mawkish, lengthy outpourings was impossible; all that the person who was forced to listen to them could do was to take in as little as possible and forget it as quickly. And even that was hard to do at times, since Yovanka physically overwhelmed her interlocutor and obstinately and relentlessly came back, again and again, to the subject close to her heart.

That was how, lately, she had been bemusing Miss Raika with her talk of Ratkovich, his honesty and probity, of his efforts to obtain the Ford dealership and the difficulties he had encountered in that task, and also of her own efforts to help him.

"You've no idea, Raika, what a sterling man he is. Goodness itself, I tell you. A volunteer and hero of the Salonika battle, but he will not take advantage of it or beg from anyone. Look at those gate-crashers who wangle all kinds of concessions and contracts from government departments, nothing but Jews and Austrians, and he can't get what he wants. Now he's put in a bid to the Ministry of Construction for some automobile parts. I went to see Velovich, the minister, whom I know very well. They said he was out of town. Later I heard he's gone to Vienna, officially on business, but actually to see his girl friend there. And that's a minister! But I told off his cabinet chief! I gave him a piece of my mind! You should've heard me. This afternoon I'm going to Mayor Karadzich, to his house. His wife and I grew up together in Vrachara. He was older than either of us, a big tall lout, and he got hold of our pigtails and chased us around like a team of horses. I'm not going to leave his house until he signs the permit."

Listening to these tales of Yovanka's, Miss Raika would remember the young man she had met one winter evening in the house of Hadzi-Vasich. And then, one day in May, Yovanka came again and complained about the difficulties and obstacles which unscrupulous competition and a rotten administration had put in Ratkovich's way.

"I wore out my toenails going from office to office in the Ministry of Finance. You really ought to see that place. You've no idea what a barn it is."

"Yes, I know," Raika said quietly.

"No, you don't. How could you! This government is a madhouse. I told them so in their faces. But poor Ratko is too good, too soft for them, so they twist him and walk all over him. Now they're asking him for taxes and financial guarantees, and some kind of affidavits they never ask of anybody. And he just looks at them horrified, instead of hitting them over the head, by way of affidavits. But I wanted to talk with you. We've got to help the poor devil. His plan is stuck now over some taxes. I've given him a little money, but he needs more. I thought you might like to be in on it. It's money well invested, believe me. All we have to do is help him get on his feet; afterwards it'll be easy. He's going to pay it back, naturally. Because you don't know what a man he is. A real brain, a heart and a soul. He'll go far, only we have to hold him up now."

The moment Raika heard it was a question of giving something to someone, everything disintegrated like smoke, the thought of Ratkovich and the memory of Uncle Vlado and the languor brought on by the stream of those words; every last fiber of her sat up as it were and stiffened into an attitude of mistrust and defensiveness. Extending her neck and dropping her eyes, with a martyred expression on her face, she began to equivocate in a faint voice.

"I have no money, Yovanka, believe me. Can't spare a dinar, believe me. I still owe the taxes here and back in Sarajevo."

"Oh, go on, don't cry to me, please. Maybe you have, maybe you don't, but we've got to help this man somehow. In fact I'm going to bring him over one of these days, so he can personally tell you about his proposition and his needs."

Had this person in front of her been anybody else, Raika

would have told her that she had no need of such a visit, and she would have turned her back. But with this exasperating creature who went by the name of Yovanka such a thing was very hard to do. It seemed to her that if she were back in her place in Sarajevo, in her old house or in her store, it might have been easier to ward her off, for no one would have dared to approach her with such a scheme, but here she felt herself tied and unresisting.

And then, one day, Yovanka really came with Ratkovich. In the full light of day, he looked even bigger and stronger. Everything he wore was simplicity itself, ample yet neat and harmonious: his shirt, suit, and shoes. Everything inspired confidence, for it suggested a man of the world, a calm and simple man of affairs who spoke little but basically knew what he wanted. The face, eyes, and smile—those were Uncle Vlado's. It was no trick of dreams or the illusion of an evening, it really was so. With this one difference: here was Uncle Vlado as Miss Raika had always wished him to be, but as he never could be—a settled businessman who knew his figures and took everything into account, yet hardly spoke about money, or did so haltingly, in a tone of voice that was almost devout and which was bound to surprise and move her. In sharp contrast to the young crowd she had got to know in the Hadzi-Vasich house, he confined himself to his own affairs and said only as much as was necessary. He talked like young men who are still generous with their strength and whose reserves of hope are enormous, but at the same time with restraint, without boasting and importunities, as though he were submitting an account of himself. Miss Raika gave him a silent and attentive hearing, and when she raised her eyes, she met Uncle Vlado's smile, easy, carefree, and ungrudging. She dropped her eyes and listened on, and as she did, his smile still played over her folded hands.

He talked about his business, which, like all beginnings, was slow and difficult; he did not gild or try to cut a figure. He spoke about her, too, complimenting her quietly and moderately on everything he had heard about her abilities, which so many men lacked. . . . Never in her life had anyone bribed her with words and won her over with flatteries, for just as she was indifferent to appearance, to dress and looks, she was insensible to human kindness or the lack of it. But here the case was different. Here in front of her was Uncle Vlado—but an Uncle Vlado who was somehow to her liking.

Ratkovich asked for nothing—either openly or by implication—but it was quite apparent from his talk that he still had before him many months of hard work and struggle, probably to the end of the year, when success would be certain, if only he had the means to hold out till then. As far as he was personally concerned, he had enough to get by, but taxes and especially the greasing of various government officials were eating him up. The problem was to prevent others from getting the Ford franchise, and this again depended on government contracts which he must secure in advance. Yovanka injected the idea of a promissory note, which she said she would be willing to underwrite if Miss Raika and one of Ratkovich's colleagues were to add their signatures. It was simply a matter of favor, because the moment an agreement was signed with the Ford company Ratkovich would receive an advance in dollars with which he would forthwith settle his debts. Miss Raika countered that she was not versed in the business of notes, that there was little money around, and then asked them for a day or two in which to think about it.

Next day Yovanka came again, and Miss Raika, against

her will and better judgment, put her signature to a note for 12,000 dinars. Later Ratkovich himself came to thank her. Sitting alone with him, she could not take her eyes off that smile which had been part of her early youth, or hear enough of his calm sober talk. And what she was gazing at prevented her from hearing and properly judging what she was listening to; what she was hearing interfered with her desire to gaze her fill at her dearest memory, now miraculously come to life.

After this, Ratkovich came a few more times. Twice he came in his car, a ramshackle old Ford that rode the Belgrade cobblestones like a twitching grasshopper, and took Raika and Yovanka for a drive in the country. But Raika liked it best when he came by himself, to sit awhile and talk to her about the progress of his important business. His talk was free of embellishment and he never patted himself on the back. Quite the contrary. To her questions, he answered sincerely and with an air of concern.

"By God, Miss Raika, there's no end to it. They're coming at me from all sides and sometimes I'm afraid and wonder if I can see it through. But we've got to fight for it."

Listening to his pure Herzegovinian accents as if they were music, she found it perfectly natural and understandable that she, too, should participate in this struggle for his good; she did not ask herself when she had made that decision and was unaware of the fact that it was in sharp contrast with all her work and outlook up to that moment. And the slow and difficult progress of his business, instead of compelling her to think about the fate of the promissory note, filled her with a deep emotion she had never known and with a desire to help him.

So it happened that one day she gave him 400 dinars,

which he needed for two long telegrams abroad. Fifteen days later he returned the money and, by way of interest, brought her a small, finely woven basket full of reddish yellow mandarin oranges. She was a little angry at the expense, and the incident revived the memory of her fond and short-lived tiffs with Uncle Vlado over his lavish gifts. Save that here everything was temperate and within reason. At the beginning of August Ratko extended the note of 12,000 dinars, and two or three days later took another cash loan of 5,000 dinars. Raika could not explain how this came about, for he had not asked her anything. It seemed to be the natural sequel to a conversation in which he had mentioned the need for a trip to Paris and Brussels, where he might personally talk to the chief European representative of Ford. Ratkovich carefully penned an IOU in his round distinct handwriting, which flowed smoothly like a melody. Maturity was set at January 1, 1921, with interest of 8 per cent. It was the lowest interest rate Miss Raika had ever agreed to in her life.

All through the month of September, Ratkovich continued to travel and send postcards to Yovanka and Raika. Once he even sent a telegram from Antwerp. During that period, Yovanka was a frequent visitor in Stishka Street. The weather that month was hot and dry. The two of them sat by the window in the cool twilight of the room. Raika would bend over her embroidery, while Yovanka fidgeted restlessly and bubbled with excitement.

"I don't like the looks of it, I tell you. First Paris, then Brussels, and now they say Nata Dabich went and told someone she'd seen him at Biarritz. Of course, Nata is a big liar, that's true. A pathological case. Then again, I keep wondering, maybe this time is an exception and she's telling the truth. Why doesn't he come back and look after his business!"

"Perhaps he can't," Raika said quietly, pleased that she could defend him. She bit the thread off with her teeth and the taste of it seemed unaccountably delicious.

"Why can't he? What do you mean he can't? He ought to write and say so. And here, this pack of vultures, they won't let up till they pick him clean. Why, his best friend and countryman's working against him in the Ministry of Finance. He's playing it canny, trying to get the contracts *and* the Ford representation. And here I am, without the faintest idea where that vagabond is, so I can let him know."

"He won't let it happen, don't worry. Not after all that hard work and the money he put in. He's a serious man."

"Hmmm-m." Yovanka shook her head. "Serious! I wish I could be sure of it. You can't trust these men further than your nose."

And they sat on, like two women whose nearest blood kin was journeying abroad and whose welfare concerned them both equally; and their common concern brought them closer together and became a bond. Save that in the case of Raika the worry was much more acute. Yovanka had a number of other young men and women besides Ratkovich whom she championed and lavished with her bountiful and inexhaustible energy. But for Raika it was the first and only such case in her life, a unique experience and a deep personal secret. She had never breathed a word either to Ratko or Yovanka about the former's uncanny likeness to Uncle Vlado.

A couple of days later, Ratkovich himself appeared in Stishka Street. He was deeply tanned, a little more haggard, more tired and thoughtful. He told them that the negotiations had been completed, that the Americans hesitated to make the final move, seeing how they were still a little unclear about the new regime and new conditions in Belgrade, but that he was the only candidate in the picture; the rest was a matter of waiting. Raika gazed at him and listened to him, concerned because he was concerned, but happy to know that he had come back alive and well.

Some days later he requested her to sign another note, this time in the amount of 9,000 dinars. He needed that much to see him through to the end of the year, by which time the whole thing would be settled and he would be able to discharge all his obligations out of the Americans' advance payment. Miss Raika gave in. Her inborn and inveterate resistance to any kind of giving or risk made itself felt even now, but it was muted somehow to a faint gnawing, and numbed as if by anaesthesia; she thought about it, she could feel it inside her, but saw that it was languid and not functioning. Had Yovanka's signature also been on the note, she might have raised some kind of objection, but this way she didn't know what to do. Moreover, she was only too glad that he had turned to her personally, and only to her, and that for once she could support him alone, without any intervention, and to help him, as a mother would her child, "to get on his feet."

That was how Ratko Ratkovich obtained, without too much talk or equivocation, what he so desperately needed at the time. He himself could not get over it as, still smiling, as though still in conversation with Miss Raika, he slammed, a little too joyously, the iron courtyard gate behind him. Miss Raika remained alone, motionless in her chair and spellbound by the odd and heretofore unfamiliar sensation that

her whole being was expanding, becoming infinitely richer
and more spacious. And the slammed gate was tangible
proof to her that this was no illusion, that she was in fact
helping a dear weak man. She could not decide at that moment whether he was some kind of infant nurtured and growing on her sacrifice and devotion, or Uncle Vlado himself, in
a new shape, willing to work and listen, for whom there was
help and salvation yet.

In the days that followed, she went to bed and got up in
the morning with this novel and bewildering sensation. Even
if she had paused to ask herself just how she happened to be
doing favors for this almost unknown young man, who was
nothing to her—favors she never would have dreamed of
granting to anyone—there would have been no answer to
give. But it never occurred to her to ask herself that question.

Fifteen years had gone by since she had started to work
and make money, single-mindedly, heedless of everything.
During that time she had not given a penny to anyone unless
she had to. She had cut herself off from the community and
the world, she had piqued everyone, brought shame on herself, sinned against the poor, the weak, and her own flesh and
blood. She had stolen and cheated (or, more accurately, done
things which by their nature and ultimate consequence
amounted to theft and fraud), and had been willing to commit even graver abuses in order to enlarge what she had, or
at least not diminish it. She had grudged her mother a loaf of
bread and trembled with inward resentment over the fact
that elderly people lost all their strength but their appetite
remained the same, and even improved. She had not only denied herself every pleasure, but also the most necessary
things, even medicines. She had done it all without a mo-

ment's hesitation, making no exceptions, and might have gone on doing it to the end of her life.

And now, here was a man who was neither kin nor destitute, neither brother nor lover, from whom she herself neither demanded nor expected anything, but to whom she gave willingly and cheerfully all that she had never given, or thought herself capable of giving, to anyone. She felt no compunction or regrets. True, when she sometimes woke up in the night, her head would reel with the sudden thought: I signed a note yesterday for 9,000 dinars! And the thought would have an edge of fear, but this would be no more than a vestige of the deep-rooted habits which, in the twilight of sleep, nagged their way to the surface. The moment she roused herself, the sense of bliss would return. She would close her eyes and imagine that the man she was helping to stand on his feet and walk was not a grownup of twenty-six years but actually a small pink baby who smiled and caused everyone around him to smile as he tested his feet for the first time. Not even in daytime, when her look was alert and she could see well, when illusions had much less of an effect on her, did she feel regret or uneasiness about the money she had given to Ratko, for in her act of giving to him she found the same satisfaction she had always felt when denying or depriving others.

Those were the weeks in which Miss Raika lived in a dream, without ever recognizing the whole power and the true nature of her dream. She went about her business as usual. Nothing changed in her way of life. And still, there was a change, even though it was visible only to herself.

Evenings, when she remained alone, she was usually tired out and disheartened by the day's errands—errands which here in Belgrade always gave the impression of going well, yet seldom found the favorable conclusion they had promised; she was exhausted by the hard cobblestones of Belgrade, which were a real bane to her unaccustomed feet and her slender ankles. In moments like those she would remember, with an emotion which in other people might be called tenderness, that this same Belgrade also contained Uncle Vlado, a more perfect version of him as it were, more sensible, who also gadded about the big far-flung city, trying to build a business of his own, so that he might begin to make money and gain financial security.

That autumn, Yovanka spent a few weeks with some relatives in the country. Ratko, too, was absent during that time. Miss Raika didn't even notice their absence, or feel how the time passed. She lived and went about immersed in her affairs, but calmly, almost without a care in the world, borne along by a feeling that might have passed for happiness had she, in her previous life, experienced something that resembled it, and by which now she might have measured and judged it.

In the middle of October Yovanka came back and reappeared, dark and restless, in Stishka Street.

"What's happening with our entrepreneur?"

"Didn't you know he is out of town, in Budapest?"

"In Budapest?"

"That's right. Evidently he's taking it easy."

"It's possible he went there on business."

"I've no idea. All I know is I don't like the looks of it." The little woman threw back her head and asked sharply, in tones of a policeman: "You did not lend him any more money, did you?"

At that Miss Raika, who ordinarily could hold anyone's stare without flinching and coolly outbargain the craftiest money-changer, became flustered and confused in a way she had never known, in the worst possible way of all, in which decent but naïve and weak people who don't have the courage to speak the truth always became enmeshed, having neither the strength to remain silent nor the skill to lie.

"I haven't. . . . That is, I have. I gave him a loan. He asked me, you know. Only till the end of the year."

"Was that before or after I went away?"

Miss Raika concentrated hard. "After . . . I believe. Yes, definitely after."

"How much did you give him?"

"Nine thousand."

"Ah! You made a mistake."

"What do you mean? You said yourself we ought to help him."

"My dear, you made a mistake. Don't do it again. You're not to give him a penny until I find out a few things. Looks as if our hero has something cooking and is not the saint and the innocent little lamb he makes himself out to be. So, I intend to find out. And if he drops in again, you act as if you know nothing and treat him well. As for money, no! I don't want you and me to look foolish before the world."

Miss Raika was left more offended than worried; more resentful of Yovanka than in doubt about the young man. It was in this mood that she received Ratko when, some days after Yovanka's visit, he appeared at the door of her house, with the old smile on his face, calm and unchanged. He explained blandly and meticulously, as always, that he had been obliged to go to Budapest where there had been a meeting of all Ford representatives in Central Europe and the Balkans, and that this had been a wise move, useful to them as well as to himself. They had wanted to hear his advice on a number of things concerning the newly formed state of Serbs, Croats, and Slovenes, as if he were already their man; and he came back firmly convinced that the matter was in principle as good as settled. There would still be some expenses and a few loose ends to attend to, but the thing would be favorably concluded by the end of the year at the latest.

At the mention of expenses, Raika started ever so slightly; she recalled the toss of Yovanka's head, and quickly thought: Am I to give, or turn him down, and how do I do that? She would find it hard to give, but to turn him down was impossible. However, Ratko didn't ask for anything. So the visit ended with the usual smiles and calm, reassuring words full of good hopes. Raika felt a little contrite about her doubts, displeased with herself, and even more cross at Yovanka.

That was on a Friday. The following Monday, Raika had some business at the town hall. After she had finished, she set off for home, whipped by the cold autumn rain and holding on to her umbrella for dear life. As she came abreast of the University, she collided with a woman who flew out through the portals as if ejected and promptly got entangled in Raika's lowered umbrella. Before they could think of excuses or start an argument, Raika found herself face to face with Yovanka, who immediately burst into excited, breathless talk, as if resuming a conversation.

"Oh good, it's you. I have to talk to you. I'll drop in tomorrow. Your fine Ratko is a good-for-nothing, a cad, and a bag of mischief. I just talked to a man. It's all clear to me now."

"What is?"

"Everything. You'll see when I tell you. Now I'm in a hurry. Going to see a school friend of mine, to check a few more details. We'll catch him red-handed. As for the money, you can forget it—it's gone! I was *one* fool who tried to help the biggest reprobate and liar on the face of this earth, thinking he was a great patriot, a fighter, and a man of the future. And you were the *second*. That's all I can tell you now. And if that lump of beauty as much as puts his foot inside your door, just shove your broom in the tramp's face. I'll see you!"

After which Yovanka disappeared in the crowd of people which, bad weather notwithstanding, milled around the wooden stands and counters on the big square opposite the university building.

Dumfounded, Miss Raika continued on her way, slowly, bending against the strong wind that lashed her with fine icy rain.

Yovanka did not come the next day or the day after, for that would have been an exception to her rule, which was surprise and disorder. But she came in the early morning of the third day and resumed the conversation she had begun in front of the University, as if she had never broken it off.

"I know it all! I have the whole story!" she shouted almost with joy. "I know his whole bag of tricks!"

Beating the table with her small but strong fist, whose tough, uncouth appearance suggested that of a delivery boy rather than a young woman's, she began to tell her friend who Ratko Ratkovich was and what manner of life he led.

One gathered from her slangy and colorful language that she had finally done what she should have done right at the start of that acquaintance. She had found a couple of Ratko's countrymen, a young professor and an industrialist. Both were more or less the same age as Ratko, had known him from childhood, met him during the last war, and were seeing a good deal of him in Belgrade at this time. The information she had got from each of them was identical and a genuine revelation to her.

It was in Yovanka's temperament not to be able to meet a person or face a fact without instantly taking a position, and thereby a position toward the rest of the world, which invariably was one of unconditional approval or extreme displeasure. In the same way, she never could reproduce the content of someone's talk without imitating his speech and his gestures, or injecting picturesque and tiring descriptions of his personality and the company he kept.

This time she was so agitated that she came out with the bare facts first. True, she had learned most of them from the industrialist, who happened to be a dry and laconic type of man, and not in the least interesting. She had learned the following.

Ratko came from a poor home, was an only son, and had shown from earliest boyhood a stronge predilection for a life of style, spending, and idleness. Because of it, his friends nicknamed him "count." In reality, he made a jolly companion and was popular among his classmates. He liked going out of his way to help others and never asked for a favor in return, but by the same token he was incapable of paying back anything that was lent to him. As a high-school student, he was thrown out of the Gymnasium at Mostar on account of poor grades, disorderly living, and forbidden machinations with other people's money. After joining up with a Hungarian, he went to Budapest and a year later returned to Mostar as an agent for a bicycle factory. When the war broke out in 1914, he was drafted and sent to the Russian front. In 1915, he did indeed manage to go over to the Russians and take with him an entire company of Serbs serving under the Austrians. It was a dangerous and bold undertaking. From Russia, he came down to Salonika, not to seek combat duty at the front, but to get himself assigned to the quartermaster's office. Here he made a connection with the quartermaster's outfit of the British. He went to England on army business several times. Near the end of the war, some irregularities were discovered in the quartermaster's office. An officer and two noncoms were taken into custody; one of the two was Ratko.

After the breakthrough on the Salonika front, they were released without court-martial. No one knew exactly why they had been arrested, nor on what basis they had been released, but there was no more talk about it. Here in Belgrade he did, in fact, perform minor services for some British firms, since he understood motorcars and knew the English language. They paid him on a "piecework basis"—that is, separately for every completed service—but there was no question, nor could there be, of his ever getting and managing the representation of any bigger firm. And the tenders he was submitting to the Ministry of Finance and the Ministry of Construction were for somebody else's account.

In reality, he had no real or clear-cut occupation, and was not likely to have one at any time, as he had no credit standing and no one would ever trust him with merchandise, for he lacked the necessary integrity and stamina. Ratko was at bottom not a bad man. On the contrary, he was goodhearted, gentle, and polished, as if he really came from a good home, but improvident to distraction and a great lover of beautiful women, entertainment, and fun of all kinds; one of those men who never settle down and become serious but spend their entire lives playing games with themselves and with the whole world. At the moment, with the exception of those more or less useless errands in the ministries, his chief occupation was sitting up at night in gay company. Lately he was to be found every night with the same party of people in a *chambre séparée* at the Casino.

The party was a mixed and colorful one, made up of men of business and politics, first harbingers of corruption, of local men as well as foreigners, lawyers, journalists, and contractors, and of assorted hopefuls still waiting to be assigned a niche in one or another social category; a bunch of men having no other ties than that fleeting companionship of alcohol which was currently spreading and proliferating throughout the capital, like wild grass at the roadside. The pillar of that company, its president as it were, was a lawyer from across the river who had opened an office in Belgrade and was enjoying a flourishing practice.

Some two weeks ago, a new cabaret had opened. It was the first cabaret in postwar Belgrade. The main attraction of this cabaret was a Parisian *diseuse* by the name of Carmencita, no longer young or in voice, but with a good deal of charm and quite skillful. She came out as *violetera*, in a Spanish costume, and sang her song of violets which even the Belgrade delivery boys had lately begun to whistle. As she sang she mingled with the customers on the floor and passed out real violets, and for every bunch received large dinar notes from the drunken guests. Several Belgrade newspapers had published photographs of her, thus creating some lively publicity. And even without it, customers came in such droves that there was never any room to sit, and they spent money unsparingly. This Carmencita had been brought to Belgrade by Ratko Ratkovich. He had met her in Biarritz that autumn and become intimate with her. On his return to Belgrade he had negotiated an engagement for her with the Hungarian owner of the Casino Cabaret. Then he had gone to Budapest to wait for Carmencita, to persuade her to come to Belgrade. Now some people were saying that he had a share in her substantial income, while others maintained that he was getting into debt on her account. At all events, he was intimately connected with her.

This was the dry but factual account the industrialist had given Yovanka. All of it had been more or less corroborated by the young professor of ethnography from Herzegovina, who taught at the University. Yovanka had arranged to meet him some days before, for the express purpose of getting accurate firsthand information on Ratkovich. The professor had made a very good impression on Yovanka. As she was listening to his quiet account, and while inwardly fuming at Ratko and his deceit, she made up her mind to take this young man under her wing and, by means of her connections, help him make his way at the University and in society. Because of that, she now felt compelled to repeat his story and to describe him and the whole course of the conversation down to the finest detail.

The Herzegovinian professor was a model of a disinterested young man and a true scientist. He was modest and led a retiring life, completely dedicated to science. (His specialty was the psychology of the Dinaric man.) He was thin and pale like a hermit. A thick short mustache covered his upper lip; strong brushlike eyebrows jutted out like a pair of eaves, shadowing his nearsighted and trusting eyes, strained by too much reading. Like all men who are devoted body and soul to a single endeavor but lack opportunities to express themselves adequately from the rostrum or through the printed word, he loved a good and lively conversation; and what he said was like a printed essay. Not knowing why Yovanka was asking questions about his old classmate, the professor analyzed Ratko's case for her with complete objectivity and without any bad intentions, using it now as an example of typical aberrations in the Mediterranean-Dinaric race, and again as a general phenomenon, characteristic of the wartime and postwar conditions of a crude and unsettled society.

"Indeed, there is such a thing as the Dinaric type," concluded the professor. "It's an interesting compound, hardly studied as yet, in which two kinds of persons exist side by side, inseparably bound. One gallant and decent, the other timid and morally unsound."

"A scoundrel and a rat!" Yovanka broke in, as if translating the scientific prose into plain human speech for someone's benefit.

"No, no, please don't misunderstand me. There are all sorts of shadings and half-tones here, and if one doesn't take them into account, then the conclusions are bound to be exaggerated and basically untrue and unfair. These two characters in a man mingle and clash in endless overlapping and interweaving, and they can often deceive not only the people around that particular person but the person himself, so that he lives with a completely wrong notion of himself, his personal qualities, moral values, and the real significance of his actions. Youth is a critical time for a man like that. His entire personality bends or breaks in one or the other direction. At that period there's a chance his whole life might veer toward genuine creative endeavor, or, just as readily, toward the point of no return along the path of indulgence and idleness."

Talking to Yovanka about the nuances and subtleties of psychological make-up and definition was like explaining light and colors to a blind man.

"He's a tramp, Professor, I'm telling you plain and clear," was her comment to the meticulous exposition of the young scientist.

The rest of his generalized exposé, by which he sought to explain the extraordinary conditions under which the youth of the day had to live, fared no better at her hands.

"In times like these," said the professor, "so soon after the hard long years of bloodshed and suffering, the young people don't see their youth for what it really is—a short phase in the natural evolution of a generation—but as a unique gift of the gods which, this one time and quite by accident, has been cast down from the heavens, a miraculous explosion of strength and beauty. Everything they experience and observe around them appears fresh and new, as though it were snatched by wildest chance from a universal deluge and allowed to live a jubilant, defiant life without measure or limits."

"I can see it all," said Yovanka. "It's a madhouse, not a country. Nothing but spongers and gamblers."

Having said this, she got up. Anything else the professor might say would be anticlimactic. She made a mental note to push and promote him over his older colleagues, who, "like the mummies they were," barred the advance of younger men at the University. First, however, she would clip the wings of Ratko Ratkovich; she would get back from him what he owed them and, what was more important, drive him out of town and into limbo.

And so, from there she came straight to Stishka Street to discuss their next joint move with Raika.

Listening to Yovanka's long account, Raika had averted her head in confusion. She had felt a cold shudder of unease arching now the back of her neck, now her spine, as it slowly penetrated her body. Inwardly she was consumed with the hope that Yovanka had made a mistake, that she had been misinformed, or that she was lying, it did not matter which, as long as what she said was untrue, but at the same time the appalling effort of will not to show and give away that hope made her freeze outwardly. The graver the accusations, the more unsavory the epithets showered on Ratko, the more unbearable grew her shudder and the stronger waxed the need, somewhere in the pit of her innards, to protect him from this terrible Yovanka, from everything and everyone, even from the truth itself. But it would have been easier to defend him against a whole legion of state prosecutors than against this creature who was relentless in her affection and frantic in her hate. All Miss Raika could do from time to time was to mumble some vague expression of doubt in favor of the culprit Ratko.

"Let's wait and see," she said. "I think the best thing would be for us to talk to him."

"Me, talk to him?" cried Yovanka in a hoarse voice. "I don't talk to confidence men. Are you out of your mind?

How can you be so naïve! I do believe you still trust that snake. I knew it. Well, you'll come along with me this evening, so you can see with your own eyes and hear with your own two ears what a precious little plum *your* fine Ratko is. You'll see it and hear it, if you don't want to believe what people are telling you. You'll find out for yourself."

Bitterness spread through Miss Raika and lapped at her throat, and on it swam the words of what would have been a logical and natural reply, namely, that Ratko was certainly not *hers* but, on the contrary, Yovanka's, that Yovanka herself had brought him along and praised him and espoused him so much that in the end she had persuaded her, Raika, to advance him the first money against a note. She wanted to tell her that, and could have proved it, but could not find the strength to do it, for she felt inexplicably weak and helpless, all but paralyzed, under the spouting of that wide-open mouth which never yet had admitted its own errors, not even the smallest, and which was capable of drowning every blessed thing in creation with its brazen, flapping sounds.

They were sounds beyond the pale of truth and lies, beyond all reality—indeed, they were an irresistible reality all their own. The moment one was left alone and could examine them detachedly, nothing was simpler or easier than to prove the glaring inaccuracy of each and every word; but exposed to them like this, one was utterly helpless and forced to back away as before a swift stream of molten white-hot lava. So Miss Raika kept quiet, although her silence required a great effort. The more torn she felt by the contradicting feelings of rebellion, shameful weakness, and unexplainable indignation, the less strength she had to resist the infuriated Yovanka. And while she was the first to wonder at her own lethargy, she was unable to find a word or gesture by which to throw it off.

Yovanka was detailing the scheme (she had apparently decided on it earlier) by which she would expose the young man to Miss Raika, so that the latter could convince herself once and for all about the nature of his "business" and see with her own eyes how he spent the money they gave him. With undiminished heat, she went over the fine points of the scheme as if it, and not their disenchantment and the lost money, were now the main problem. She had arranged it all, she said. At the Casino there worked a man called Joshka, who was employed as a night electrician and technical assistant and who during the day worked in a mill owned by one of her relatives in the suburbs. She had come to an agreement with Joshka. Tonight after eleven, the two of them would enter the courtyard at the back of the Casino. Joshka would lead them in through a side entrance, to a small unused gallery from which they would be able to look down unobserved on the *chambre séparée* where Ratko caroused and scattered money every night with his fine-feathered friends. They would also see Carmencita, who at that hour went from *séparée* to *séparée* and collected her baksheesh. And afterwards they could sneak out unnoticed and unrecognized, just as they had come.

Miss Raika listened as if her friend were telling her about a foolish dream, not an actual plan to be put into effect that very evening and in which she was to take part. And if anyone had asked her whether she really intended to go and prowl along dark galleries in some nightclub where extravagance and every sort of debauchery were the fashion, about which she could not even bear to read in books, she would have denied it firmly as a mad, offensive, and inconceivable project. She did, in fact, decline it now, only it did not help her much. Yovanka was in one of her "white heats." Words came pouring out of her, one sparking another like a thick bundle of rockets, going off with loud volleys that deafened Miss Raika's will and smothered every thought of resistance. And still, unable to stomach Yovanka's spiteful proposal, she made a last fainthearted attempt to bow out of the witless expedition.

"You know what, Yovanka? I'd rather not go."

"What now? Why wouldn't you?"

"I don't want to. You go if you want to."

"What do you mean, you go?" cried Yovanka. "I wore off my feet for a whole week for your sake and now that I have the thing out in the open you tell me, 'Go yourself, I don't want to go!' Well, you have to go with me, you simply have to. What nonsense is this? You're going to let the crook take all that money and make fools out of us, and not lift a finger? Certainly not! He's going to pay dear, that rat, but I want you to see for yourself first. You have to see for yourself."

At the mention of money, Raika once more felt a weak pang of loss and regret deep down in her chest. She found it hard to believe that it was she who had foolishly given away so much money through a deception, just as she could not see herself dallying in shabby cafés in the dead of night. But she already felt herself breaking down and giving in, powerless as in a dream, while Yovanka's "You have to!" sliced the air around her like a whip.

It was a little before ten when Yovanka reached the house in Stishka Street and knocked on the window nearest the door, in which there was light. Miss Raika went to let her in.

The two girls sat for a while in the weak light of the unshaded bulb and made forced, desultory conversation. As it was cold in the room, they both wore their overcoats and looked like two poor women waiting for a train at a railway station. Yovanka kept puffing at her coarse and pungent French cigarettes, meanwhile recounting tidbits from the lives of the various people who at that moment were the object of her attention and protection. Miss Raika listened, coughing now and then. Half an hour later, Yovanka rose and suggested that they go.

Outside, the October night was damp and chilly and a strong wind was blowing. As she carefully locked the door and glanced at the windows of the house which she was abandoning at such an unusual hour, Miss Raika shivered with cold and suppressed agitation. She walked slowly and with difficulty over the pitted cobblestones along the wet and badly lighted Alexander Street. She stumbled and held on to Yovanka, who marched like a recruit with her sturdy practiced legs. It was nearly midnight when they reached Terazye Square in the center of the town. Here, there was more light and traffic. Muted sounds of music, singing, and talk came from Topola and other ground-floor cafés on both sides of the street. One could see from the thickly steamed windows that these places were filled to overflowing with hot crowds bent on drink, song, and dancing. Lashed by the wind, the two girls turned the corner of Alexander Street and entered the gate at the rear of the Casino.

The dark courtyard was illuminated only by the glow of the kitchen windows; one of these was open and spewing white clouds of steam. The air was heavy with the odors of greasy food and a stable somewhere nearby. From the kitchen came the sounds of waiters shouting their orders, the cries and bickering of women cooks and dishwashers, the clatter of plates and pots. Miss Raika clutched Yovanka's elbow. Out of a door, suddenly flung open, burst a big aproned woman with a huge caldron in her hands and narrowly missed soaking them with the slop which she emptied into the courtyard with a powerful swing of her entire body. They entered a narrow hall and began to climb a poorly lighted stairway. Looking awkwardly in front of her, Miss Raika heard her friend inquire of someone: "Where's Joshka?"

"Upstairs by the boxes," replied a boy's voice. Yovanka pressed on with tight lips, dark and intent like some goddess of justice and retribution. Miss Raika staggered after her through several gloomy narrow rooms piled with crates, barrels, canopies, and stage sets, and she kept banging her knees and elbows against invisible objects. The place smelled unaired and heavy with dust and the odor of carbide.

On climbing to the first landing they found, in a long, somewhat better lighted corridor, a man with reddish hair and mustaches, dressed in an oil-stained workman's overall, with the sleeves rolled up to the elbows. Yovanka exchanged a greeting with him, whereupon he promptly led them to the far end of the corridor. Miss Raika had the impression that his face wore a faintly mocking expression, like the smile of grownups taking a turn at a children's game. The man cautiously opened a small door and let them both inside. Once more they found themselves in almost total darkness. In a far corner, however, as if from behind some draperies, they saw a slender crack of light. Somewhere from down below there came mingled cries and the knocking of glasses. Moving on tiptoe, both women approached the light in the corner. The side, indeed, was a panel of curtains of a heavy fabric. Yovanka parted them a little and looked out, then stepped back and, without a word, pushed Raika toward the crack.

Peering out, Raika at first saw only blinding light and a wall in the distance. She almost choked with the hot and heavy air which was full of tobacco smoke and multiple vapors. As she lowered her gaze, she saw down below her a narrow cubicle which was filled almost entirely by a long table strewn with plates, glasses, and assorted dishes of food. Around the table sat five or six men. She knew then that she was on a gallery and that the place down below was the *chambre séparée* which Yovanka had mentioned.

In the great excitement of the first few seconds, everything seemed to blur and shiver in front of her eyes, but as she took hold of herself the picture before her began to coalesce and grow steady, and from then on she could follow everything, the faces, gestures, and voices, as on a movie screen. The first figure she made out was Ratko's—fair, almost boyish among those other corpulent men. He was more restrained than the others, but threw his head back every now and then and laughed out heartily and loudly. This gave him a blithe and radiant look such as she had never seen on him. The others kept up a chorus of shouts, waved their arms unnecessarily, laughed almost to tears, clapped their hands. A few nibbled constantly at the food before them and drank wine out of slender glasses.

Observed from that unusual perspective, the whole scene had an air of madness and unreality. Holding her breath and forgetting where and who she was, Raika watched the men who evidently were well in their cups. At the head of the table sat a fat man with a sallow complexion, black hair, and a thick, black, trimmed mustache. He was the quietest of the lot and from time to time he mopped the sweat on his bull-like neck with a large handkerchief. The lawyer from the other side of the river! thought Miss Raika. She could now follow the conversation much better—if indeed this cheerful noisy riot of tossing heads, laughter, and shouting could be called a conversation. She heard every word, even though the men kept interrupting one another, roaring with laughter and stamping their feet, not allowing anyone to finish a sentence.

"Let the man recite for once," said the lawyer in his easy, rich voice, waving good-humoredly toward a strapping pale-faced man wearing big spectacles, who had got up at the other end of the table and stood with a sheet of paper in his hand, waiting in vain to get a word in.

"Come on now, let's hear it!"

"Oh, sit down, brother. Never mind the verses. I didn't care for them when I was at school. . . ." This from a small, fat, lively man, flushed with drink.

"Oh, come on, let him!"

"Forward, poet, march!"

Perfectly sober and tense like a gun at the ready, the large poet took advantage of the moment's comparative calm and, while some of the others were still talking, eating, and clinking their glasses, started to recite his poem in a booming baritone:

"BELGRADE

"My town beside the twin rivers.
A swelling line of dark silhouettes
nudging the Milky Way.
When the young moon, silvery cuirassier,
rides the stellar garden path,
the breath of my town,

whimsical, stormy and free,
rising o'er all, soars on aloft
and betwixt the planetary orbs
boldly spins the great daring curves
of its wondrous architecture to come. . . ."

"Oh, it makes me want to die!" cried the small fat man, who had never been fond of verses.

Several voices tried to hush him up all at the same time. "Be quiet, please!"

"Sit still, you drunken fool. Ignoramus! Let the fellow make a fiver!"

"Excuse me, gentlemen, excuse me," cried a thin, long-haired, very nattily dressed man, "excuse me, but there's some confusion here. The question here is not one of money. Our friend's not in that kind of predicament. He's not asking anything of us. On the contrary, he wishes to give us a rare pleasure. He's our leading poet of the cosmos. And today when we, too, aspire to culture . . ."

"Enough, enough, for God's sake. You think because you're an apothecary . . ."

"Ah, let the poet speak!"

"Now whose idea was it to drag in poetry and spoil the party?" asked a deep unruffled basso, as if he had just woken up.

This elicited a round of laughter. But the lean and natty long-haired gentleman, who was known as an apothecary, remained obdurate. He presently got to his feet and shouted at the tops of his lungs: "Gentlemen, I beg of you, don't pick on poetry! Poets are extraordinary people and ought to be respected!"

"What, what?" yelled the small man, pushing forward

around the table. "Why should we respect him? I don't respect anybody. I'd like you to know that! There's no one can
impress me, understand? Not even the good Lord. And I refuse to listen to this crashing bore, understand? I—will—
not—listen, so there!"

The lawyer at the head of the table kept waving his hand,
rocking with laughter and wiping the sweat from the nape of
his neck. The poet, solemn and unshakably grave, hesitated
briefly, then sat down and folded his paper. Between the
apothecary and the vociferous little man who did not care
for verses and who, as it transpired from the talk, was by
profession a customhouse agent, there developed a loud argument about culture and poetry. Their shouting made it impossible to hear what the others were saying. Then the
hubbub and the talk suddenly died down. They all turned to
the invisible door, which was somewhere beneath the gallery
on which Miss Raika was standing, and their faces lit up and
broadened into grins.

Rustling in her rich wide dress of crude silk the color of a
walnut shell, a high Spanish mantilla of black lace on her
head, a big bunch of violets pinned to her breast, Carmencita
slowly came forward. Hooked over her left arm she carried
a shallow basket, hugging it against her crinoline. The basket
was full of big and by now quite withered Parma violets, tied
in small bunches. Behind her came a little girl with a similar
basket, in which there was a whole pile of paper money in
large denominations.

Miss Raika clutched the curtain convulsively with both her
hands.

Only then, when the last man in the drunken company had
fallen silent, could one hear Carmencita quietly singing her

melody, to Serbian lyrics which she pronounced mechanically and without understanding.

> "Oh, señores, señoritas,
> Buy from Carmencita
> Little blue violets
> as a pledge of happiness
> perchance even tonight."

Her voice was thin and sweet, her pronunciation slurred and unclear, her movements, to the rhythm of the song, graceful and poised. Before she ever approached the table, the dissolute revelers around it were thoroughly tamed.

Still singing, she took the bunches of violets from the basket and stuck them, one after another, in the buttonholes of the men, while they tossed dinar bills into the basket carried by the little girl. Carmencita seemed not to be aware of the existence of the little girl and her basket. The small man who didn't care for verses was now staring in front of him, meek and deflated all of a sudden; and to cover up his awkwardness he pulled out of his wallet a whole sheaf of bills and tossed them with an impetuous movement to the girl. The smile glistening on her white teeth and in her half-lidded eyes never left Carmencita's porcelain face as she slowly made her way between the chairs and the wall in her wide, wide skirt of stiff silk. They all made room for her, their eyes bulging with admiration and respect. Only Ratko was freer and more natural. Having contributed his bill, he bowed slightly to enable her to pin the violets to his lapel, and then, taking her hand and raising it to his lips, he covered it with kisses up to the elbow. Carmencita interrupted her low-pitched song and spoke out loudly and musically: *"Laisse-moi tranquille, Ratko! Voyons, laisse-moi passer, méchant gars!"*

Her face gleamed with make-up and with the practiced assured smile of an experienced tamer of beasts. With a smooth graceful movement, she withdrew her hand and in a twinkling reached the other side of the table, where she resumed her quiet song and the distribution of violets. And when she was finished, she made a deep theatrical bow to all of them and vanished together with the girl, whose basket was now heaped to the rim with bills. Ratko, his eyes flashing, called after her and spoke a few phrases in rapid French.

At that point, the entire room with its drunken company reeled in front of Miss Raika's eyes. The curtain fabric, which she was clutching and pressing to her cheeks, scorched her as if it were on fire, but she dared not let go of it, for it seemed to her that the floor had fallen away from her and she was suspended over a chasm and only her desperate clutching of the curtains kept her from sinking.

This tossing of money, the shameless hand kissing, the wide grin which seemed to her at once hideous and moronic and depraved, apart from looking incongruous on Ratko's face, all, all this was disgraceful and painfully ugly. And that unfamiliar foreign tongue, so lively and brash, full of melodious vowels and brittle lapidary phrases that flew through the air like sparks tied in necklaces and bundles of lightning, in glaring contrast to her own dull husky Bosnian speech, that, also, sounded to her like corruption personified, a corruption unaware even of the idea of sin, one that revealed the full measure of Ratko's fall and perfidy.

She thought of loosening her grip on the curtain and

slumping to the floor, into the chasm, anywhere, only not to have that image before her eyes. But she felt Yovanka's hot breath behind her like a warning.

When the mist of fury, pounding blood, and shame that hung over her eyes thinned a little, the drunks were back in their chairs. The violets in their lapels were the only tangible sign that Carmencita had been there. But now they were joined by two girls from the cabaret, both blond and pretty and like twins in their evening dresses of pale green taffeta. Both were spinning wooden swizzle sticks in the champagne glasses in front of them. They were all convulsed with laughter over a joke told by the customs agent who hated poetry—which he delivered in a high voice and with much energetic waving of his hands above the table. Only the poet sat motionless, like a horned owl, with his great round spectacles of thick glass. An amiable alcoholic discussion was going on between Ratko and the customs agent, which brought on another explosion of general laughter.

"The champagne is on you," Ratko was saying. "On you, brother. And don't worry about it. Just tell the customs inspector to look the other way a couple of times, and anything that's silk you just mark up as cotton and in the morning there'll be a thousand-dinar bill under your pillow."

"Shut up, you lady killer. It's easy for you to talk. All you have to do is go and snuggle up to that midwife of yours somewhere in Stishka Street, or wherever, and its cash in hand for you."

The gasp of mirth around the table was so great that for a split second they all seemed transfixed and speechless, after which they began to slap their thighs with their palms and roar at Ratko, who laughed heartily right back at them.

Here Miss Raika let go of the drapery and backed into Yovanka's strong arms.

It was only when they found themselves again in the dark courtyard that Raika fully came to and realized that she was leaning with the whole weight of her body on Yovanka, who led her along with her arms about her, like a war casualty. Mortified with shame, she broke away with an agonizing effort and freed herself from the embrace. But Yovanka clutched her arm again, whispering: "Easy, easy now."

As they came out of the gate, Miss Raika jerked away again and, breaking the hold on her upper arm, said sharply and hoarsely: "Thank you, I'll go alone. I'm all right."

"What? Am I to leave you now when you most need help? No, no, I'll take you home. Come now, slowly. The air will brace you."

Miss Raika halted. Crushed though she was, she could feel a sudden wave of new and unexpected strength rising in her, sharpening into an irresistible urge to thrust away any kind of help, even the smallest, every last sound and gesture that had the remotest semblance of sympathy and pity; a strange, obstinate, destructive, and healing kind of strength that found its gratification in living anguish to its bitter end, in lengthening every fall to the very bottom, to reach the ground and there either smash itself to pieces or land on its feet and stand up again.

"Thank you. Not necessary." Miss Raika pushed the smaller woman away quite unceremoniously.

"Why? What on earth?" stammered Yovanka, unable to believe her eyes, her protector's pride clearly wounded. She was flabbergasted—something that happened very rarely in her life—and she stood as if stricken, frail and unwanted, before this thin woman who suddenly needed nothing.

"That's right. Leave me alone. I don't need anybody. I can manage myself."

Yovanka wheeled around as if whipped and without another word strode off sharply in the direction of Knez-Mihailo Street. Miss Raika set off in the opposite direction.

She walked against the wind, slowly and laboriously, as one walks in a dream, but as she turned the corner into Alexander Street she felt that she had overestimated her strength, that her knees were giving way, and that she was about to faint. To stop herself from falling, she leaned against a iron post on top of which a great electric lamp of milky glass was swaying to and fro in the wind. The lower end of the post was of cast iron, hollow and pierced here and there by artillery shrapnel of the last war. Through these holes the high wind soughed and whined, its whistle mingling with her sobs and tears. This brought her something like relief, and the icy touch of the iron was pleasant. She wanted to stay and cling to the pillar, but was taken aback by the inexplicable shouting and loud laughter which seemed to be waxing stronger behind her. The shocking thought occurred to her that she was still in that room with the drunken party. When she stirred and let go of the post, she found herself facing a group of hack drivers gathered in front of their fiacres, guffawing and cracking jokes about her, evidently under the impression that she'd had too much to drink.

"How about a fare? Thirty dinars."

"Want a ride, lady?"

"Lady, let's see you stand up," yelled a third driver.

Miss Raika summoned all her strength and walked away.

Going up the long Alexander Street seemed like an eternity. The wind shook the big electric lamps strung out at intervals over the street. In time with their motion, large scarves of weak light drifted to and fro across the muddy crumbled pavement. The scene gave Miss Raika a distinct feeling that the earth was moving and sinking under her feet. From time to time, she trembled with the fear that she was going to totter and fall, but she kept on walking, driven onward by the coarse laughter and unspeakable catcalls of the hack drivers which still echoed in her ears. That tramping through the night was endless. The road looked weird, as though she were walking on it for the first time; the night was full of snares and dangers.

Struggling like this up interminable Alexander Street she was racked, as by a poisoned thorn buried deep in the flesh, by a thought she hardly dared to face and admit into her consciousness. What had come over her, she asked herself, that in her mature years she went and lost her head over a smile that reminded her of Uncle Vlado, that she felt motherly pity for a good-for-nothing adventurer and gaily showered him, as if in a game, with huge sums of money— *her* money, which to her was dearer than her eyes, more precious than blood? Where *were* her eyes, her experience, and her good sense? What possessed her to get embroiled with that unpredictable intriguer Yovanka? How could it happen that she, who had never once set foot in a café, now in her middle age went sneaking down squalid doubtful alleys and spying on a young man who was nothing to her and about whom, in fact, she cared no more than about a picture in some illustrated magazine that might remind her of Uncle Vlado?

As if shaken awake, she saw these questions before her and they contained all her inexplicable folly, irreparable harm, and great shame; if she wanted to keep her sanity and continue walking along this accursed road and get home alive, it was best to silence them and not face them for the time being. Choking with gall and shame, she sobbed dryly and talked to herself, wordlessly, in a mute but eloquent language which she alone understood, one that made sense and had a clear significance only in the context of her unusual life but otherwise had no logic or palpable connection with real life like children's weeping or the private mumbling of a person plunged in despair.

Addressing her dry tears and her disjointed, unfinished sentences to that grave in Sarajevo, she begged it to forgive her for what she was unable to forgive herself, to have patience with her, to try to understand how very hard it was to live without another soul and to deal with people.

. . . The world is so riddled with traps, Father, there are so many changes and surprises wherever you turn that a woman can go mad trying to cope with them and survive. I know and remember all those things you told me and asked me to hold on to, but what good are they when life is such that lies and humbug are stronger than everything? I've done everything I could think of for my security. But what use is it when they sneak up on you from a side you never expect? And even if no one deceives us, we deceive ourselves. Forgive me for being so lost and helpless after all these years and hardships, but I didn't break my pledge to you—people broke faith with me. You know how hard and how long I've worked. I thought that your advice, together with my will and effort, would be sufficient protection, but it was not so. There's no such thing as protection in this world. It is much worse, Father, than you imagined. Only those who live long enough, only they can see the world and the people in it for what they are. If you're a have-not, they walk over you. If you have, they take it away from you. . . .

This, more or less, was the gist of Raika's interior monologue as she went on complaining like an irrational child about everything and everyone, addressing her complaints to the distance and to the grave in that distance, but there was no comforting echo from that quarter either. Then she turned her gall on the living and thought about Ratko and Yovanka and her recent experience. She asked herself: Isn't there a man who can be clean and decent at least for a little while; are there no exceptions to the rule? It seemed there were not. Was it not possible for people to approach one another without hidden motives and intentions? How was one to spot and protect oneself from all the walking lies and dissimulation, from the vile, perilous, and inexplicable instincts which lurked in people and over which you had no control whatsoever, since they themselves knew little about them, let alone controlled them.

Her mind spun faster and faster with these questions; they came flocking, pelting, and clashing. She staggered under their pressure, which kept mounting unbearably, but was unable to find an answer. Indeed, she never would find it, for people like her, confronted with this kind of situation, are unable to understand anything and can see and hear nothing of life but its shortcomings and their own resentment of them.

Reaching the corner of her street, she paused unconsciously and turned into it. She unlocked the front door, slowly, awkwardly, like a stranger, and entered the house. She barely managed to take off her long black overcoat, but at the first movement her strength gave out. All her laborious restraint of the past hours suddenly loosened and came undone like a knot. She sank to her knees, her arms and head on the edge of the bed; she could no longer stand or keep her eyes open, or contain herself. The earth pulled her down irresistibly. But greater and stronger than anything else was her need to lament the lost money and her own unaccountable blindness, to moan like one wounded. Her throat contracted with the misery that pressed on her chest like a dark mountain and struck her down. The moaning washed away some of the wretchedness; what remained seemed to grow lighter and more bearable. She no longer talked and ranted aloud. Deaf to her surroundings, she existed only as a ball of pain and misery from which a thin wisp of moans uncoiled itself like a thread.

When she came to herself and recognized the lighted familiar room, she made a strange discovery. For a while she struggled with disbelief, but as her head cleared it became more and more apparent to her that her mother was sitting on the floor and that she, Raika, was in her lap. This was something neither of them would have thought possible even in a dream. It was unbelievable that the frail old woman could support her tall bony frame; yet she did. Mothers have unimagined strength and fall into instinctive postures. Holding this thin limp body, folded at the waist and knees, in her lap, like the Mother of God with her dead Son in an old icon, the old lady propped her head with one hand and with the other moistened her forehead and open mouth. The moans coming out of that mouth had become a steady, muffled sobbing. And, like a pair of clocks ticking at different rhythms in the room, Raika's sobs were punctuated by the gentle whispering of her mother: "Don't, Raika, darling. Don't, my child. There, your mother's with you. It'll be all right."

GETTING OVER HER LOSS AND BITTER DISILLUSION CAME hard to Miss Raika, but she bore it in silence. Her mother nursed her without a word of reproach, without questioning, with a love that asked no explanation or reasons.

Next day she called the doctor, a quiet man who walked on soundless feet and was altogether gentle and soft-spoken, as if made entirely of rubber. The thought of the doctor's bill kindled a brief fire in Miss Raika, but she was too weak and exhausted to resist the examination. On his way out, the doctor informed the old lady that the illness itself was nothing to worry about but that, besides her condition, her daughter had a congenital heart murmur which only a specialist could handle. This ought to be seen to as soon as possible. In the meantime, she was to avoid excitement of any kind.

On the fourth day, however, Miss Raika got up from bed, like one of those people who revive miraculously. She pushed her mother away and informed her coldly that she was not sick and didn't need medicines or care. She firmly declined to go see a doctor about her heart.

Standing on her feet once more, she looked at herself and around the room, and at the autumn sky outside with its filigree of bare tree branches, and then, like a man trying to clear his head after a bad blow, articulated her first full-fledged thought: So be it! After they've all betrayed and ruined you, there's still thrift! That doesn't depend on anyone. I'm going to save. Saving will help me get back at least a part of what they've taken away. In the end, maybe, it'll give me what all my slaving could not give me. Who knows? And even if it doesn't, I'm still going to save with all my strength, in spite of everything and everyone. Better and more than I have so far . . . The thought sent a deep, violent tremor through her body, as if she were shaking off everything that had crushed and oppressed her in the last few days. Afterwards, though still trembling within, she was indeed restored to health. Pale and frowning, she resumed her normal life with its old habits.

A day later, a breathless Ratko arrived at Stishka Street. Raika received him calmly, without anger or excitement. It was apparent at once that he had learned from Yovanka about their night visit to the Casino. The handsome young man gave the impression of a cat surprised in mischief. He tried to explain and justify himself, but Miss Raika gazed at him as on a puppet with a painted smile and his voice passed her by like an empty rattle. She had recovered from him, burned him out with her fever and got him out of her system forever—him and his smile, as well as her lost money. She could find no connection between this prattling young man and her memory of Uncle Vlado, which remained intact in her mind, vivid and dear as it had always been.

He came several times more, asking questions, wheedling, offering his services, his explanations and regrets; everything, in fact, save the loaned money. True, he swore that he would soon establish his business, start earning money, and repay the loans, but Raika had learned what the oaths of weak and unstable people were worth. She looked upon him as a loss that had been written off; not even the thought that there was a faint possibility of saving some of her money could persuade her to listen seriously or to see him in another light. At last he stopped coming altogether.

The affair with Yovanka was more difficult. She could forgive neither Ratko nor Miss Raika. She had never forgiven anyone who made a mockery of her role of protector, one she nurtured with so much care and enthusiasm, so devotedly and selflessly, over such long periods of time.

After that strange night, which had produced a great emotional shock for her instead of a triumph, Yovanka immediately and violently recoiled not only from her good-for-nothing protégé but also from her friend. And the same passionate zeal with which heretofore she had lavished attentions and favors on her friends and championed their causes as if they were her own, now became fuel for her malice, slander, and persecution of them.

"The scum that's pouring into town these days, why you'll never believe it," Yovanka kept saying to her various other protégés who had not yet toppled from grace.

And she would launch with flashing eyes into her tale of disillusionment with Ratko and Miss Raika, and all of her body would quiver with inner fury and bitterness. She maintained that Miss Raika "got hooked up" with the young man, that she had been an Austrian spy in Sarajevo and had to leave Bosnia on account of it, that Ratko had been a white-slave trader at Salonika. Every day she added some new detail to the story. She obtained from Sarajevo the back issues of newspapers that contained derogatory articles about Raika, and showed them jubilantly to their common acquaintances, who naturally had no time to read them. She called Ratko a "forced volunteer" and "apache," and Miss Raika a "black-and-yellow* usurer," a spy, and a vampire.

It was only five or six weeks later that she put her newspapers away and took her hands off Ratko and Miss Raika, in order to lay them on someone else.

None of this could touch or move Raika who, beginning with that terrible night and during her illness, had squared her accounts and mercilessly written off the whole thing once and for all. Now her life flowed quietly again, barren and colorless in the eyes of other people, but rich and well filled in her own, occupied entirely by petty chores and her all-encompassing thrift. She kept in touch with the exchange offices from London to Belgrade, studied the behavior of currencies, and checked the daily rates of those that were publicly announced on the blackboards in front of shops at Kolarats, as well as the confidential ones that were communicated in whispers. She bought and sold little, and even more cautiously than before. She visited the few banks with which she was still connected. She shifted her money from one account to another, or took it out of one bank in order to put it in another, at the same rate of interest. She moved it around, like a cat her kittens, from one place that seemed doubtful to her to another which, immediately after she put down the

* Colors of the Imperial Austrian flag.

money, began to look insecure in her eyes. In doing that she never even noticed the air of boredom and wonder on the faces of clerks and managers, or the pitying, sarcastic smiles with which even the doormen saw her in and out. She carried on a correspondence with Veso. He had remained the same as ever. Just as he had refused to be daunted by the last war, so now the unprecedented boom of the years after liberation could not ruffle his calm or budge him from his steady habits, or persuade him to give up his petty trading, his small but assured income, or the great satisfaction he derived from such work and such a way of life.

It was in these activities, in her consuming passion for ever greater, more perfect thrift and in her struggle against any kind of expense, that Raika's life frittered away, a life on which the encounter with Ratko and Yovanka had left no mark or sign of change, for nothing apparently could change or upset its course any more. Only her heart defect, accidentally discovered by that quiet-voiced physician during his fleeting examination, gave her trouble and unpleasantness. Quite often these days she would wake up in the night with a feeling that she was stifling for lack of air. And, apart from that, the least fright or surprise could bring her heart into her throat with such a deafening rush that her eyes would dim and the ground would sink under her feet. Her mother, who noticed these attacks no matter how much Raika tried to hide and deny them, urged her in vain to go see a specialist. And when all Raika's attempts to shrug it off failed, she tried to turn it into a joke: "It's nothing, Mother. You remember, they always said I had an evil heart."

Actually, she resented her mother's concern and felt exasperated with herself and with her heart which needed doctors and medicines. (What good is a heart that costs money?) She was determined not to admit her weakness, to die if need be, only not to be bedridden and to have to undergo a cure. Her mother hovered around her with that brooding and questioning look with which mothers watch an ailing, moody child. And yet, the first one to fall sick was not the daughter but the mother. In the spring, two years after their arrival in Belgrade, the old lady went to bed one day and did not get up again.

After that autumn night when she had discovered Raika unconscious on the floor and had gathered her up and set about nursing her, the relations between mother and daughter had continued as they had always been, dry, studied, without warmth or intimacy. It was as if the two of them had dreamt the same extraordinary dream, which the daughter promptly erased from her mind and the mother dared not mention. So the whole incident remained like an unspoken secret between them, a thing apart, swept under the rug, as if unreal. And the sickness of the old lady did not change it in any way.

Her illness was brief and embarrassing to her, and she tried to ask as little as possible from her daughter. At times she would give way to loud moaning, but as soon as she heard steps coming nearer she would restrain herself and fall silent, no matter how much this worsened her suffering. She would meet all questions with the answer that she was feeling better than the day before and that all this would pass. They debated for a long time whether to call a doctor, and when at last they called him it transpired that the pneumonia was far advanced. At that point even Miss Raika took fright. She engaged a woman to help her around the house and she herself looked after her mother conscientiously and devotedly, although even then the peculiar coolness and strange self-consciousness that had marked their relationship all these years did not vanish altogether. But this, too, did not last long. On the ninth day, the patient's heart weakened and she fell into a coma and died.

Miss Raika was staggered more by the swiftness and ease with which a living being could be transformed into a frail and shriveled corpse than by feelings of sorrow or loss. No matter how earnestly she searched her heart and thought about everything, she could not summon up anything that resembled a deep and true sorrow. She found that disconcerting. As she lay in bed in the dark, she repeated to herself the words she had used during the day before other people: "Poor mother! May God have mercy on her!" But tears would not come at night any more than they did by day.

The funeral was attended by a few women from the neighborhood and by the entire Hadzi-Vasich family. Master George was deeply grieved. The high pallor of his face gave an inkling of the great sorrow within him, which an occasional small tear and his decorous businessman's manner could not convey fully. After the funeral ceremony Raika did not even ask them to coffee at her home. Taken aback by this extraordinary behavior, which was beyond all decency and custom, her relatives invited her to come to their house and share with them the sorrow and burden of those most trying moments, but she replied flatly that she didn't need it and would prefer to be alone. And so she remained.

The event marked the beginning of Miss Raika's real life —a life she had always craved, even if subconsciously, one that so far she had been prevented from living by one thing

or another. Even her mother, with her slavelike submissive-
ness, had managed to keep some trifles in the house right up
to the last moment, some vestigial old habits that had been
hard to uproot. All that disappeared now.

To begin with, Raika gave away the big tomcat Gagan, a
big eater and loafer, over whom she'd had endless quarrels
with her mother, right up to the last day. She sold all her
mother's books. (She herself had stopped buying books some
time before, including German travel books, once her favorite reading, for she neither had the time nor felt the need to
read.) She threw out the flower stands, the one luxury the
old lady had stubbornly insisted on having. With a sense of
vindictiveness, she emptied the flowers and the soil into the
garbage box, but kept the stands and the boxes in order to
sell them at the first opportunity. She stopped the big wall
clock, which also had been a bone of constant and lengthy
contention between her mother and her. Raika had maintained that the ancient clock was an expensive and superfluous gadget and that two pocket watches in the house should
be sufficient, while her mother had claimed that the clock
came from her father's home, that she had spent a happy
childhood and even happier years of marriage to its ticking,
that she wanted to hear it tick to the end of her days, and
afterwards they could do with it what they pleased. Raika
never could understand what possible connection happiness,
as mother called it, had to do with the ticking of an antique
clock; and now, with a certain malicious eagerness, she
yanked at the chain and stilled it forever, so that never again
would it need repairs or winding or oiling. She took off the
last tablecloths and antimacassars which her mother had kept
in her room, and covered the furniture with newspaper. She

removed all pictures from the walls, except her father's. The house was now utterly denuded of that superfluous bric-a-brac which detracts and consumes our attention and without which most people do not consider life worth living. There was no color, no sound, not a single token to suggest a delicacy of feeling or expensive leisure. And so at last, after so many years of petty yieldings and surrenders, Miss Raika was truly free in a house that best accorded with her deepest needs and desires. Free and alone.

Every genuine, great passion seeks solitude and anonymity. A person wishing to gratify his passion wants to remain unseen and unknown, alone with the object of his passion, and he would rather talk—can talk better and at greater length—about everything under the sun except the thing which is the main subject of his thoughts and cravings. Even vice has its own code of discretion and shame, perverted and strange though it may be. And Belgrade at that time was an ideal environment for a person who wanted to be alone in the multitude, unnoticed in the milling throng. In that warm and exuberant welter, in the coursing flood of diverse and ever new humanity, of new patterns of life and custom, in the headlong and fitful transformation and ripening of all things, in that life without pause or respite, it was possible for a man to withdraw and live alone and invisible, according to his will, as in a thick forest or a megalopolis. Miss Raika, too, found her place there.

With time, conditions in the land and in the capital began to settle down and money transactions found their own level, without that wild seesawing in which speculation flourished, without abrupt changes and jumps. Those money-changing establishments on Terazye Square vanished one after another. With them, too, vanished the possibility of secret and ever-changing games which a man might play in complete anonymity, the chance of losing or winning according to how much stronger, more cunning, or luckier he was than other men, without having to give an account to anyone of his gains and losses, or of the passionate ups and downs that accompanied them. The great floodtide of universal speculation that had been raging for some few years subsided now and was transformed into the routine activities of banks and various authorities; there was no longer room or opportunity for petty speculation or quick killings.

Even without that, however, Miss Raika had been growing more and more cautious; she found it increasingly difficult to make business decisions, even the most innocuous, until in the end she concentrated all her attention on thrift. Lending money at interest in this new, unfamiliar, and hazardous environment was something she dared not even think about. She did assay a few transactions, if such can be called the timid pecking and scratching which she ventured on the fringe of the big currency game and the stock market, and she undertook them only when they were of a nature that was almost identical with thrift—that is to say, when they were safe, swift, and without intermediaries, regardless of how piddling the gain might be. She resigned herself to the fact that her yearly income, which came from the rent on the house in Sarajevo, from several kinds of stock and interest on commercial investments, was more or less static, and more likely to decline than rise should there be a change; and because of that she tried desperately, while cutting down her needs and expenses, to save as much as possible of that income and add it to the capital, which lay there and multiplied, modestly and slowly, but steadily and securely. And, dedicating herself entirely to that cause, she plunged into it silently, obeying only her instinct, deaf to everything, like a worm in the woodwork.

So another ten years went by amidst changes and events, which were felt perhaps more deeply and strongly in Belgrade at that time than elsewhere. Miss Raika did not follow these changes; she barely even noticed them. And when during the holidays she would go to visit the Hadzi-Vasich home and hear all the personal and family news, it would seem to her that they came from another planet.

Madame Seka had grown fatter and heavier, if anything; her eyes were still bright and lively, but her skin had become yellow, the soft black down on her upper lip almost a real mustache. She had married off both her daughters, and very well. The girls had married neither the young playmates nor the liberal poets they had adored in the early 1920's. Danka's husband was the well-known banker Stragarats. She had inherited her mother's mustache, but her fight against corpulence was more successful; she had two children. Davinka had married an architect and professor at the Technical Faculty. The son Misha had married a daughter of the Stragarats family, so that there was now a double tie between the two families. He had made a reputation as a financial expert and served on various international commissions. Master George had suddenly become old, though without any marked outward changes. Remaining his old self, he just seemed to wear away quietly and shrink by the day.

It was in one of those family gatherings during a holiday in the Hadzi-Vasich home that Raika heard about Yovanka's death. She had died of typhoid fever somewhere in the interior of Serbia, where she had gone on somebody else's business; having caught the infection, she was treated for the wrong illness, received inadequate care, and succumbed. And the following year, 1928, during another holiday season, Raika learned from a chance conversation that took place in her presence that Ratko Ratkovich had become manager of a large government model farm in Slavonia, where he acted the host to visiting notables and gave receptions and arranged conducted tours of the farm, which were written up in the newspapers and caused much talk.

All of this reached Miss Raika's ears by purest accident; she heard it without the least excitement and afterwards promptly forgot it, relapsing into her calm world in which there were no marriages, no illnesses, and no deaths. (Indeed, it might be more accurate to say that this was true only of marriages and deaths, for illness certainly was part of her life. There was no doubt now of her coronary defect, which, judging by all signs, was growing more acute. But she acknowledged this bit of bad luck only during the moments when she actually suffered from it, and as soon as the attack was over she resolutely pushed it out of her mind and didn't let it disturb the peace she had created within and around herself.)

The great depression and monetary crisis of 1930 shattered this peace and forced her, not into new efforts to make money, but to protect what she had. When the first tremors of panic reached the banks, she was among those who withdrew their deposits and saved them from being frozen. She even had to close up her house and travel to Zagreb to save the money she had there in the Serbian Bank.

It was a difficult and stormy time. Once more the old energy and spirit of enterprise revived in her, fanned by the same old terror: not to remain on the losing side, never, not at any price, not for a single moment. In those days she felt keenly that she was indeed alone in the world, more so than she had ever imagined, that she had no close friend or trusted person whose advice she might seek, at least in her financial problems, as she had once done with Konforti, director Paier, or with Veso. One could practice thrift all alone, without anyone's help, but to carry on business and try to protect oneself in those circumstances was very difficult, and becoming more difficult as the years went by.

Fearful, her confidence shaken, she went from bank to bank and pestered them and lied stubbornly, and often transparently, that she needed money in a hurry to pay off some very urgent debts. With thick wads of thousand- and hundred-dinar bills tied like armor around her fallow chest, or sewn into her dress, she stole uneasily along the streets, turning around constantly for fear that someone might be following her. She put on an elaborate and conspicuous act of depositing her safe box at the Danube Bank, in which she kept her gold ducats and valuable papers, announcing that she no longer needed the box since there was hardly anything left worth putting in.

At home, she had no end of trouble devising new ways to hide the stacks of money bills and the bag of gold. She bought American locks for both the house door and the door to her room; she obtained them at Zagreb, so that the locksmith here, who was to fit them on, would not be able to duplicate the keys. At that time, also, she had iron bars put on all the windows. She worried a long time about the best hid-

237

ing place for the money, so that she might tuck it away in several nooks at once and all of them would be perfectly safe. She bought tin safe-boxes and divided up the bills, gold, and valuable papers among them, then hid them in the tile ovens throughout the rooms or stuffed them into secret crannies which she then boarded up. And even at that she often woke up in the night at hearing suspicious noises that sounded like human footsteps, or from the terrible thought that there might be a fire. Her heart beat violently in her throat and her ears. She would jump out of bed and, undressed as she was, unboard the holes and pull out the tin boxes, after which, shivering with cold and from all kinds of thoughts, she carried them from one room to another, not daring to put them back in the old places and unable to find new crannies that were more reassuring. In the end she would get tired and, unable to think of another solution, return to bed, still cradling the cold boxes, her anxieties unresolved. She would have trouble falling asleep; and when she did, she slept badly. Even though she had made sure that there were no prowlers and no danger of fire, she had no peace, for whether she was awake or asleep and dreaming, it seemed to her that the wretched dinars were slipping and falling, the valuable papers losing their value, while fear waxed and spread and thickened on all sides like a curse.

This went on for months. However, a strong will and painstaking care overcome all things. In those sleepless and terror-stricken hours, Miss Raika also made new resolutions. She plucked up her courage and began to buy small quantities of Swiss francs in the black market, thus transforming her unwieldy stacks of dinars into a score or so of blue thousand-franc notes and russet five-hundred-franc notes.

The francs took up little space and just two months later she could have sold them at a profit of five to seven dinars per franc. But she wouldn't think of doing that. She kept them in a new hiding place which, for the moment anyway, seemed perfectly safe. In that place, bundled together with thick rolls of other foreign currencies and valuables, they took on the character of a familiar and dear and ever-fresh realm, one she could visit often and gaze at for minutes on end at various times of the day and night, in the light of an electric bulb, in the light of day, or in the calm glow of a candle.

Here lay those precious Swiss bills in picturesque disarray beside loose sterling notes in denominations of five and ten pounds, fair as love letters. And behind the mounds of this precious colorful paper there was a glimmer of gold and assorted jewelry which was either heirloom or had been bought or left as pledges for loans. And over all of it, as if scattered accidentally, were piles of American twenty-dollar gold pieces, four hundred and eleven of them. They were all alike: wide, heavy, almost fleshy and warm, as if throbbing with the sap of life, as if breathing and growing. Only the sharp relief of their letters and heads showed that they were money and inanimate metal. On one side the huge figure of Liberty with her name graven above her head, on the other the Seal of State with its tiny but legible motto *E pluribus unum*. Everything was always the same, but one could go on reading it for hours, days, and years, like a book of wonders that repeated and perpetuated itself. How these strapping Americans spread out in their meandering files: a golden army marching up the hillocks of pink, white, and violet bills, and down the dales of jewelry and bills! Along their flanks marched the columns of straggling and seemingly (but only seemingly) shabby Turkish liras and Hungarian kronen. They were darkened with age and so frail and light that if you laid them out on a marble slab their sound would be more like the rustle of leaves than the clang of metal; and they looked chipped and scraped along the edges. This was so because over the years they had suffered much biting and testing and gnawing at the insatiably covetous teeth of Sephardic and all other kinds of baptized and unbaptized money-changers throughout the Balkans and the Ottoman Empire.

These Turkish ducats, dating back to the critical years 1908, 1912, and 1913 (and how well she remembered them!), had been bought unbelievably cheaply from various young Moslem sparks and spendthrifts, or from widows of Turkish functionaries, who used to burst into tears so easily but were just as apt to turn away, slam the door, and spoil the transaction. There was no more profitable business in the whole world than dealing with those kinds of people. Their contempt for bargaining and figuring was every bit as great as their need for money. Driven by that need, and at the same time hamstrung by a mysterious but powerful sense of inner shame and personal consideration, they were easy and rewarding prey for a businessman who knew how to see through them, understand them, and make skillful use of them. As often as she glanced at those Turkish ducats, Miss Raika had a blurred and distant recollection of the proud and awkward customers and the generous profits she had made on them. In those moments she would often experience a renewed flutter of that strange "other heart" of hers, but it was a far cry from the stormy elation she had once felt in her moments of great triumph; the flutter was quieter now, as if in the distance, a mere echo of the erstwhile heartbeat.

Flanking and bringing up the rear of the first and second gold legions were a hundred or so napoleons, frisky diminutive French cockerels of a bright and well-defined cut. They were like a detachment of Circassian skirmishers and advance scouts. They had a lovely name and a sound one could never hear enough of.

This was the sight Miss Raika enjoyed every day, her "window to the world," her company and edification, her faith and her family, her nourishment and leisure. After every count and scrutiny the view recomposed itself into another aspect, and she could not decide what was better, more beautiful, and more potent, the view itself or the things it offered. Therein lay the foundation, the meaning, and the goal of life.

Miss Raika lived next to that treasure—calm but ever alert, watchful as a dragon. She did not let anyone into the house, and locked everything before dark. She had insured every single thing, twice and three times over, and taken every precautionary measure. There remained, of course, her daily worry about her stocks. She lived on their dividends. These were shrinking, but thrift made up for the loss of income and was a good thing even when everything else went awry. Thrift survived all things and filled one's existence completely; one could live with it to the last breath, and curtail and save even a little of that.

Now it was the winter of 1935. Life had ceased being anything else but thrift. A vast, splendid, and death-bringing desert of thrift, in which a person lost himself like a grain of sand and in which no other thing could or did exist.

She had long since stopped having those night dreams of "a million," from which once she had wakened in a warm glow and trembling with excitement. (During the best years of her business she had indeed been worth a million kronen, but those had been the anaemic Austrian kronen of the inflation after the war; the real, solid-as-gold million about which she had dreamed so often, the *first* million that was to have been a Pied Piper to a procession of other millions, still eluded her grasp.) And that grave in Sarajevo was not as vivid as once it had been; it had paled and cooled long since, especially from this distance. She had forgotten nothing of what had been, but none of it exerted any more power over her either. She still remembered the vow she had made to her father on his deathbed, but now that pledge seemed to her like an ancient, incomprehensible, and useless game from childhood. With it or without it, her life was as it was, as it had been from the beginning. Reality had long overtaken it and left it far behind. Everything had turned out to be harder, different, and more complex than her father could have dreamed, than she herself had anticipated in her young years of enthusiasm. Her bonds with the dead, as well as with the living, were becoming weaker.

Every year, on All Souls' Day, she would go to visit her mother's grave. In the town she saw no one. She had no need of people, they passed her by; they were born, they grew up and died, but never amounted to more than one of the elements, harmful or useful, favorable or hazardous, in her pursuit of thrift; otherwise she was not aware of their existence and had nothing in common with them. Not even Time existed for her; all that existed were the dates of receipts and disbursements. There was no future, and the past lay buried. Once in a while she would remember Uncle Vlado, her father, and her childhood. This would untangle the skein of memories and the thread would uncoil further and vividly

fore she reached the front door, however, her hand still outstretched and fumbling in the dark before her, she suddenly
came across—someone! She let out a short hoarse scream,
so weird that it terrified even her. Rigid with horror, she
found just enough strength to pull back a little. Her fingers
had unexpectedly touched a moist rough cloth. Still bemused
and distracted by her long remembrance, she was convinced
that there in front of her stood someone who had just entered the door from outside. She wanted to scream and call
for help, but she had no voice left. Her heart swelled and
billowed out into every part of her body. In the next instant
she had the feeling that all of her was suddenly draining
away, crumbling into icy pins and needles. There remained
only the mortifying thought that she was alone, that here in
the dark someone was facing her, that Someone who, unknown and invisible, forever preyed on the likes of her, the
one who sooner or later came to take the money. A thousand
times in the past, she had shuddered like this in the dark at
the thought of him, and a thousand times her fear had proved
to be unfounded. But this time, it seemed to her, he really
had come and was standing there in the middle of the hall,
in a soaked overcoat, ready at any moment to begin his rob-
ber's work. And tonight of all times, she could not recall
what she was supposed to do, in what way she was to defend
and protect herself. She made a strenuous, brief-as-lightning
effort to remember what that might have been, but did not
succeed. All she did remember was that she had always been
afraid of theft and prowlers, and how times without end she
had jumped in the dead of night at a suspicious noise or a
strange shadow and then sat up for hours wondering what
she would do if someone, in spite of all her precautions,

sneaked into the house and attacked her. All her life she had done her best to leave her money in a safe place, to hide and secure it, to remove every trace of it; all her life she had thought and done nothing else, so that in the end her existence had come to be the sum total of such precautionary measures. All that she remembered.

But the thing that was happening at this moment was as unexpected, as terrifying and new as if she had never been afraid or taken precautions, as if she had never done anything to safeguard and protect herself. It seemed to her as though she had spent her entire life in unforgivable and wanton carelessness, making no provisions of any kind, and that now she was about to lose her money and her life, stupidly, dismally, unnecessarily, simply because of her folly and want of good sense. *Now*, it seemed to her, she would know exactly how to save and conserve, how to hide and protect—but it was too late. The vile bandit stood in front of her, in the dark, this side of the door lock. It was all over. She expected the unknown voice to say, "Hand over the money!"—after which the murderous fists would slide out of the rain-soaked sleeves. But she neither heard him nor had the time to feel his hands. Inexorably, with a tightening clutch, her own heart strangled her. Sound drained out of her ears, the staring eyes blacked out, the gaping mouth went dumb. Her knees became like putty.

Toppling forward, she grabbed the air once more with her outstretched arms, as if to swim, and knocked over the coat stand on which hung her own winter coat of coarse cloth, still wet from the rain.

Sprawling on the floor, she tore with the last of her convulsive strength at the woolen blouse on her chest, in a desperate attempt to make more room for her stifling breath. Oh, a little more air, one more breath, and then perhaps all would be saved—life, money, and possessions. She would gladly have paid with gold for a breath of air. But no breath came. The knees twitched in a spasm, the top of the head was about to burst open. The blood stream came to a stop, it lay coiled inside her like molten lead. The next breath never came. The movements grew weaker, until they, too, were stilled. For a few more seconds, a hoarse rattle marked the last stage of the death struggle. Then that, too, passed. The body grew limp and quiet and remained outstretched in the gloom and the silence.

Belgrade,
December 1943–October 1944

A NOTE ON THE TYPE

THIS BOOK was set on the Linotype in *Bodoni Book,* a print-
ing type so called after Giambattista Bodoni (1740–1813),
a celebrated printer and type designer of Rome and Parma.
Bodoni Book as produced by the Mergenthaler Linotype
Company is not a copy of any one of Bodoni's fonts, but is a
composite, modern version of the Bodoni manner. Bodoni's
innovations in printing-type style were a greater degree of
contrast in the "thick and thin" elements of the letters and
a sharper and more angular finish of details.
*Composed, printed, and bound by The Haddon Craftsmen,
Scranton, Pennsylvania. Typography and binding design by*
HERBERT BAYER

A NOTE ABOUT THE AUTHOR

Ivo Andrić was born in 1892 in Travnik in northern Bosnia. At the outset of the First World War, while he was still a student, Andrić was arrested for his participation in a revolutionary movement which opposed the Habsburg regime and sought unity and independence for the South Slavic peoples. He was in prison for three years. After his release, he completed his studies, and received a doctorate in history from the University of Graz in Austria. He then entered his country's diplomatic corps and served in a number of European capitals, including Berlin, where he was stationed at the outbreak of hostilities between Yugoslavia and Germany in 1941. During the Nazi occupation of Yugoslavia, Andrić remained under virtual house arrest in his Belgrade apartment, and devoted himself to writing. The publication of his Bosnian Trilogy in 1945 firmly established his reputation in his native land. In 1961 he was awarded the Nobel Prize for Literature.